"Victoria Malvey a
and new verve

—Roman

Praise for the Delightful Novels of
Victoria Malvey

WEDDING OF THE YEAR

"Engaging and entertaining."

—*Romantic Times*

"A happy ending for everyone. Brava, Ms. Malvey, for a story well told."

—*Old Book Barn Gazette*

"A lovely escapist read. . . . This story has more twists and turns than a roller coaster."

—TheRomanceReader.com

"An eminently pleasant read. . . . Deftly crafted."

—AllAboutRomance.com

"An amusing historical romance. . . . Victoria Malvey provides her audience with a humorous tale with a pinch of suspense."

—Harriet Klausner, AllReaders.com

A PROPER AFFAIR

"Exhilarating. . . . A truly sparkling work. . . . It was great fun."

—*Affaire de Coeur*

"An engaging battle of wills."

—*Romantic Times*

"[A] deliciously sensual story. . . . A novel that delights the mind and heart."

—CompuServe Romance Reviews

"A very nice read. . . . [The] secondary characters are so well-drawn that I wouldn't be surprised to find them in a sequel."

—*Old Book Barn Gazette*

FORTUNE'S BRIDE

"Ms. Malvey crafts a tapestry of intrigue, broken promises, and misunderstanding, paving the road to true love with a mixture of laughter and heartbreak. With a unique blend of humor and sensuality, she serves her readers a delicious romantic treat. It's the stuff that fuels dreams and carries you off into the clouds. Climb aboard and enjoy the delightful journey."

—*Rendezvous*

"An energetic and amusing tale, perfectly suited to fans of Regency romances."

—*Publishers Weekly*

"A delightful and entertaining regency romp that will bring laughter to your heart. . . . I highly recommend curling up on a cold wintry day with *Fortune's Bride* to bring warmth into your heart."

—*Romance Reviews Today*

A MERRY CHASE

"Malvey delights with her charming characters and witty situations, and the many plot twists add a dash of spice and suspense to this romantic chase."

—*Publishers Weekly*

"You'll find yourself enjoying every minute. . . . Delightful, delicious, and delectable. Her intelligent, witty characters are easy to like and their comical antics bring a quick smile and genuine laughter. Don't miss the fun."

—*Rendezvous*

TEMPTRESS

"Victoria Malvey gives classic romance a fresh and exciting new voice."

—Teresa Medeiros, author of *The Bride and the Beast*

ENCHANTED

"Delightful and alluring. . . . This is the kind of tale that brightens the day and brings back memories of first crushes and the wonderful feeling of falling in love."

—*Romantic Times*

"Written with skill and humor—a delight to read. . . . A compelling story about the endurance of love."

—*Rendezvous*

"An enthralling tale of mystery and intrigue. Splendid."

—*Bell, Book & Candle*

PORTRAIT OF DREAMS

"A new star has burst upon the romance horizon. Victoria Malvey's *Portrait of Dreams* [is] a sensually sweet tale of love found and fought for. The spark that makes a book a best-seller is present on every page of this beautiful story."

—*Affaire de Coeur*

"Heartwarming and tender—a truly unforgettable story."

—Julie Garwood, author of *Mercy*

Books by Victoria Malvey

Portrait of Dreams
Enchanted
Temptress
A Merry Chase
Fortune's Bride
A Proper Affair
Wedding of the Year
Chasing a Rogue

Published by POCKET BOOKS

VICTORIA MALVEY

Chasing a Rogue

SONNET BOOKS

New York   London   Toronto   Sydney   Singapore

The sale of this book without its cover is unauthorized. If you purchased this book without a cover, you should be aware that it was reported to the publisher as "unsold and destroyed."   Neither the author nor the publisher has received payment for the sale of this "stripped book."

This book is a work of fiction. Names, characters, places and incidents are products of the author's imagination or are used fictitiously. Any resemblance to actual events or locales or persons, living or dead, is entirely coincidental.

An *Original* Publication of POCKET BOOKS

 A Sonnet Book published by
POCKET BOOKS, a division of Simon & Schuster, Inc.
1230 Avenue of the Americas, New York, NY 10020

Copyright © 2002 by Victoria Malvey

All rights reserved, including the right to reproduce
this book or portions thereof in any form whatsoever.
For information address Pocket Books, 1230 Avenue
of the Americas, New York, NY 10020

ISBN: 0-7434-1885-9

First Sonnet Books printing November 2002

10   9   8   7   6   5   4   3   2   1

SONNET BOOKS and colophon are trademarks of
Simon & Schuster, Inc.

For information regarding special discounts for bulk purchases,
please contact Simon & Schuster Special Sales at 1-800-456-6798
or business@simonandschuster.com

Front cover illustration by Alan Ayers

Printed in the U.S.A.

To my niece
Christina Noelle Malvey
Born 12/31/01

Our newest angel—
With Christopher and Lindsey to watch over you.
Blessing be upon you, Christina.

Chasing
a Rogue

Chapter One

London,
January, 1817

*H*arriet Nash was going to Hell.

As she sat there, quietly sipping her tea, she became more and more convinced of that inevitability. After all, what sort of person was she that she felt envious of her dearest friend's happiness? Watching Laurel hug her two-year-old son, Harriet felt another wave of envy wash over her, leaving her utterly convinced that she was bound for Hades.

"He's quite the handful," Laurel admitted as she kissed Ryan's cheek before handing him off to his waiting nanny. "But then again, so am I," she finished with a laugh, smoothing her hands down her rounded stomach.

"I'm certain you've not heard a word of complaint from Royce," Harriet insisted, setting down her cup, "as you are even lovelier than usual when you're enceinte."

"That's very sweet of you, Harriet, but I assure you I'm feeling anything but lovely these days. I waddle like a duck, my back aches every day, and my ankles have all but disappeared." Lifting up her skirt, Laurel stuck out a foot in order to prove her point.

"And you wouldn't trade one miserable minute of it."

Laurel grinned broadly. "Of course not, but that doesn't mean I can't complain about it." A wicked gleam lit her gaze. "Especially to Royce."

"That only seems fair as he's partly responsible for your condition."

"Precisely." Glancing around the drawing room, Laurel remarked, "Speaking of responsibilities, where are your aunts?"

Harriet couldn't help but laugh at the question. "I convinced them they needed to shop for my parents' visit."

"Your parents?" Laurel's eyes widened. "You shall have both your parents and your aunts directing your days now?"

Glumly, Harriet nodded. "My parents are absolute dears, and I adore them, but they are so . . . so . . ."

"Overprotective?" Laurel offered.

"Exactly. They shall follow me to every social event, hovering about, trying to ensure I have a marvelous time, and, in the process, scare away any of the few gentlemen who might ask me to dance."

"It is a problem," agreed Laurel. "Even now, your aunts, dears that they are, tend to intimidate all but the most stalwart gentlemen. Why, you hardly danced at the last few balls."

Much as Harriet would like to blame her lack of popularity upon her two aunts, she knew they weren't entirely at fault. "I've never danced much, Laurel," Harriet pointed out softly. "I'm well received by most of the ladies in society, but hardly spared a glance by the gentlemen. My aunts merely provide a convenient excuse upon which to blame my lack of appeal."

A scowl darkened Laurel's face as she immediately leapt to Harriet's defense. "You are far too harsh on yourself, Harriet," she protested loyally. "You are . . ."

"Yoo-hoo!" The loud, singsong call interrupted Laurel. "We're home, Harriet dear!"

A moment later, Aunt Agatha burst into the room, her short, round figure swaying under the weight of her packages. "Just wait until you see what I bought," she said from behind a stack of boxes.

Rising to help her aunt, Harriet reached for the top four boxes. "Why didn't you ask the footman to carry these in?"

"Because he's carrying in the rest." Aunt Agatha's smiling face appeared as Harriet removed her boxes. "Oh, my, that is much better," she pronounced brightly, before glancing over toward Laurel. "My darling Laurel, what a pleasant surprise to see you." With no concern for their contents, Aunt Agatha tossed the remaining boxes onto a nearby wing-back chair. "I didn't know you were going to call upon us today," she said, sending a reproachful glance at Harriet. As Laurel struggled to stand up, Aunt Agatha waved her back down into the chair. "Oh, no, my dear. Don't get up on my account," she said as she hurried over to press a kiss upon Laurel's cheek.

"Thank you, Lady Agatha," murmured Laurel. Patting her stomach, she said ruefully, "This belly of mine makes it difficult to stand."

"Mine does as well," Aunt Agatha admitted with a laugh, "and I can't even blame my width upon a baby."

"A few more shopping trips like this, Aggie, and I vow

you'll be thin as a post," pronounced Aunt Hilda as she sailed into the room with regal grace. "Good afternoon, Harriet, Laurel," she said, smiling at them. "I'd advise both of you to avoid the shops for a few days . . . in order to give them time to restock."

"Don't be an old pooh," Aunt Agatha chided as she reached up to remove her hat. "Not only were all my purchases absolute necessities, but they were wonderfully priced as well."

Peeling off her gloves, Aunt Hilda smoothed her hands down the front of her dove gray walking dress. "I hardly consider those ivory combs a necessity and, I assure you, Aggie, that they were not a bargain."

Aunt Agatha's peacock blue gown fluttered out behind her as she hurried over to where she'd tossed her packages. Digging through the smallest box, she retrieved two pretty ivory combs and held them up for everyone to see. "These will match my new ball gown perfectly, so how can you say they aren't necessary?"

Harriet stifled a smile at the exasperated sigh that broke from Aunt Hilda. "Really, Aggie," she returned dryly with a shake of her head. "With the way you fritter away your funds, it's no wonder you have little monies left."

"I beg to differ, Hilda. Might I remind you that I still receive my monthly stipend, thank you very much," she retorted crisply.

"Which is spent within a day, leaving you fairly penniless for the remainder of the month."

Aunt Agatha shrugged her shoulders. "It is my money to do with as I please."

"That's quite true, but have you considered if you were less of a spendthrift, you would be able to settle a larger portion upon Harriet," Hilda pointed out quietly.

Guilt warred with distress in Aunt Agatha's expression as she turned toward Harriet. "Oh, my dear, darling niece, I'm being so dreadfully selfish, aren't I?"

"Of course not," Harriet rushed to assure her. "You've already settled a portion upon me. Besides, it is your money, and I would prefer that you spend it in a manner that pleases you."

Stepping forward, Aunt Agatha laid a gentle hand upon Harriet's cheek. "Having you live here with me and Hilda for these past few years is what has pleased me more than anything."

Love warmed her. "I feel the same way, Aunt Agatha."

"Yes, yes," Aunt Hilda interrupted tartly. "We know that you love us, just as you know we adore you, Harriet, but that has absolutely nothing to do with the fact that if you had a larger portion, it might entice a gentleman of breeding."

"If I need a fortune in order to attract a gentleman, Aunt Hilda, then he's not someone I wish to marry anyway," Harriet asserted without hesitation. No, she wanted what her friend Laurel had: To be adored by her husband, to feel overwhelming love for that special someone, to know that they were bound to each other for eternity. "I don't want to have to purchase a husband."

"Don't be crass, dear," reprimanded Aunt Hilda. "Besides, you are scoffing at a time-honored reason for marrying."

"Because the notion deserves to be mocked." Laurel levered herself out of her chair. Slipping her arm through Harriet's, she faced down the aunts. "Our Harriet deserves to marry for love, don't you agree?"

"Just because a marriage is arranged, doesn't mean that love can't form," protested Aunt Agatha. "Why, my marriage was arranged by my parents, yet I grew most fond of my dear Roland."

"I fear 'most fond' is a far cry from 'in love.'"

Harriet's soft remark fell upon deaf ears. "Good Heavens, Harriet, must you be so impractical? Can't you see that liking your husband, being compatible with him, is far more important than that flash of heat most women mistake for love?"

Hiding a smile, Laurel cleared her throat. "Excuse me, Lady Agatha, but I beg to differ. I'm madly in love with my Royce."

With a wave of her hand, Aunt Agatha dismissed the statement. "I know, dear, but you are the exception, not the rule."

"Especially here in town," added Aunt Hilda. "The gentlemen of the town are a jaded, cynical lot who want nothing more than to marry someone of good breeding and heritage, beget her with child, then resume their debased pastimes, secure in the knowledge that they've done their duty to their name and title."

Both Harriet and Laurel blinked at the surprisingly vehement outburst. While her aunt had often made caustic remarks about any gentleman she'd shown an interest in, it was the first time Harriet had heard such harshness from her aunt. "But I thought you wanted me to marry," Harriet finally said.

"Indeed, I do. However, I feel it best if you return with your parents to the country and find an honorable gentleman there."

With a few simple words, Aunt Hilda had knocked the

breath out of her. Struggling to remain calm, Harriet shook her head. "I have no wish to return to the country. I'd prefer to live here in town with you and Aunt Agatha until I marry."

"I quite agree with Harriet," Laurel stated firmly. "It would devastate me to lose my best friend in the world."

"You wouldn't be losing her," Aunt Hilda assured her. "Hartsdale Manor is only a day outside of town, and you could visit her there whenever you wish."

"But I don't want to return to the country," Harriet repeated, this time in a firmer voice. "Growing up, I never had the slightest interest in any of the gentlemen around me. Their conversations centered around crops and farms and other dreadfully dull things that bored me to tears. The gentlemen I've met in town are urbane, charming, and much more interesting than their country peers."

"I agree with Harriet," announced Aunt Agatha, shooting her sister a quelling look. "Besides, this is a discussion that can wait until Sally and Lionel arrive."

Suddenly, all the pieces fell into place: The unexpected visit from her parents, Aunt Agatha's sudden urging for her to marry, and the negative remarks from Aunt Hilda about any gentleman who happened to show even the slightest bit of interest in her.

Oh, Lord, everyone wanted her to leave London.

Everyone but Laurel and Aunt Agatha that is.

Desperately, Harriet tried to think of a way to use that to her advantage. There simply had to be a way to stay in London. If she was forced to return to the country, her dreams of finding what Laurel had found with Royce would shrivel and die beneath the weight of horrid conversations about fertilizers and the like.

No, she needed to remain in London.

Whatever the cost.

Lord, he despised the city.

Steven pulled back on the reins and the well-matched bays came to a halt like the perfectly trained carriage horses they were. Of course, he'd expect nothing less for the bloody fortune he'd paid for them.

Alighting from his newly purchased tilbury, Steven paused to brush off his jacket. While the dashing open carriage was a pleasure to drive in the country, it left one somewhat unprotected from the soot and stench so pervasive here in London. The city's smells invoked memories of his days of folly after Royce's marriage to Laurel. Steven winced as he thought of the depths of his debauchery during that first year after his best friend's marriage. All the women, liquor, and gambling had done little to ease his guilt over having fallen in love with Royce's wife. It was only after he'd sobered enough to spend time with Laurel again that he'd realized that his feelings for her had mellowed into deep affection. The guilt was finally assuaged, he'd retreated to the country to reclaim his sense of honor . . . and he'd been doing a fine job of it until this little mess had occurred.

Indeed, he'd been perfectly content, nay, joyful even at his country estate. All the repairs were progressing splendidly, and the cottages he was building only added to the appeal of his property. When the hunting lodge, the bathing house, and the fishing cottage were completed, he was positive they would only enhance his enjoyment of his private sanctuary.

Which is precisely why he hated every blasted minute

he had to spend away from his home . . . especially when it involved coming into town.

Yet, he'd been left with little choice when his landscape architect, John Nash, the premier arborist in all of England, had informed him that Mr. Tyler, Steven's solicitor, had been unable to honor his marker for payment. Though embarrassed, Nash had informed Steven that he couldn't progress on his design for the grounds without payment.

Stunned, Steven had ordered his carriage brought around and headed into town to straighten out the matter. He'd gone to Tyler's place of business only to be informed that Tyler was ill and had remained at home. Sick or not, Tyler was going to provide some sort of explanation for the blunder he'd made in turning away Steven's marker. After all, Steven knew his financial status was secure. Tyler was bloody well going to set things aright . . . and issue a formal apology to Nash for the mistake.

Steven secured the reins to the post in front of Tyler's home and took the steps two at a time to reach the dark wooden door on the well-maintained brownstone. His knock was answered promptly, and he was shown into Tyler's parlor. Tapping his fingers against the windowpane, Steven waited impatiently.

A loud sneeze heralded Tyler's arrival. Bleary-eyed and pale, Tyler looked as miserable as he sounded. "Good day, my l—l—l . . ." Another sneeze punctuated the greeting. ". . . my lord."

Steven might have felt guilty at dragging the fellow from his bed if he weren't so blasted annoyed. Instead, Steven waved Tyler into a nearby chair. "Sorry for the intrusion, sir, but the matter is of the utmost importance."

"Yes, yes, I know," Mr. Tyler assured him, pausing for

a moment to blow his nose. "I'd hoped to be well enough to call upon you and bring this matter to your attention."

Steven looked sharply at his solicitor. "What matter?"

A baffled expression crept over Mr. Tyler's countenance. "Why, your lack of finances, naturally, my lord."

"Lack of finances?" he repeated slowly, before shaking his head. "You've obviously made a mistake."

"I'm afraid that's not possible," Mr. Tyler advised him glumly. "After I received the notes of debit from your mother, I . . ."

"My mother?" Steven tried to grasp what his solicitor was saying. If the man were speaking a foreign language, he might have had an easier go of understanding him.

Mr. Tyler nodded once. "Her debts were exceedingly large and when combined with your own recent expenditures . . ." He trailed off, leaving the obvious conclusion unspoken.

"But I had more than adequate funds to cover my mother's jaunt through Europe along with repairing my estate," Steven protested.

"That's true, my lord . . . but then I doubt if you anticipated the sum of your mother's expenditures."

"Good God, man! How much could fripperies cost?" When Tyler mentioned the amount, Steven shook his head in denial, unable to get his mind around the sum. "I still don't understand how she could have gone through so much money," he murmured.

"That is a question only Lady Heath can answer."

Steven fisted his hands, fighting to hold onto his control. "How much is left?"

Tyler coughed into his handkerchief. "Lady Heath spent a fortune, my lord . . . your entire fortune."

Steven flinched as if he'd been struck, but he remained standing straight, unwilling to let his solicitor know how devastated he was at his sudden reversal of fortune.

"I loathe to be the bearer of even more unhappy tidings, my lord, but I feel it only right to inform you of the entire truth of the matter." Tyler hesitated a moment. "I've received a second set of markers due and owing, markers that cannot be covered."

"This can't be possible," he muttered, more to himself than to Tyler.

"I assure you it is, my lord," Mr. Tyler replied somberly. "And if you don't find a way in which to cover the additional markers, I fear you might face debtors' gaol."

As Steven stalked out onto the street, he wished he was at Minton's so he could pound out some of his frustrations. Mr. Tyler stood, wheezing, at the door, concern darkening his features, but Steven was too angry even to manage a farewell.

Bloody Hell. He was a damn pauper! No, he was worse; he was a debtor.

Grabbing hold of the reins, Steven vaulted into his carriage. How ironic that only moments before, he'd looked upon his conveyance with pride, noting the gleaming trim and smart horses; but now all he could see was yet another debt. A wave of anger toward his mother crashed over him, making Steven glad that she was still traveling back from the Continent. He needed to regain control of his anger before he saw her.

The thought of heading for his country estate, seeing all the work in progress and knowing that he could lose all he possessed, was unbearable. The last thing he needed right now was to see all he stood to lose. What he needed was to get royally drunk. Thinking it was the best idea he'd had all day, Steven headed for his club, determined to lose himself in brandy.

When he arrived outside the hallowed doors of White's Gentleman's Club, Steven tossed his reins to the footman and strode inside. As he entered the elegant rooms, he wondered if this would be the last time he'd be welcome, a thought that only strengthened his determination to get mindlessly inebriated.

Heading back to the rear of the smoking room, Steven spied his friend, Royce, comfortably ensconced in a leather chair, enjoying a cigar and brandy. "Steven!" Royce exclaimed, raising his hand. "What the devil are you doing back in town? I thought it would take a minor miracle to get you out of the country."

Steven shrugged, not wanting to get into all the nasty details. "Looks like you were mistaken."

"Come, join me," Royce bade as he gestured toward a nearby chair. "I'll welcome your company as you aren't female and irritable like my wife or two years old and demanding like my son," he added with a broad grin that belied his words.

Steve shook his head. "I fear I'm far worse company than either Laurel or Ryan could ever be."

Royce's brows lifted. "That bad?"

"Worse."

"Well, now I'm afraid I'll have to insist you join me. Misery loves company and all that rot." Royce straightened in his chair. "You can't toss out that bit and expect me to swallow my curiosity."

Torn between wanting to talk about his recent trouble

and wanting to keep the horrid news private, Steven remained standing. "I'd rather get drunk than talk."

Instead of being insulted, Royce tossed back his head with a laugh. "Now that's what I like to hear!" he exclaimed. "I thought you'd turned your estate into a monastery and given up all earthly pleasures." He pointed to the chair across from him. "Now plant your arse there and tell me what brought on this return of the old Steven."

"The old Steven?"

"Yes, you remember him, don't you?" Royce asked with a grin. "He was the amusing fellow who used to set the tongues of the ton wagging with his exploits. Hell, Steven, your reputation for excess in all things is legendary." He slanted up one eyebrow. "And, I'll be the first to tell you, you were a hell of a lot more enjoyable to be around than when you left London behind and lived your monkish existence in the country."

"It was hardly monkish," Steven protested.

"When was the last time you got drunk?"

He couldn't remember. "Lord, I have become a monk!" Lifting his hand, he ordered a decanter of brandy before taking his seat. "Luckily I'm just in the mood to correct that failing." When the servant set the brandy down next to him, Steven refilled Royce's glass as well as pouring himself a full snifter. Taking a long draw on the amber liquid, Steven savored the taste. "I'm going to miss the taste of fine brandy."

"What are you talking about?"

"I'm going to have to give up these little pleasures," Steven admitted, anger simmering inside of him. "I'm bloody destitute."

"What?"

"On my way to debtors' gaol in the very near future if I don't sell off my entire estate." He tipped his glass toward Royce. "Lovely little turn of events, isn't it?"

"What the devil happened?"

With anger coloring his voice, Steven poured out the entire confusing chain of events. ". . . so as you can see, I'm in debt with no means of repaying the creditors without bankrupting myself."

"Hardly," Royce said, rejecting Steven's assertion. "True, you're in a bit of a rough patch, but you're hardly going to be hauled off to gaol or be forced into selling your home." He set his glass down upon the table. "I'll cover your markers."

"I'm not taking your money, Royce," Steven retorted, his gut twisting at the thought. It was bad enough to admit to his financial ruin; there was no way Steven would give up his honor by accepting financial assistance from his friend.

"If you're worrying about paying me back, don't. It wouldn't be a loan, but rather a gift." He waved dismissively. "Let's call it repayment for your help with Laurel." As Steven opened his mouth to protest, Royce cut him off. "I know what you're going to say," he began. "And while I understand that you only spent time with Laurel to torment me and make me jealous, well, it worked. I can hardly complain about your methods when the results were so overwhelmingly satisfactory; so I do indeed owe you."

"If you think I'm going to sit here while you insult me, you're sadly mistaken," Steven ground out as he slammed his brandy glass down onto the table.

"Insult you?"

"Absolutely." Steven leaned forward. "It's my mess; I can figure out a way to clean it up myself."

Lifting both hands, Royce grinned. "Didn't mean to insult you, Steven." He took a sip of his brandy. "If you insist on keeping hold of your debt, I suppose there's only one thing to be done." He pointed the tip of his cigar at Steven. "You, my friend, have got to catch yourself an heiress."

Steven groaned at the suggestion.

"What's wrong with the idea?" Royce leaned forward, resting his elbows upon his knees. "It's time you marry and secure an heir anyway, so why not fulfill all your needs in one fell swoop?"

"Because it's so . . . so . . ."

"Wise?"

"Repulsive," Steven corrected his friend. "I've already explained to you about this mess my mother has caused. The last thing I need is another female muddling up my life."

"You know what your problem is, Steven? You've been locked away at that country estate too long." Royce settled back in his chair, a broad smile upon his face. "You've obviously forgotten what delightful creatures females can be."

"Oh, I'll admit they're delightful, in certain circumstances. But marriage?" Steven lifted his glass to Royce. "I shall leave that to you."

Royce's expression sobered as he leaned forward, glancing around to ensure their privacy. "Is your reluctance toward marriage because of your feelings for Laurel?"

"Absolutely not," Steven assured his friend. "I long ago realized that what I feel for your wife is nothing more than the deep affection of friendship." He lifted a shoulder. "My reluctance to wed is the dread I feel every time I imagine shackling myself to one woman."

"Personally, I find marriage suits me perfectly."

"Perhaps, but even you, my friend, who wed for love often find yourself on the outs with your wife," Steven pointed out.

Royce grinned widely. "Arguments serve to spice up our wedded bliss. At least I'm never bored."

"Now there's an inducement to wed," Steven drawled.

"Then marry one of those young chits who won't murmur a cross word."

Steven shivered at the thought. "And be followed about by a brainless twit? No thank you."

"Quite honestly, Steven," Royce began, leaning back in his chair and propping a booted foot against the table, "I don't see where you have much choice."

Blast and damn, but Royce was right. If he was going to save his estate, retain his honor, he needed to find an heiress and wed her before his financial ruin came to light. As distasteful as he might find the idea, he was willing to do whatever it took to preserve his honor and name. "You're right," he finally ground out.

"Of course I am. You find a wealthy wife and your future will be secure." Royce laughed softly. "In fact, I think we should make a game of it."

"Pardon me?"

"You heard me. Remember how you challenged me to apply my theory that finding a proper bride was like running a fox to ground?"

"I remember," Steven retorted with a chuckle. "Know your quarry, scent her, then give chase until she wearies, and you catch your bride."

"Precisely." Royce tapped his finger against the side of his glass. "Well, the chase invigorated me, and I strongly recommend you enjoy the hunt as well."

For the first time since learning of his empty coffers, Steven laughed. "But that theory is ridiculous!"

"Don't scoff at it, Steven. After all, you can't argue with its success." Before Steven could protest, Royce lifted his hands. "I know that there were areas of the theory that needed to be tuned and shifted, but overall, it was a sound application of logic."

"If I remember correctly, your courtship didn't go nearly that smoothly."

"Ah, yes, but I learned quite a bit along the way, and I think this time we could perfect the hunt." Royce's eyes gleamed brightly. "So, what do you say?"

Steven couldn't help but smile at Royce's unabashed enthusiasm and arrogance. Still, what did he have to lose? Royce was correct that an heiress was the perfect solution to his current problems, and it was time for Steven to secure an heir. So, why not kill two birds with one stone? Instead of fuming over his fate, why not accept it? If he agreed to Royce's scheme, Lord knows, it would be overwhelmingly entertaining at the very least. Besides, if he used logic to find an heiress, it might be far quicker than any formal courtship, and he could leave this blasted town behind. The way he saw it, he could approach the matter of finding an heiress in one of two ways: gloom and doom or as a lark—continuation of Royce's half-baked theory.

Put that way, there really was no choice.

"I'm in."

Chapter Two

❧

*H*arriet's chances of being asked to dance were decreasing by the minute.

"Harriet, dear, Lady Whimple just asked how your embroidery was progressing," Aunt Hilda said as she pulled Harriet's attention from the lovely swirl of dancers.

Forcing a smile upon her face, Harriet turned toward her maidenly aunt and equally elderly companion, Lady Whimple. "I'm quite pleased with it," she murmured vaguely, trying to inject enthusiasm into her response. "The thread you gave me for the flowers is such a vivid addition to the piece."

A pleased expression smoothed Lady Whimple's lined cheeks. "I'm so glad to be of assistance. Nothing would delight me more than if you would join your aunts for our weekly visits."

Images of a life filled with embroidery gatherings and stilted conversation flashed before her eyes in alarming clarity. Harriet shot to her feet, needing to get as far away from that future as possible.

"Is anything wrong, dear?" asked Aunt Hilda.

Regaining her composure, Harriet shook her head. "No, Aunt Hilda. I'm merely parched."

Aunt Hilda peered around the room. "There's no need to fetch your own punch, Harriet. A waiter should be along soon with refreshments."

Leaving her stranded in her chair, conversing with her dear, sweet elderly aunt. Unacceptable, Harriet decided firmly. "While I'm quite certain you're correct, I find myself far too thirsty to wait even for a moment." Knowing her aunt well, Harriet snapped open her fan, and began waving it briskly. "It's a bit warm in here this evening. I wonder that the Van Housands haven't opened the doors to the veranda as of yet."

Alarm filled Aunt Hilda's gaze as she gasped and clutched her kerchief to her chest. "Open the doors? Good heavens, child, that would never do." Turning toward Lady Whimple, Aunt Hilda began her rant on the dangers of exposing oneself to the chill of night air . . . just as Harriet had predicted she would.

"If you'll excuse me," Harriet murmured softly, though she knew her aunt, caught up in her diatribe, probably didn't even hear her. Smiling to herself, Harriet made her way along the edge of the ballroom toward the parlor where refreshments were being served. She would fetch a glass of lemonade to fortify herself, then she would find the most prominent position in the room and stand there with her still-unmarked dance card in clear view.

Glancing down at the crisp card, Harriet wondered if

perhaps it might be better if she added a few names. After all, it wouldn't do to appear so . . . well, so desperate. Indeed, it would be far better for a gentleman to believe he'd been fortunate to find a spot upon her dance card. Satisfied with her decision, Harriet began her search for a writing implement. But her footsteps faltered as the most glorious man strode into the ballroom.

Steven Morris, Earl of Heath.

A flush warmed her as she beheld his handsome form standing beside Royce. Though she hadn't seen Lord Heath in years, she'd not forgotten how he'd made her heart flutter. From the first moment she'd met him during Royce's unconventional courtship of Laurel, Harriet had been drawn to him. Yet he'd been too enamored of Laurel even to notice her. Even after Laurel's marriage, when Lord Heath had slipped beyond the pale, she'd looked for him at every event, feeling utterly foolish for becoming breathless whenever he stepped into a room. It stunned her that even now, with years between them, all those emotions rushed back over her, making her feel almost giddy.

Eager to renew their acquaintance, Harriet stepped forward. "Lord Heath," she began, trying not to sound overly familiar. "How delightful to see you again."

Lord Heath's smile began slowly, then bloomed into a gloriously warm grin. "Miss Nash." Lifting her hand, he pressed a kiss upon her glove-encased fingers. "The pleasure is all mine." He squeezed her hand before releasing it.

"I haven't seen you for many years now, my l-l-ord." Silently, Harriet cursed herself for having stammered.

"Business on my estates has kept me away from town."

"Oh." Harriet could have kicked herself for her uninspired response. Oh? Couldn't she have replied with a little more spirit?

Luckily Royce's greeting saved her from any additional response. "Good evening, Harriet. You're looking most fetching this evening."

"Thank you, my lord," she returned warmly. She'd grown to love Laurel's husband over the years.

As the quartet sounded the start of the next quadrille, Royce nudged Lord Heath. "Why don't you ask Harriet to dance, Steven? It will be a wonderful way to announce your return into town." Royce glanced at her, before smiling ruefully. "Not to mention the pleasure of enjoying such a wonderful partner."

"Naturally," Harriet replied dryly, taking little liking to being an afterthought.

"If Miss Nash is free," began Lord Heath as he reached for her humiliatingly empty dance card.

Snatching back the card before he could see it, Harriet smiled brightly. "I believe this dance is indeed available," she murmured casually as if she'd been dancing the entire evening and he'd been lucky to find an open dance.

"I am most fortunate then." Proffering his arm, Lord Heath led her out onto the dance floor.

And for Harriet, the night became magic.

As she stepped onto the same dance floor that she'd gazed at longingly all evening, praying for someone to ask her to join the elegantly clad couples, Harriet struggled to maintain her composure. "When did you arrive in town, my lord?"

"Yesterday." Lord Heath gifted her with another of his dizzying smiles. "And what of you? As I recall, your family resides in Essex."

The knowledge that he remembered that detail after all these years thrilled her. "Though my parents still live there, I have remained here in town with my aunts, Lady Agatha Dalrymple and Lady Hilda Amherst."

"Remained? Since Royce and Laurel wed?"

Cocking her head to the side, Harriet gazed up into Steven's handsome face. "Naturally. Don't you remember seeing me at all those functions after their wedding?"

A corner of his mouth tipped upward. "My dear Miss Nash, how could you believe otherwise?"

"You handle your missteps quite nicely, my lord," she remarked, knowing perfectly well that he obviously hadn't noticed her at all . . . and trying to ignore the spark of hurt that realization caused.

"Ah, but you mistake me, Miss Nash," he murmured softly, tucking her in closer until her skirt flowed around his legs. "I never forget a lady."

The well-practiced line set her heart pounding. "Your reputation testifies to that claim, Lord Heath."

"Been listening to gossip, Miss Nash?" he asked slyly as he bent toward her. "I didn't think well-mannered ladies such as yourself stooped to such levels."

The brush of his warm breath made her shiver. "I don't gossip, my lord," she answered.

"Then how do you know of my reputation?"

"I'm hardly blind, my lord."

His teeth flashed brilliantly as he grinned down at her. "Don't tell me I was so obvious before? Shame on me." Bending his head, he brushed his cheek against hers as he whispered in her ear. "I shall have to take more care in the future."

If his arm hadn't been wrapped around her waist, Harriet was quite certain she would have melted into a pool of liquid heat right onto Lord Heath's gleaming Hessians. Memories of how often she'd sat next to her aunts and their elderly friends and watched as Lord Heath danced with one lady after another filled her thoughts. Never had she imagined that she'd be the one in his arms, having him focus his charm and warmth upon her.

"Then again," he began conversationally as he straightened to look into her eyes, "I doubt anyone would dare whisper a word about Miss Harriet Nash behaving in a less than proper manner. If my memory serves correctly, you are the epitome of a refined lady." As the music swelled to its final crescendo, Lord Heath spun her around in a series of dizzying moves, making her feel even more light-headed than before. The final note reverberated upon the violin strings as he pulled her up against him and gazed into her eyes. "All the matrons are undoubtedly wondering what you're doing with such a dastardly fellow as myself." He held her against him for one more moment before stepping back to press a kiss onto her fingers. "You might want to become more discriminating about your escorts in the future, Miss Nash."

Was she mistaken, or was he flirting with her? "I assure you, my lord, I am most capable of caring for my reputation."

"I'm quite certain you believe that, Miss Nash," he said as he straightened, still retaining a hold upon her hand. "But what you fail to comprehend is just how devious we gentlemen can be when it comes to enticing a lovely young lady such as yourself." The words had no sooner left his mouth, than he lifted her hand and pressed a soft kiss into the palm of her hand.

A gasp broke from Harriet as she jerked back her hand without conscious thought . . . and cursed her own actions a moment later. Lord Heath was grinning at her. He was teasing her. First flirting, then teasing. What on earth could he be up to?

"I warned you we were quick." Without another word, he tucked his hand under her elbow and escorted her off the dance floor.

Loath to lose his enticing company, she was about to ask him to escort her to the refreshments when her aunt Hilda pounced upon them.

"I'm feeling a bit fatigued, Harriet," she stated in firm tones. "I think it's time for us to leave."

Flushing slightly at her aunt's rudeness, Harriet tried to smooth over the awkward moment. "Of course, Aunt Hilda, but first may I present you to my escort?" Without awaiting her aunt's response, she turned toward Lord Heath. "Aunt Hilda, this is Steven Morris, Earl of Heath. He is a dear friend of Lord Tewksbury." She gestured toward Lord Heath. "My lord, may I present my aunt, Miss Hilda Amherst."

Lord Heath held out his hand. When Aunt Hilda slipped her gloved fingers onto his, Lord Heath bent over her hand in proper fashion, his blond hair gleaming in the candlelight. "It is an honor, my lady."

"Most gracious of you to say, my lord," Aunt Hilda said stiffly. As soon as he straightened, she withdrew her proffered hand and looked pointedly at Harriet. "Bid Lord Heath farewell, my dear, so we might be off."

Her aunt's behavior puzzled Harriet. "Certainly," she murmured, before offering a smile to Lord Heath. "Thank you for the dance, my lord. It was truly an enjoyable experience." One that left her flustered, for Harriet wasn't used to being flirted with or teased; if she was honest with herself she'd have to admit she quite liked the experience.

"It is I who should thank you, Miss Nash," he murmured, with a wicked glint in his blue eyes. "Perhaps I should leave as well, for I doubt I shall be able to find so charming a dance partner." A corner of his mouth slanted upward. "I fear you've quite ruined me."

A laugh that sounded distressingly like a giggle escaped Harriet. Dear Lord, she needed to leave before she began to simper over the man! "If you fear for your good name, Lord Heath, I suppose it only fair to warn you that I shall be at Almack's tomorrow," she murmured teasingly.

"Then I shall toss my reputation to the wind and be there as well to claim another dance."

"You are a brave soul, my lord," she retorted with a laugh. "'Til Wednesday, my lord."

Lord Heath pressed a hand to his chest. "I shall spend the next two days devising a way to get the patronesses of Almack's to allow a waltz."

The image of Lord Heath sweeping her into his arms and whirling her around Almack's floor made her want to shout for joy in a manner completely unfitting for a lady. She settled instead for a smile. "How perfectly scandalous, my lord."

"Indeed it is," sniffed Lady Hilda. "Not that you will have any luck persuading the ladies to permit a waltz, but even if you did, my niece would not be allowed to dance in such a bold manner."

"Aunt Hilda!"

Lord Heath ignored her shocked gasp as he laughed out loud. "Bold, perhaps, but highly entertaining, Lady Amherst." Leaning forward, he smiled rakishly at Aunt Hilda. "Perhaps I'll arrange for Almack's to play two waltzes, and I'll save the second one for you. That way you can see for yourself how enjoyable it is to waltz."

A corner of Aunt Hilda's mouth twitched. "You have a clever tongue, my lord."

"It matches my wit quite well," he countered.

"And your arrogance," Aunt Hilda returned, unable to hold back a laugh.

Harriet couldn't believe that Lord Heath had managed to draw laughter from her dour aunt.

"Come along now, Harriet, before this young rapscallion manages to wrangle an invitation to call upon us."

Lord Heath's head tilted to the right. "Is there a possibility of that happening?"

"Yes."

"No."

Frustrated, Harriet looked at her aunt. "I would like to extend an invitation to Lord Heath."

"I understand that, dear, but unfortunately, we haven't a spare moment over the next few days." Before Harriet could murmur another word of protest, Aunt Hilda grasped her arm and began to steer her toward the door. "Good eve, my lord."

"I shall look forward to your company on Wednesday," Harriet called over her shoulder, uncaring if anyone found her overly brazen.

Lord Heath lifted his hand in a farewell salute. "As shall I."

Facing forward, Harriet allowed her aunt to pull her

from the ballroom. And to think that she'd begun to give up hope of ever finding a gentleman she might like to marry.

Steven couldn't hide his grin as he watched Miss Nash being virtually dragged from the room by her dragon of an aunt. And to think he'd believed it would be hard to find someone he'd be even remotely interested in wedding.

As he made his way back to Royce, Steven imagined how neatly his life would fall into place. He'd wed the charming Miss Nash as quickly as possible, then leave this dreadful town and head back to his country estate with his new bride in tow. Together, they could use her fortune and build a wonderful life for themselves.

"Good God, Steven!" Royce exclaimed, his eyes narrowed. "What were you thinking? You don't dance with a lady like that."

"Like what?"

Royce looked like he wanted to burst. "Like you would with a mistress when alone in your rooms!"

Since the memory of Harriet's lithe body pressed against his chest was still fresh in his mind, Steven gave Royce's admonishment credence. "Perhaps I was a bit intimate with her."

"There's no perhaps about it," Royce ground out. "Harriet is a proper lady . . . who just happens to be my wife's best friend."

"She's also a delectable armful." As Royce's features grew taut, Steven raised his hands, warding off his friend's anger. "But your point is well taken, Royce. Guess my old habits kicked in. However, in the future, I shall be more respectful of the place."

His reassurance calmed Royce. "That's all I ask."

"Besides, I owe you for this," Steven said, clasping a hand upon Royce's shoulder. "She is perfect."

Royce nodded easily. "She is charming in her own unique sort of way, isn't she?"

"Indeed," Steven agreed, releasing his hold upon his friend. "She is more than I'd hoped for."

A frown lowered Royce's brow. "What are you talking about?"

"I'm speaking of the purpose for which we came to this party—to find an heiress."

"You think Harriet is an heiress?"

Royce's question raised Steven's wariness. "Of course. You urged me to dance with her, after all."

"And I said I'd introduce you to the most eligible heiresses." For a moment, Royce closed his eyes and rubbed at his forehead. Sighing, he finally met Steven's gaze again. "I'm afraid I misled you, Steven. Harriet isn't an heiress. While she has a modest portion settled upon her, it isn't even close to the kind of monies you need to replenish your coffers."

"But you urged me to dance with her," he reminded Royce.

"I only did so because she's Laurel's dear friend, not because she's an heiress." Royce's expression grew heavy with regret. "I thought you knew."

"No, I didn't." Odd how he could feel a sense of loss for a brief fantasy. It wasn't as if he were one of those poppycock-headed dandies who imagined himself in love at a glance; rather he'd found it unbelievably easy to imagine Harriet fitting into his life.

Sighing, Steven pushed aside his regret and focused

upon the task at hand—finding himself an heiress. "Very well then, Royce," he began, straightening his shoulders, "whom shall you introduce me to first?"

"That's the spirit." Royce scanned the room, before allowing his gaze to rest upon a blonde beauty standing near the garden door. "I believe you'd enjoy meeting Lady Arabella Pinchley. She's the daughter of the Duke of Arlington and comes with a very generous portion."

Steven stood firm. "What's wrong with her?"

"Wrong with her? Nothing."

"She is beautiful, wealthy, and titled, so why isn't she surrounded by gentlemen vying for her hand?"

Royce shifted beneath Steven's searching gaze. "Perhaps some gentlemen find her a bit . . . vapid."

"Wonderful," Steven said dryly. Life was certainly full of wicked twists these days. Why couldn't Harriet have been the one who glittered with riches? Harriet. Good, solid, sensible name. But no; he wasn't that lucky. Instead he found himself having to approach Lady Arabella Pinchley, the vapid daughter of a duke. Arabella. Lord, even her name sounded like a frothy bit of nothing.

"Come on now." Royce gave Steven an affectionate slap on the back. "Remember you need to look upon this as a game and Lady Arabella merely another player."

Steven raised an eyebrow. "Do you suppose she even knows how to play games?"

Wincing slightly, Royce gave Steven an apologetic smile. "Wouldn't care to wager on that one, my friend, but unfortunately you don't have much choice. Believe it or not, Lady Arabella is the best of the lot."

"What a comforting thought." Tugging down on his

waistcoat, Steven took a deep breath. "Let's get this over with."

"That's hardly a gaming attitude," Royce reprimanded him lightly.

"Tally-ho."

Royce grinned. "Now, that's the spirit!"

Yes, Royce is right; that is the spirit, Steven thought to himself. "Lead onward, Royce."

"I do believe this is going to be most entertaining," Royce murmured, before heading across the ballroom.

Steven paused for a moment. Like any well-played game, to the victor go the spoils.

Here's to hoping Lady Arabella wasn't spoiled as well.

Chapter Three

~

"Harriet, dear, it is so wonderful of you to help me out like this," said Lady Whimple as she handed Harriet another jumble of embroidery threads. "My eyesight isn't what it used to be, and I have a difficult time sorting out the colors." She peered over the rim of her spectacles. "I fear I've made a mess of it."

"Nothing that can't be undone," Harriet assured her aunt's friend as she set to untangling the threads.

Lady Whimple reached out to pat Harriet's arm. "You are such a good girl."

"Thank you," she replied, trying not to wince at the sentiment. After all, there was no denying she was a 'good girl'; just this morning, she'd already visited with Lady Hampton to help her plan her next dinner party, helped Lady Hammersmith choose fabrics for her new clothes, and visited with Lady Howard, who was recovering from a dreadful cold. All contemporaries of her aunts, none of the ladies was a day under sixty, but Harriet truly enjoyed their company. She'd spent nearly every day of the past few years the same way and thought her time with these elderly women well spent.

Only lately, she'd begun to chafe under the duties of a 'good girl'; she'd begun to yearn for more.

And last night, she'd found just what she wanted. Steven Morris, Earl of Heath.

Working on the knotted threads, Harriet hoped that her task would go quickly, so she could be off to Laurel's house. It was her final stop of the busy day, and Harriet couldn't wait to tell Laurel about her dance with Steven.

"I really do appreciate this," Lady Whimple said again.

Harriet tucked away her thoughts and refocused on the elderly lady beside her. "It is my pleasure," she murmured, before smiling at her companion. "Last week you were telling me about a romance brewing between your grandson and Lady Hampton's granddaughter. Will I be hearing an announcement soon?"

Lady Whimple's eyes began to sparkle. "I believe you might."

Settling back in her chair, Harriet prepared to enjoy her afternoon chat with Lady Whimple. "You must bring me up to date," she said, still working on the thread. "And don't leave out any tiny detail. You know I love to hear about romance."

"I'm telling you, Laurel, I've never seen Aunt Hilda behave so rudely." Harriet began to pace in front of the fireplace in the Van Cleef's parlor. She'd left Lady Whimple to her late-afternoon nap and come to see Laurel straightaway. "And when I tried to talk to her about her behavior in the carriage, she simply closed her eyes and told me she was far too fatigued to discuss the matter."

"Why didn't you wait to speak with her this morning?"

"I had planned on doing just that, but she never came down for her morning repast, and I had an early meeting with Lady Hampton." Harriet fiddled with a ribbon dangling from the front of her high-necked bodice. "It's almost as if Aunt Hilda's avoiding me."

"It sounds as if there is no 'almost' about it," Laurel pronounced. "Did Steven behave in a forward manner that would put off Aunt Hilda?"

"Perhaps." She couldn't hold back a smile.

Laurel's brows lifted. "Do I detect a note of interest?"

"More than a note," Harriet admitted, feeling her cheeks warm.

"Oh, Harriet."

Hearing the concerned note in Laurel's voice, Harriet stopped her pacing to stare down at her friend. "You don't approve?"

"Steven isn't the sort of gentleman I would have chosen for you."

Laurel's admission stunned Harriet. "Why ever not? I thought the two of you were friends."

"We were . . . we are," she corrected herself. "It's just that Steven has become somewhat of a . . ."

"Rake?" Harriet interjected when Laurel stammered into silence.

"Exactly."

Harriet shrugged lightly. "I'm well aware of his reputation, but it doesn't worry me. Some of the best husbands are former rogues." She gave Laurel a pointed look. "Yours included."

"That's true," Laurel conceded. "However, I believe Steven's past might be even more colorful than Royce's ever was."

"Why do I care? I'm interested in his future, not his past."

"But his past can determine his future."

Taking a seat across from Laurel, Harriet leaned forward. "Very well then, Laurel, let's look at Steven's past," she began earnestly. "He helped you when Royce was behaving poorly. He was the perfect gentleman."

"Who then turned into the perfect rake," Laurel reminded Harriet. "You can't forget his outrageous behavior—how he enticed Lady Anna to lift her skirts past her knees when she danced at Almack's or how he made a wager with Lady Emily that if he could juggle three oranges she would grant him a kiss."

"I'm perfectly aware that stories of his scandals abound, but that doesn't take away from the fact that Steven is, underneath it all, a fine gentleman who helped you out in your hour of need," Harriet finished with dramatic flair.

"No, I suppose it doesn't." Laurel's eyes darkened as she looked solemnly at Harriet. "Promise me you'll be careful."

"I promise." Slipping onto her knees, Harriet reached to clasp her friend's hands. "I just want to find some of the happiness you've found with Royce. You've inspired me to seek out my perfect match." She rose to her feet. "And for the first time, I truly believe I'll be able to find him."

"Lucky, lucky Steven," murmured Laurel.

Harriet merely smiled. No, lucky, lucky me, she corrected silently, feeling like a giddy schoolgirl.

"If you're determined to catch Steven's notice, we need to decide upon your outfit tonight. After all, we want all eyes trained upon you." Laurel tapped her finger against her chin before finally snapping her fingers. "I have just the thing. You should wear your white organza and I'll lend you my embroidered wrap and the Tewksbury sapphires."

"I couldn't . . ."

"Nonsense," pronounced Laurel, cutting off Harriet's protest. "Now help hoist me out of this chair, and we'll go raid my armoire."

Before Harriet could even cup her friend's elbow, Laurel stood and headed from the room at a pace that belied her advanced pregnancy. "Hoist, indeed." Smiling, Harriet followed Laurel from the room.

Handing his overcoat and hat to the butler, Royce caught a glimpse of blue silk as it disappeared along the upstairs corridor. "Is my wife resting?"

"No, your grace," murmured Harton. "I believe she is entertaining Miss Nash at the moment."

"Good God." Royce gestured frantically at Steven. "Give Harton your outerwear and let's head to my study."

"What's the hurry?"

"None . . . if you're prepared to explain why you won't be asking for a waltz this evening," Royce countered.

Swiftly, Steven stripped off his coat and hat, then followed Royce down the hallway into the large, wood-paneled room. "I didn't realize that Miss Nash would be here," Steven said to Royce the minute he closed the door to the study.

"Neither did I." Royce poured them both a brandy and retrieved two cigars from his humidor. "If I'd known, I would have suggested we go to your town house." Passing off the drink and cigar, Royce settled into an oversize leather chair. "So how are you going to handle your problem with Harriet?"

Steven lifted a shoulder. "I'll simply inform her that the patronesses won't allow a waltz." Coming up with an excuse was easy; the real problem lay in the fact that Steven wanted to waltz with Harriet. He wanted to pull her into his arms, mold her body against his, brush his cheek against the softness of her hair, and spin her until they were both dizzy with desire.

Shaking his head, Royce tipped his cigar toward Steven. "I have to hand it to you, Steven; you're even better at the game than I was."

"I've applied myself most diligently to pleasurable pursuits; getting myself out of unfortunate predicaments is not new to me," Steven returned, taking a sip of his brandy.

"And was it these unfortunate predicaments that drove you to the country?"

"Not at all. I simply grew bored with the game." Steven sipped at his brandy. "You understand that, Royce; otherwise, you wouldn't be so blasted happy with marriage."

"True enough," Royce murmured, a corner of his mouth tilting upward. "Guess it happens to the best of us."

"Indeed it does. My only wish is that I can find an heiress more palatable than the dreadful Lady Arabella."

"Wishes only count when you're two." Royce blew out a stream of smoke. "I take it you found the Lady Arabella less than enchanting?"

"I'd say. All evening I tried to entice her into actually conversing with me, but the longest string of words I managed to pull out of her was 'thank you, my lord.'" He rolled his eyes. "Not exactly scintillating conversation."

Royce sipped his brandy. "I believe I mentioned that failing to you, Steven, but as I said before, she's the best of the bunch."

Lord, if he believed that, then he'd really be doomed. Refusing to accept Royce's opinion as gospel, Steven rose to his feet and went to Royce's desk. "Perhaps you're mistaken and some of the other heiresses will hold more appeal."

Royce looked doubtful, but Steven simply couldn't believe that Lady Arabella was the best the ton had to offer. "Why don't you let me be the judge of this matter?" Retrieving paper and quill, he gazed expectantly at Royce. "Why don't you give me the names of the heiresses available on the social market this season, and I'll make a list?"

Royce shrugged. "Then you should put Lady Arabella on the top, along with your thoughts on her. It will ensure that you have a complete list."

Steven laughed at the thought of listing the ladies' attributes or lack thereof. "Why don't I just make two columns and list what I like and don't like about each heiress?"

"Even better."

"I was jesting, Royce."

"Well, I wasn't. What's rule number one in fox hunting? Know your quarry." Gesturing toward the sheet, Royce continued, "Making a list of heiresses, including the pluses and minuses about each one, will narrow the field and help you pinpoint your quarry."

In for a penny, in for a pound, Steven decided, forcing his reservations aside. Making three columns on the sheet, he then wrote Lady Arabella's name in the far left-hand column. In the second one, he added the words "dull-witted, stiff, pompous" before moving on to the third column. There, he hesitated. "I don't know what to add to the positive attributes column."

"How about wealthy?"

"If this is a list of heiresses only, then all of the ladies would have that attribute."

"True." Sipping at his brandy, Royce fell silent for a moment. "How about attractive?"

"As long as you don't try to speak with her," muttered Steven. But as soon as the words left his mouth, he realized he wasn't being fair. Compromising somewhat, he wrote "attractive if silent" in the positive attributes column. "Done. Why don't you give me the names of the others, and I'll add them to this sheet?"

Dutifully, Royce began to rattle off names. "Lady Portia Hammelson—short in stature and quite the chatterbox. Lady Margaret Brendan—pleasant enough in a poorly lit room. Lady . . ."

Raising his hands, Steven stopped Royce midlist. "I'd prefer if you simply gave me their names and allowed me to form my own opinions."

Royce drained his brandy glass before listing five more names. ". . . and those are the only ladies wealthy enough to provide you with the funds you require."

"How the devil do you come by this knowledge?"

"Easy," he returned with a grin. "I asked my solicitor to compile a list of wealthy heiresses." Royce pointed his cigar at Steven. "I thought I'd help you in the first step toward knowing your quarry. Doing your research on each of these ladies will ensure that you don't waste your efforts on someone who won't suit your financial needs."

"Like Harriet," Steven murmured.

"Exactly."

Steven studied the list, trying to ignore the feeling that he was selling himself. It wasn't as if he was doing something that hadn't been done for generations. Indeed, it was a time-honored tradition for titles to seek fortunes. Steeling himself for what he must do in order to protect his home and family, Steven asked Royce, "Might you introduce me to Lady Portia this evening if she is at Almack's?"

"Steven, my old friend," Royce began with a huge grin, "I wouldn't miss it for the world."

"Are you certain you wouldn't prefer to sit?" asked Aunt Hilda for what must have been the hundredth time.

"Positive." It was perfectly clear to Harriet that her aunt was planning on staying by her side all evening.

Aunt Hilda gave a long-suffering sigh. "Then you leave me with no choice but to stand here with you until my tired bones begin to ache."

"Stop being such an old ninnyhammer," chided Aunt Agatha, giving Hilda a sharp elbow. "You are just bound and determined to completely spoil this evening, aren't you?"

"Why, I never . . ."

But Aunt Agatha cut off Aunt Hilda's sputterings. "You most certainly did! The entire ride here we heard nothing but how tired you were and what an imposition it was that you had to come to Almack's when you knew perfectly well that I could easily escort Harriet by myself."

"You?" Aunt Hilda sniffed with disdain. "You're so eager to marry the girl off that you'd probably wish some rake well as he swept our dear innocent off into the garden."

Unwilling to have her aunts sour her evening, Harriet lifted both of her hands. "Enough! Good heavens, the way you two carry on, it makes me wonder as to your age." She drew in a calming breath and lowered her voice. "Aunt Hilda, you are incorrect about Aunt Agatha. She has escorted me to many an evening and is a most conscientious guardian."

Aunt Agatha gave a satisfied sniff. "Thank you, my dear."

"However, you are incorrect as well, Aunt Agatha, for Aunt Hilda only made one remark about her desire to remain at home this evening."

"Thank you, Harriet," said Aunt Hilda as she glared at her sister. "I'm so pleased to see that you inherited my good sense . . . unlike someone else I could mention."

"Please, Aunt Hilda, I really wish that you would refrain from . . ." But Harriet could no more finish her thought than stand on her head. Steven Morris had entered the room.

"Harriet?"

Aunt Agatha's question snapped Harriet from her daze. Blinking twice, she struggled to regain her composure. "Forgive me, Aunt Agatha. I lost track of my thoughts."

Perceptive as ever, Aunt Agatha gave Steven a pointed look. "Lost track of them or merely was overwhelmed by new ones?"

There was no deceiving her clever aunt. Pressing a hand to her warming cheek, Harriet admitted, "I suppose I was distracted by Lord Heath's arrival."

Obviously intrigued, Aunt Agatha turned her full attention on Steven. "Lord Heath?" She squinted at him. "He must be Harold's son then."

"I'm uncertain," Harriet admitted. "I know him only as Royce's dearest friend."

"And the gentleman who wishes to waltz with you this evening," Aunt Hilda added coolly.

"Waltz?" Aunt Agatha rolled the word over her tongue like it was a rare and utterly delicious delicacy. "How positively scandalous."

Aunt Hilda gave her sister a stern look. "Why is it you can say the very phrase that I'm thinking, yet have it sound like a good thing?"

"One of my special talents, I suppose," Aunt Agatha said with a dismissive wave. "Now, do hush, Hilda, for I wish to hear more about this handsome Lord Heath."

"There's not more to tell," Harriet began. "I met him when Laurel and Royce were . . ." Her words trailed off and her breath caught in her throat as Steven turned his gaze upon her. Their eyes met across the room and, for Harriet, everything else faded away.

Finally, she thought, as she waited for him to approach

and claim her for a dance. He would hesitate for another moment, then he would . . .

. . . turn and walk away from her?

Harriet couldn't believe her eyes. Why would he turn away from her? She couldn't imagine a reason . . . unless he'd wanted to arrange for the waltz first! Relief flooded her at the thought. Of course! He'd promised to convince the patronesses of Almack's to permit a waltz. It was only natural that he wouldn't approach her until he'd succeeded in his quest.

With her smile firmly in place, Harriet settled back on her heels and watched the dancers. While she would prefer to keep her gaze fixed upon Steven, it wouldn't do to appear so forward. No, as always, she'd conduct herself as the sedate, proper lady she was . . .

. . . regardless of how it was beginning to chafe.

Bloody hell, Steven thought, as he turned away from Harriet. He felt like a perfect heel; no, he was a perfect heel! He'd caught her eye unexpectedly, but he'd have to have been blind not to see the expectant, eager expression upon her face. She'd been waiting for him.

And why not?

After all, he had promised to arrange for a waltz to be played simply to have the pleasure of holding her in his arms. Though he'd like nothing better than to fulfill that promise, he needed to remain focused upon his task of finding an heiress, or he stood to lose all. Later in the evening, he would seek out Harriet and inform her that he couldn't arrange for a waltz.

Steven tapped Royce upon the shoulder. "Would you mind introducing me to Lady Portia now?"

Royce grinned broadly. "Eager to find your bride?"

"No; I'm eager to be done with this business," Steven countered.

Slapping a companionable hand upon Steven's back, Royce led the way into the gaming room, finally coming to a stop next to a table where four ladies sat playing cards.

Before Royce could utter a word, the smallest of the women tossed down her cards. "You've bankrupted me," she pronounced in a nasal tone. "Now I shall have to talk my father into advancing me my allowance."

"But I thought you did that last Wednesday," remarked one of her companions.

"Bloody hell. I suppose I'll have to ask for an advance two months ahead," the lady finished with a laugh. "Not that Papa will mind. He gives me anything I want because I'm his princess. Unlike your father," she said to the lady to her right. "I wouldn't be able to stand it if my papa was as miserly as yours."

Steven hoped this unlikely lady was not his quarry of the evening. The last thing he needed was to attach himself to a spoiled spendthrift. He'd learned all too well recently how easy it was to run through a fortune. As Steven reached out to draw Royce away, the lady turned her attention upon them.

"Why, Lord Tewksbury," she began. "I didn't realize you'd joined us." Her gaze swept over Royce in a manner befitting a trollop. "How perfectly delicious. Since your wife isn't here, would you like to play with us?"

The lack of subtlety in her question caused Royce's features to harden. "I don't wish to interrupt your game, my lady." He gestured toward Steven. "May I present my friend, Steven Morris, Earl of Heath." His eyes sparkled with an odd mixture of sympathy and ill-concealed mirth as Royce finished the introduction. "And Steven, it is my honor to present Lady Portia Hammelson."

Lady Portia held out her plump hand to him. "Charmed."

As Royce had done moments before, Steven bowed toward her. "The pleasure is mine."

Her giggle scraped along his nerves. "I must say, Lord Tewksbury, you do have the most interesting friends," Lady Portia said boldly as her eyes raked over him in a most forward fashion, making Steven feel rather like an unplucked rooster being sized up for his meat. The glint in her gaze made Steven shift uncomfortably upon his feet. "It sounds as if they're going to play a quadrille next," she continued. "Since I haven't danced all evening, I wondered if you might escort me in this next dance, Lord Heath."

Calling upon all his charm, Steven proffered his arm. "Nothing would please me more, my lady."

Like a starving dog, Lady Portia latched on to his arm, her nails digging into the fine linen of his coat. "I often have gentlemen asking to make my acquaintance because of my fortune. But in your case . . ." She paused meaningfully as she swept her gaze over him once again. ". . . I don't mind one whit."

It was unfortunate that he couldn't return the sentiment. Managing a halfhearted smile, he led her onto the dance floor . . . and prayed that the evening passed swiftly.

Chapter Four

"Good evening, Lord Heath."

"Miss Nash," he murmured, drawing out each syllable like a caress.

Encouraged, she was thankful that she'd finally gotten up the courage to approach him. "Are you enjoying the evening's festivities?"

"Indeed I am; it's been a while since I've entered the hallowed halls of Almack's. And you, Miss Nash?"

"From all accounts, you preferred more . . . colorful haunts while in town," she returned teasingly.

"Lies, all lies."

The gleam in his eyes belied his words. "Doubtful."

Crossing his arms, Steven turned until he faced her. "Why is it, Miss Nash, that every time we meet you mention my reputation as a rake?" He leaned closer to her. "Are you seeking to stain your own pristine reputation perchance?"

Her face heated at his taunt. "Certainly not."

"Are you positive?" He arched a brow. "You do seem unduly interested in my personal pursuits."

"Perhaps I am merely trying to help you keep out of trouble."

"Or perhaps you are seeking a bit of adventure." Lifting a hand, he stroked a finger along the curve of her jaw. "Is that it, Miss Nash? Are you yearning for a taste of the darker pleasures?"

Her stomach fluttered, but she held her gaze steadily upon him. "And what if I am, my lord? Are you offering to appease my hunger?"

Desire flashed in Steven's eyes, bringing a soft gasp from Harriet. For the first time, she felt as if a man truly wanted her. Her heart pounding rapidly, she reached out to smooth Steven's wrinkled jacket. "I believe you promised me a waltz, my lord."

Something in his eyes shifted as he offered her a polite smile. "I most certainly did," he murmured, subtly shifting his arm until her hand fell free. "Unfortunately, Lady Jersey was most adamant that no waltz be played this evening."

Though disappointed, Harriet remained undaunted. "Then I suppose I shall simply have to settle for a quadrille."

A silky blond lock fell onto his forehead as Steven shook his head. "While I would like nothing better than to escort you to the next set, Miss Nash, I . . ."

"Yoo-hoo, Lord Heath!" The braying call sent a shudder through Steven as he squared his shoulders and turned to face Lady Portia Hammelson. "There you are, my lord," she said as she approached them. "Come along now; I've arranged for a waltz to be played."

"You arranged for the waltz?" gasped Harriet.

Pausing to look at Harriet as if she were a hideous, unwanted bug, Lady Portia cut her off without another glance. Instead, she dug her fingers into Steven's already wrinkled jacket and tugged him toward the dance floor.

Resisting the tugging, Steven looked over his shoulder, remorse filling his gaze as he lifted his shoulders in a dismissive gesture before allowing himself to be drawn away.

Harriet watched in disbelief as Steven whirled past her on the dance floor, waltzing her promised dance with another woman.

The rogue had lied to her!

Anger sustained Harriet as she finished out the remainder of the evening, ever aware of Steven. The fact that he hadn't tried to approach her, to apologize for blatantly lying to her, enraged her further. She'd sat with the matrons, safely ensconced within their affectionate fold, separated from the action in the room by more than just distance.

This evening, however, instead of finding comfort in the familiar conversation of her elderly friends, she found their natterings only increased her fury toward Steven. Instead of sitting with the matrons, she'd been looking forward to waltzing with a handsome gentleman, swept off her feet by him.

Worse yet, mingled with her rage was confusion. One moment he was seducing her with his words, a soft stroke of his finger, then the next he was allowing himself to be dragged off by that dreadful shrew, Lady Portia Hammelson . . . who was no lady, Harriet knew, regardless of her title.

Could that be the problem? Was she just simply too innocent for Steven's taste? Earlier, when he'd been teasing her, she'd blushed. Perhaps he had no desire for innocent young girls.

Then why had he gazed down at her as if he wanted to kiss her?

Her jumbled thoughts continued on the ride home. Harriet handed off her wrap to the butler, wanting only to retire to the peace and quiet of her bedchamber.

"Harriet!"

"Mama?" Harriet opened her arms as her mother hurried down the hallway with her father in tow. "You're here."

Her mother's plain face shimmered with happiness as she pulled back from Harriet's embrace. "We couldn't wait another moment and decided to come early. Isn't that right, Lionel?"

"Indeed it is," he agreed as he tugged Harriet into a fierce hug. "Your mother and I missed you far too much, moppet."

Harriet smiled over the familiar endearment. "I'm glad to see you," she admitted as she stepped out of her father's arms and waited until her parents had exchanged greetings with her aunts.

"You're glad to see us, but not that we've come?" her mother asked shrewdly.

She'd never been able to hold back her intimate thoughts from her mother, Harriet realized. "It's not that I'm unhappy you came; I'm simply concerned about the reason behind your visit. I worry that you're going to ask me to return home with you."

"Well of course we are," her father said firmly. "You've

dallied long enough here in town, and it's time you returned home to find a suitable husband instead of trifling with these spuddling snoutfairs here in town."

Harriet rolled her eyes at her father's habit of using archaic words. He'd even begun a book filled with the most remarkable English words ever forgotten. Unfortunately, his habit made it difficult to understand what he was saying half the time. "Spuddling snoutfairs?"

Father waved his hands. "Yes, you know, those handsome dandies who prance about town, enticing innocents into unsuitable behavior."

"Oh, Father," sighed Harriet, feeling far too weary to have this discussion yet again. Every time her parents came to town, they urged her to return home to the country, where she'd be doomed to a life of stifling boredom.

"Come, Harriet darling," her mother began as she led her, Father, Aunt Agatha, and Aunt Hilda into the nearest salon. "You've been in town for a number of years now and still haven't found a gentleman of interest. Why don't you return with your father and me to the country? I believe you'll find many of our young gentlemen have grown into fascinating fellows during your absence."

If one found manure thrilling, then Harriet had no doubt that she would indeed. However, since her interests lay elsewhere, she highly doubted she would meet anyone as interesting as . . . well . . . as Steven. Even with this evening's debacle, she couldn't deny that he'd made her feel more alive, more desirable, than she'd ever experienced before. She wasn't about to walk away from those feelings. "Perhaps I would," Harriet conceded in order to appease her mother. "However, I prefer town life and would like to remain here with Aunt Agatha and Aunt Hilda."

Stepping forward, Aunt Hilda placed a hand upon Harriet's cheek. "As much as I adore having you here with us, Harriet, I remain convinced that you should return home to the fine gentlemen in Essex. You'll not find a gentleman of worth here in town."

"You did," Harriet pointed out.

Bitterness deepened the lines around Aunt Hilda's mouth. "Not one of worth."

Before Harriet could respond to that remark, Aunt Agatha stepped forward, pushing her sister aside. "Don't bore the girl with that old tale," she reprimanded Aunt Hilda. "I'm a perfect example that a love match with a town gentleman is possible. I can't imagine anyone more perfect for me than my Roland, God rest his soul."

Grabbing hold of that argument, Harriet nodded toward Aunt Agatha. "You see? It is possible to find a respectable gentleman here in London."

"I'm not disputing that fact," Mama stated, her voice firm. "However you must remember that Agatha met her husband during her first Season and married him shortly thereafter. You, on the other hand, have not been successful in finding a suitable gentleman in more than three Seasons." Kindness and concern softened the harsh words. "I'm worried that if you continue to search for a husband here in town, you'll end up an unhappy old maid."

"If I marry without love, I'll simply be an unhappy married lady," Harriet countered.

Her father crossed his arms. "Now you're just being fratchy. Your mother and I can't wait forever for you to grow disquixotted with town. It's time you came home."

In her head, Harriet translated her father's odd speech, substituting the word "quarrelsome" for "fratchy" and "disillusioned" for "disquixotted." "I'm not arguing simply for argument's sake. In fact, I have recently met a very interesting gentleman who, I believe, finds me equally interesting." Or, rather, he'd found her interesting last night. Still, that wasn't something she was about to admit, for it didn't aid her cause.

Aunt Agatha and Mama wore matching expressions of delight. "Really?" asked Mama. "How wonderful."

"It is," Harriet agreed. "But if I return to Essex, I'll never know for certain if he was the one for me or not."

Worrying the folds of her plain gray dress between her fingertips, Mama considered this. "Even if your father and I insisted you return with us, you would pine away for your town gentleman, and I'm certain no country gentleman could compete in your mind."

Mama indeed knew her well. "I fear you are correct."

Undoubtedly seeing he'd lost the battle, her father tried to win the war. "Very well then, Harriet. If your mother and I agree to let you remain in town, you must promise that you will return home at the end of this Season if you haven't found a fiancé." He leveled a stare at her. "Agreed?"

She knew her father had yielded far more than he'd wanted. "Thank you, Papa," she murmured, leaning in to kiss her father's cheek before turning to hug her mother. "I appreciate your understanding."

Clearing his throat, her father tugged down on the overly tight waistcoat that he insisted upon wearing because he refused to acknowledge he'd put on weight.

"Yes, well, now that we've reached an agreement, I'm heading off to bed. These late hours aren't good for a man's digestive system."

As her aunts scurried to make her parents comfortable, Harriet dropped into a chair, tired from the trying day. She'd been granted a reprieve, but the clock was ticking. Now, more than ever, she needed to understand why Steven had lied to her this evening . . . and to make certain he never did it again.

In the morning, she'd call upon Laurel again to ask her friend's advice on how she should confront Steven. She might be a 'good girl,' but that didn't mean she was someone he could flirt with and toss aside without a thought.

Tomorrow she'd devise a way to make Steven realize that there was more to her than meets the eye.

Having managed to escape Lady Portia's claws for a moment, Steven strode into the gentlemen's gaming room and ordered a brandy. As soon as the footman delivered the glass, Steven drained it in two swallows.

"That bad, eh?" Royce asked as he came to a standstill beside Steven.

"Worse." He fixed a gaze upon his friend. "Surely Arabella and Portia aren't the best heiresses to be found."

"For you they are."

Steven frowned at Royce's comment. "What do you mean for me?"

"Just that," he countered, pausing to help himself to a cigar. "There are other heiresses, shy, sweet young things, but their parents wouldn't let you within an inch of them . . . even with an introduction from me."

"That's ridiculous."

"Not to them, it isn't." Royce lit his cigar. "Take Lattley. This is his daughter's first Season, and while she's received plenty of offers, he's refused every one for her. He's determined to marry his girl off to—and I quote—'a gentleman of true breeding.'" Grinning, Royce propped himself against the mantel. "He's chased off men with far less of a reputation than you, Steven, so I didn't think it necessary to add her name to your list."

Determined not to feel defeated, Steven straightened and set his glass on the nearby table. "We'll only add it if none of the others is acceptable. If it comes to that, I'll find a way around her father."

"Damnation, Steven, you truly are better at this game than I was," Royce said with a laugh.

Steven slanted a glance at his friend. "Let's just hope I win in the end like you."

Steven's head pounded by the time he headed up the steps to his town house. It had taken all his skill to outwit Portia, but he'd managed to avoid her for the latter part of the evening. If only he could have found a way to avoid his thoughts of Harriet as easily.

All evening, his finger had itched with the feel of her skin, making him wonder if she was as soft all over. Though he could see the innocence shining in her gaze, she met his flirtations with boldness, enticing him to be more outrageous than ever. Despite her delightful blush, she'd stood her ground, challenging him in a way no other woman had.

His thoughts of her were starting to get in the way of his heiress hunt. He'd be better served to avoid her in the future. It wouldn't do to be distracted from his focus. If he indulged himself in his desire for Harriet, he would lose everything he held dear.

No, he needed to remain firm on his goal, Steven told himself as he stepped into his home.

"Good evening, my lord."

Handing his topcoat to his butler, Steven returned the greeting.

"Lady Heath awaits you in the library."

Steven froze at his butler's remark. "My mother is here?"

"Awaiting you in the library," Graves repeated with a nod.

"Thank you." Taking a deep breath, Steven slowly made his way to the library, vowing to hold on to his temper.

Immediately, his mother jumped up from the settee, her still-beautiful face showing both her happiness and worry. "Steven," she whispered, a tremulous smile curving upon her lips.

Normally he would have opened his arms and welcomed her home after her long tour of Europe, but now it was all he could do to be civil. "Mother."

His mother's lips trembled as she clasped her hands in front of her. "It's so wonderful to see you." She looked up at him with tear-filled eyes. "I'm just so sorry to burden you with my debts. I don't know what happened." She shook her head, spreading her hands wide. "I just don't understand."

Steven thrust his hands into his breeches. "How can you fail to understand the fact that you lost a fortune?"

"A fortune?" Her hand trembled as she pressed it to her cheek. "Was it that much?"

Fighting off the wave of anger, Steve stared at his

mother in disbelief. "You don't even know how much you spent?"

Tears slipped softly down her face. "It all just happened so quickly, so unexpectedly." She shook her head. "I never stopped to figure out how much I owed."

"You owe more than we have, Mother," Steven said as he struggled to remain calm. "Not only is all the money gone, but we are now in debt. Even if I sold off all our property, every possession, it would not be enough to cover the remaining amount due."

His mother staggered backward, sinking into a chair. "Dear Lord."

"I rather doubt prayer will help us much at this point."

At his cutting remark, his mother buried her face in her hands and broke into a torrent of sobs. "I'm so sorry," she said between hitching breaths. "It's just that your father always took care of things for me, so I don't have much experience with money."

Steven handed his mother a handkerchief. "I know." And that was the simple truth; his father had done everything for his mother. Despite the twenty-year age difference, his parents had truly loved one another, been openly affectionate toward one another. Still, his father had left his mother unprepared for the world's challenges.

"I probably shouldn't have gone on the tour." Mother dabbed at her eyes. "But I've been so lonely without your father. After his death last year, I couldn't bear to stay at our home without him."

"Thanks to your spending, Mother, I don't think you need to worry about having a home anymore. I'll have to sell the country estate along with everything else."

More tears slid down her cheeks as she gazed up at him. "I'm sorry," she repeated.

But her apology didn't help at this moment. Steven strode over to his desk, wanting to put distance between them. "What precisely happened in Europe? How on earth did you run through a fortune? Did you spend too heavily at the gaming tables?"

Her blue eyes glistened with tears as she dabbed at them delicately. "I don't know," she whispered, confusion darkening her eyes. "It's all just one big, confusing blur."

"You run through a fortune and you don't even know how?" Steven demanded, unable to hide his anger. "I need more explanation than that, Mother!"

"But I don't have one," she wailed, burying her face in his handkerchief. "Your father always took care of everything."

And there lay the crux of his problem. Even if his mother did have more information, it was obvious that he wasn't going to be getting it out of her tonight. He knew he should try to comfort her, to calm her sobbing, but he just didn't have it in him. His anger was too raw, too near the surface.

"I'll call for your maid, Mother," Steven said as he strode from the library. "She can see you to your room."

Before he reached the door, his mother sprang up and caught him by the arm. "I can't tell you how sorry I am," she said again.

He looked down at her, searching for something to comfort her. "I know, Mother," he said, before stepping from the room.

Chapter Five

"*I*'m tired of being good."

Laurel's tea sloshed over the edge of her cup. "Pardon me?"

"You heard me perfectly," Harriet pronounced as she stood in Laurel's parlor. She'd come over shockingly early, but Harriet hadn't been able to keep her plans to herself one more moment. "I'm convinced Steven lied to me about the waltz. What I don't understand is why. I've thought about this all night, and I believe that despite his flirtations, he's just not attracted to me."

"From what you've told me of your intimate conversation, I'd say he was attracted," Laurel pointed out.

But Harriet had thought it all through. "That's what I thought at first, but then I realized that he probably flirted with me out of habit. We've spoken of his past before and how it affects his future. Well, this is a perfect example of that theory." She felt confident with her logic. "He's the consummate rake, so it's simply his nature to flirt. The next conclusion is that the reason he didn't wish to waltz with me is because he's not attracted to me." As Laurel opened her mouth to protest, Harriet raised her hands. "Please don't dispute this fact, Laurel. If we don't acknowledge it, we'll never find a way around it. And, as I said, I know the reason Steven's not attracted to me."

"Because you're too good?"

"Precisely."

Laurel's brows drew together. "Is there such a thing?"

"When you're hoping to attract a gentleman, absolutely," Harriet exclaimed firmly. "The only innocent misses who receive offers are those with huge dowries. Since I possess neither fortune nor great beauty, I need to utilize my finest asset—my brain." She dropped into a chair beside Laurel. "If I approach the problem of Steven logically, I realize that he's naturally drawn to more experienced ladies such as Lady Portia, so if I wish to capture his interest, I need to be more . . . wicked."

Reaching for a scone, Laurel frowned at Harriet. "That's a fine plan if you wish to be his mistress. However, it leaves much to be desired if you want him to marry you."

"I know, which is why that is only one part of my plan," Harriet replied smugly. "In addition, I'll use Royce's theory to catch Steven."

"What?" The normally elegant Laurel sent crumbs flying across the front of her gown. "Not that idiotic fox hunt theory of his."

"I'll admit that the wager part of his plan was quite ridiculous," Harriet conceded, unquelled by Laurel's less than enthusiastic remarks. "However, the theory he had of applying the rules of fox hunting seem quite sound." Lifting her hand, she began to tick off the points. "First,

Royce said you need to identify the quarry." She grabbed hold of her index finger. "Steven," she announced, wiggling the finger. "Then you have to know your quarry, understand their habits, their lives, their strengths and weaknesses." Her hand dropped back into her lap. "So, that is how I shall move forward with Steven. I'll get to know him, everything about him, and come to understand what appeals to him."

Laurel's brows drew downward. "Harriet, I . . ."

But Harriet continued with her explanation as if Laurel hadn't tried to interject her opinion. "At the same time, I'll transform myself into the type of woman he finds naturally attractive. I shall become more sensual and seduce him into marrying me."

"Not to be less than encouraging, Harriet, but what do you know about being sensual?"

"Not much," she admitted, before offering Laurel a brilliant smile. "So aren't I lucky that my best friend is well versed in feminine wiles and will help me develop some?"

Laurel laughed as she set down her teacup. "You want me to teach you feminine wiles in my condition?" she asked, waving her hand over her rounded stomach.

"Yes," Harriet returned emphatically. "After all, you must have used yours in order to get in that condition."

"You have a point there," Laurel said with a grin.

"I most certainly do." Reaching out, she clasped Laurel's hand. "I know I can do this, Laurel. Whenever I'm around Steven, I feel as if every part of me is alive and in tune with him. I know he's the one for me, and I'm confident my plan will work. All I need is your help."

"Well, if he's affected you so completely, of course I'll help you," Laurel said without further hesitation. "When we're through, you'll be so appealing to Steven that he won't have a prayer of resisting."

Once home from Laurel's, Harriet paused in the hall-way, pulled off her gloves, and handed them to her maid who had accompanied her to the Van Cleef town house. As the maid left, Harriet started toward the salon, only to draw up at the sound of an ongoing argument.

". . . see that the best place for Harriet is in the coun-try." Aunt Hilda's comment resonated into the hallway.

"Poppycock," retorted Aunt Agatha.

Sighing, Harriet headed forward again to stop her aunts from arguing yet again about the same, tired subject.

"I quite disagree, Agatha." Her father's comment brought Harriet to a skidding halt. "Everyone knows that town gentlemen often suffer from satyriasis."

"That's correct," agreed Aunt Hilda.

"Oh, for heaven's sake, Hilda. You don't even know what that means!"

Aunt Agatha's derisive remark caused yet another voice to join the fray. "I believe it means gentlemen who have an excessive need for . . . for . . . "

"Disvirginating."

"My!" gasped Aunt Hilda. "I'd say the meaning of that word is quite clear, Lionel."

"As well it should be," returned Harriet's father. "The lack of moral fiber in these gents is shocking."

Rolling her eyes, Harriet spun on her heel and headed for the glass doors leading out to the gardens. She'd had quite enough of listening to the dire predictions of her ruination and disgrace. She'd finally found someone who interested her, someone who made her feel that lovely little hiccup inside, and she wasn't about to allow her parents or her aunt, well-meaning though they might be, to ruin her plans.

And even if Steven didn't prove to be the "the one," she now knew that she could feel that spark for a gentleman. If nothing else, she believed she would indeed find her special someone.

Despite the open air of the garden, Harriet still felt closed in, trapped within the well-intentioned smothering of people who loved her. She knew her parents and aunts only wanted what was best for her; the problem lay in the realization that they didn't know what was best. She wished her parents would return home and leave her to find her own way.

Without conscious thought she'd wandered to the rear door of the garden that led out onto the street. Needing to escape the overwhelming feeling of being stifled, Harriet slipped out the door, ignoring the improprieties of wandering the streets unescorted. After all, this was hardly a dangerous part of town; she'd be perfectly fine. Besides, there were some advantages to being ordinary, nearly invisible Miss Nash.

Feeling lighter already, she took off at a brisk pace, determined to enjoy her freedom. Her life was finally heading in a positive direction and with a bit of careful planning, she could at last achieve all of her dreams of finding love and happiness just like Laurel had. All Harriet needed to do was get to know Steven, learn his likes and dislikes, study his habits, understand his desires. A shiver raced over her at that last thought. Yes, indeed, she'd love to understand his desires.

The unfamiliar frisson of feminine excitement made

Harriet feel almost giddy as she rounded another corner. Lost in her images of Steven leaning in closer to kiss her, to hold her tightly against him, to claim her for his own, Harriet slowed to a stop.

Blinking, she looked around her, surprised to find herself in front of the town house belonging to none other than the Earl of Heath. Subconsciously, she must have headed for Steven's house. In an instant, she realized she was gazing up at his house like a love-starved fool. Dear Lord, what if he looked out a window at this precise moment and saw her gawking!

Alarmed at the mere possibility, Harriet dashed around the corner and out of sight of the main house. Unfortunately, it brought her in front of the drive leading to Steven's stables. Glancing up the cobbled path, she gasped in disbelief as she caught sight of Steven grooming a horse. An earl grooming his own horse?

Even with his jacket discarded, his cravat missing, the top few buttons of his shirt opened, and his sleeves rolled up, Steven looked every inch the earl, for he couldn't rid himself of his commanding presence.

"Miss Nash!"

Bloody Hell, she'd gone and done it now. She'd been so caught up in her thoughts that she hadn't even realized he'd paused in his grooming and had glanced her way. Now what was she to do? Though she desperately wanted to turn on her heel and race away, pretending that he hadn't seen her, she had far too much pride.

Which left her with no choice but to brazen out her foolhardiness.

Lifting her chin, Harriet strolled forward, forcing a smile onto her face. "Good day, Lord Heath," she said pleasantly, as if there was nothing out of the ordinary about her walking without an escort or purpose.

"Good day," he returned. "I must say, Miss Nash, this is quite a surprise." He gestured toward his disheveled clothes. "As you can tell, I wasn't expecting company."

Unbidden, heat flooded her cheeks. The way she saw it, she could either lie and give him some ridiculous story, or she could tell him the equally ridiculous truth. The decision was easy to make. "I apologize for my unexpected appearance. I truly had no intention of calling upon you," she informed him, relieved that she could at least say that truthfully. "I was merely out walking. I didn't even realize this was your home."

Well, perhaps she wasn't being completely truthful.

"I'd paused at the base of your drive because . . . I'd gotten a pebble in my shoe and had to remove it." Just stop talking! she ordered herself silently, knowing she was a horrid fibber.

If he saw through her fabrication, he was too much of a gentleman to remark upon it. "I hope the stone didn't injure you."

"No, I'm fine." She took a bracing breath. "I was far more injured by your lie last night."

Steven met her gaze unflinchingly. "I do apologize, Miss Nash. It was rather poorly done."

"I'd rather have had the dance than your apology."

A side of his mouth quirked upward at her bold statement. "Unfortunately, that's all I have to offer."

Anger sparked inside Harriet, but she pushed it away. It would hardly suit her plan to demand an explanation for his lie. Steadying her nerves, she gestured toward his horse. "Your mare is quite lovely."

Immediately, a smile played over his lips. "She is, isn't she?" Walking over to the horse, he patted her gently. "She's called Athena."

"After the huntress," Harriet murmured, joining him next to the beautiful horse. "Very clever, my lord."

"Steven," he corrected her.

Warmth rushed through her at the thought of publicly addressing him in such a familiar form. "Very well . . . Steven," she replied, stumbling slightly. "I'd be pleased if you'd address me as Harriet."

His smile broadened into a grin. "Your name suits you."

"I'm afraid it does," she agreed with a sigh. "A perfect name for an unremarkable old maid."

Sunshine glistened off his blond hair as he tossed back his head in laughter. "Old maid? You? Hardly. As for being unremarkable, I'd have to say nothing could be further from the truth."

His immediate denial pleased her more than he could ever know. "You flatter me."

"Not at all." He gestured toward himself in a down-ward-sweeping motion. "You see before you a simple country gent who lacks the golden tongue necessary to sweep a young lady off her feet with glib words."

Oh, but he was wrong. Steven possessed a charm that made young ladies' hearts flutter. She knew that for a fact. "I beg to differ, Steven," she said lightly, running a hand along the horse's neck.

Reaching out, he trapped her hand beneath his. "If I'm not careful, you'll discover all my secrets."

"Have you so many?" she whispered.

"A few." His warm breath rushed over her face as he

tipped his head toward her. Breathlessly, Harriet awaited the touch of his mouth, excited to receive her first kiss. Before their lips could touch, Athena shifted, bumping into them and breaking the moment.

Shaking his head, Steven untied his horse's reins from the post and gestured toward the stable. "I need to put Athena back in her stall. Would you care to see my other horses?"

While she wanted to do nothing more than scream in frustration at the missed opportunity, Harriet smiled softly. "I'd love to," she replied, before falling into step next to him. "How many horses do you keep here in town?"

"Five including Athena."

She lifted her brows. "That many?"

"At home, I keep four times as many." Stepping ahead, he led Athena through the double doors of the stable.

As Harriet entered the sunlit area, she smelled the unique fragrance of horse, straw, and leather that she remembered so well from childhood. "When I was young, I'd often watch as my father's stable master groomed our horses." She looked around the airy room as she followed Steven toward an open stall. "Though our stables at home are nothing as grand as this."

"If you think this is fine, you should see my stables at home." Steven's steps slowed as he glanced around. "I wonder where all the stableboys got off to."

"I don't know, but it looks as if we're the only ones here."

Steven frowned.

"What's the matter?" she asked. "Do you need help with something?"

"Athena doesn't enjoy having her hooves picked, so I need one of the stableboys to hold her reins and keep her calm while I clean them out."

"I can help," Harriet volunteered, reaching out to pat Athena's shoulder. "You'd like it if we became friends, would you, Athena?"

Surprise widened Steven's eyes. "You wouldn't mind?"

"Of course not." Harriet couldn't help but grin at Steven's expression. "Haven't you ever heard that saying about you can take the girl out of the country, but you can never take the country out of the girl . . . much to my dismay." She leaned forward to whisper. "Just don't tell anyone."

Steven crossed his index finger across his chest. "Your secret is safe with me," he replied with a smile as he handed over Athena's reins. "Why don't you lead her into her stall and stand by her head while I clean her hooves?"

Accepting the proffered reins, Harriet began to talk to Athena as she led the horse into her stall. "You're a sweet girl, aren't you? And you'll be good for me, won't you?"

Steven chuckled as he retrieved the pick. "You're right at home here, Harriet."

"Well, that's a fine thing," she joked. "I agree to help you, and you insult me."

"I never claimed to be a gentleman," he taunted, giving her a wicked smile before returning his attention to the horse.

Grasping Athena's rear left hoof, he straddled the horse's fetlock, bent over, and began to clean out the muck and small stones caught in the hoof, presenting

Harriet with a most interesting angle of his backside. And a fine backside it was, she decided, indulging herself with a lengthy look.

Almost as if he'd felt her gaze upon him, Steven glanced back over his shoulder. "How's she doing?"

Her cheeks flamed with heat as Harriet snapped her attention back to Athena. "S-s-she's fine," Harriet stuttered, praying Steven hadn't caught her staring at his posterior. Hoping to cover her nervousness, Harriet ran her hand down Athena's nose. "Aren't you, sweetheart?"

As Steven finished the first hoof and moved onto the next one, Harriet continued to croon to Athena, forcing herself to keep her attention focused on the mare. ". . . you're so silky and soft, aren't you, Athena? It feels so good to pet you, and I bet you like it too, don't you? I could . . ." Harriet broke off her calming murmurings as she became aware of Steven standing next to her, frozen in his tracks. She glanced down at his now-empty hands. "Are you done already?"

He swallowed—hard—before nodding.

Offering him a bright smile, she held out Athena's reins. "That was quick."

Just as he reached out to accept them, Athena shifted on her feet, butting her head against Steven's back and sending him sprawling forward. A gasp broke from Harriet as he bumped into her, causing her to stumble backward against the wooden wall of Athena's stall. Her breath rushed out of her as Steven landed against her, sandwiching her between him and the wall.

"I'm so sorry," he murmured as he braced himself against the wall behind her and levered himself away. "Are you all right?"

Mere inches away from him, Harriet couldn't breathe, much less speak. Her gaze lifted to his as she remained spellbound.

"Harriet?" he asked softly, his warm breath washing over her upturned face. As she beheld him silently, caught in a sensual trance, she watched as his eyes darkened into a deep indigo blue. "Harriet," he said again, but this time his voice was a harsh rasp that scraped along her sensitive nerves.

Without conscious thought, she parted her lips, praying, hoping, for a sweet kiss from this glorious man who had haunted her dreams of late.

Harriet waited while Steven lowered his head toward her. When his lips were a mere whisper away, she tilted her head, angling her mouth to align perfectly with his, welcoming the feathering touch of his lips as they captured hers for her first kiss.

The sweetness of his touch brought a sigh to her lips as she arched toward him, deepening their kiss. Mouths blended, melding together, as he molded her to his will, awakening tingling sensations inside of her. In all of her dreams, she'd never imagined a simple kiss could affect her so much.

A soft moan escaped her as Steven's hands left the wall and curved along her back, drawing her into him, pressing her against his welcomed hardness. Desire bursting to life within her, Harriet curled her arms around his neck, angling her head to further deepen their kiss.

When Steven stroked into her mouth with his tongue, she began to tremble as her body softened into his chest. Over and over again, he tasted her, driving in deeply, then stroking softly, each hungry thrust further igniting the passion within her. Unbidden, she began to mimic his actions, tasting deeply of his desire, satisfying her longing for more.

An unrecognizable need spread through her, making her breasts tingle, her stomach tighten. Steven's arms pulled her closer still until there wasn't an inch of her that wasn't touching him.

Steven began to move a hand up across her back, curving around to her breast. Eager to feel more, to ease the ache inside of her, she turned slightly, inviting his touch, his caress. Slowly, he drew closer until she wanted to beg him to hurry. Just as his hand slipped onto the curve of her breast, Steven froze.

Abruptly, he lifted his head, breaking their kiss, and instead of pulling her closer, he took a few stumbling steps backward, spinning around until all she could see was the movement of his back as he tried to catch his breath.

"Steven?" she whispered, reaching out to touch him.

"Quiet," he rasped in a low, raw voice. "Someone's coming."

Feeling as though she'd just awakened from a dream, Harriet forced herself to focus on the sounds beyond the small stall.

"The stable hands must be returning," Steven explained as he took one last deep breath and turned to face her. "Harriet, I . . ." He broke off, obviously at a loss for words.

His loss for speech mirrored her own, making her realize that he'd been as affected by their passionate embrace as she'd been. Suddenly, his lie at Almack's made sense. He'd been afraid to waltz with her, to touch her so intimately; he'd been uncertain of his ability to control his desire for her.

She'd never imagined a kiss could affect her so deeply. Her entire body tingled with unknown, but utterly delicious sensations. "It's quite all right, Steven," she murmured softly. "I understand perfectly."

"You do?" He shook his head as if trying to clear his thoughts.

His reaction confused her somewhat, but he was undoubtedly still unnerved by the abrupt ending to their embrace.

Glancing over his shoulder, Steven shifted on his feet. "I'll head off the stableboys and get them into the tack room, so you can leave without anyone seeing you."

"Very well." Unable to hold back the need to touch him once more, she laid her hand upon his arm, causing him to jump as if she'd prodded him with a hot iron. Confused at his reaction, his inability to look her in the eye, she allowed her hand to fall back to her side. "When will I see you again?"

"I don't know." Finally, he turned to face her. Thrusting both hands through his hair, he sighed deeply. "I just don't know."

Before she had a chance to ask him what he meant by that, Steven hurried from the stall, calling to the approaching stable hands, then leading them back down the main corridor to a small room at the far end of the stables. Left with no other option, Harriet slipped from Athena's stall, making sure to secure the gate behind her before hurrying out to the street.

While Steven's reaction to their kiss wasn't quite what she expected, she supposed she shouldn't be offended.

After all, they'd nearly been caught in a very delicate situation, so it wasn't surprising that he'd been unnerved. Instead, she focused on their kiss.

And what a kiss it had been!

Uncaring that she was grinning like a fool, Harriet hurried home, well pleased with this new development in her plan to become the next Countess of Heath.

Chapter Six

Good God! What in the name of all that was holy had he been thinking?

Steven paced across the rear lawn as he struggled to understand how he'd gone from conversing pleasantly with Harriet to kissing her senseless.

Thrusting his hands into his pockets, he tried to calm his still sizzling nerves. He'd always been in control of his desire, his emotions. He was the ultimate rake, enjoying women, treating them well, then bidding them farewell without a backward glance. Yet Harriet had been plaguing his thoughts far too often for comfort . . . and now this.

He still couldn't believe that he'd lost his control, that passion had swamped him, sweeping aside the decision to walk away from her. She wasn't what he needed . . . but she was what he now craved.

She wasn't even his type! He thought fiercely. He'd always preferred buxom women who knew how to handle a man's desire. Yet with Harriet he'd felt more with just one kiss than he'd felt while making love to other women. Unbidden, she stirred something within him, something he'd never felt before, something that bothered him more than he cared to admit.

When she'd gazed up at him with such longing, such naked desire, he'd been unable to resist kissing her just once. So much for his control. Again, fool he was, he thought one soft kiss would be enough to satisfy his yearnings, but the moment he'd touched her lips, he'd been lost.

Lost within her embrace. Lost in her sweetness. Lost in her.

Steven's body tightened at the memory. If the stable hands hadn't returned at that moment, he doubted he would have been able to stop with just an embrace.

There was only one thing left to do—avoid her like the plague.

He knew she wouldn't understand, but he couldn't allow himself to care. Too much was at stake—his lifestyle, his respect, his pride. He couldn't pursue this unyielding interest in Harriet, so he needed to push it aside, to forget how she felt in his arms, forget how she tasted like the finest wine, forget that he . . .

Groaning, Steven forced himself to break off those tormenting thoughts. Harriet didn't suit his needs . . . regardless of how much he wanted her to.

As Harriet entered the Lansdownes' town house, a rush of anticipaton flowed through her for she knew Steven would be at this musicale as well. Laurel had sent her a note earlier in the evening informing Harriet that both Royce and Steven would be in attendance. Handing her wrap to the butler, Harriet ignored the whispered bickerings of her aunts and murmured admonishments from her parents as she glanced about the room for Steven.

The sight of his blond hair glinting in the candlelight brought a smile to her face and, with an excited leap of her heart, she started toward him. Memories of his heated kiss stole her breath as she watched him converse with Lady Camilla Tullane. Her steps slowed as details of what she was observing began to sink in to her consciousness.

With his hand cupping Lady Camilla's elbow and his head bent toward her, Steven appeared to be quite intimate with her. Harriet stumbled to a full stop. He'd kissed her that very afternoon, yet here he was, wooing another lady altogether. It was time for Steven to put his roguish ways behind him.

Briskly, she strode up to him, ignoring the fact that he was trying to converse with Lady Camilla. "Good evening, Steven."

His eyes widened in surprise as he turned toward her. As she watched, a bevy of emotions colored his expression from happiness to remorse to guilt before his expression settled into a cool mask. Only the heightened color staining his cheekbones gave him away. "Miss Nash," he began politely . . . as if he hadn't pressed her against the wall of his horse's stall that very afternoon. "This is a surprise."

"I'll wager it is," she returned tartly. He'd had no problem calling her Harriet when he'd been kissing her senseless, but now that he stood here paying court to the proper Lady Camilla he acted as if he hadn't had his hands roaming all over her body. Well, she'd have to do something about that! "I wanted to thank you for the tour of your stables earlier. I found it quite . . . enlightening," she finished in what she hoped was an intimate tone.

For an instant, heat flashed in Steven's eyes before he banked the fires. Clearing his throat, Steven gestured toward his companion. "Lady Camilla, may I present . . ."

"We've met," Harriet interrupted. "I'd much rather continue our discussion from this afternoon."

Steven swallowed . . . hard. His reaction brought a bright smile to Harriet's face. "Ah, I see you remember it well."

His features darkened into an interesting blend of annoyance and desire that Harriet found utterly fascinating. It was amazing what a few well-placed words could achieve.

Lady Camilla's eyebrows rose slightly, but she was far too ladylike to point out Harriet's social shortcomings. "It is perfectly fine, Miss Nash," she said in a melodious tone. "If you'll excuse me . . ."

As soon as Lady Camilla stepped away, Harriet returned her attention to Steven. The flush upon his cheeks had deepened as he'd gone from embarrassment into anger.

"Well, that was entertaining," she said pertly.

Without a word, Steven cupped her elbow, not in the charming fashion he'd clasped Lady Camilla's, but rather in a tight hold, and led her down the hallway without uttering a word.

At least I have his full attention, Harriet thought, refusing to be daunted in the face of his anger. If anyone had the right to be peeved, it was she. After all, she wasn't the one who'd been flirting with someone else!

"What were you thinking?" he demanded the moment after he shut the door to the salon.

"Of our kiss," she replied easily.

He thrust a hand through his hair. "How have you survived in town if you bandy about all your improprieties?"

"Since this was my first, I haven't found it to be a problem."

He stilled. "Your first social impropriety or your first kiss?"

"My first kiss," she assured him, pleased at the way color stained his cheeks. "Since I found the experience most wonderful, I'd love to do it again."

Shaking his head, Steven took a step backward, knocking into a chair. Suddenly, as if the bump had jolted something inside of him, he seemed to shift—everything from his expression to the way he carried himself. "While I'd love to indulge your fantasies, I'm afraid I've settled upon another lady at the moment."

The rake was back in full force. "I don't think that will do at all," she said gently.

"You don't have a choice in the matter, Harriet," he scoffed, easing onto the arm of a chair. "You can't tell me where I can find my pleasure."

Despite her belief that he was hiding beneath his rakish facade, Harriet couldn't help but feel hurt at his mocking tone. Still, she held fast. "I beg to differ, Steven, since we are . . ."

"We are what?" he interrupted bluntly. "There isn't a we, Harriet. A kiss doesn't hold any deep meaning. It is simply a pleasurable pastime."

Her chest began to tighten. "I thought you desired me," she whispered.

"I did," he replied, "but I wouldn't have indulged myself if I'd known you didn't realize how the game was played."

"I wasn't playing a game."

"Of course you were," he retorted with a short laugh. "You just happened to be passing by my home—alone—and then you approach me and follow me into the stable. You were most definitely playing, my dear Harriet." He lifted a shoulder. "But as I said before, I wouldn't have kissed you had I known you were unaware of the rules."

"Rules?" she asked, her confidence badly shaken.

"There are rules of conduct to an affair."

Unable to hold back her gasp, Harriet struggled to maintain her calm exterior.

"Isn't that what you were offering? No, I can see by your expression that you didn't have an affair in mind at all." Rising, he walked over to her, cupping her cheek in the palm of his hand. "Sweet, naive Harriet, don't tell me you were thinking in terms of marriage!" His fingers caressed her neck as he trailed his hand downward. "You've spoken to me of my reputation on a number of occasions, Harriet." He gazed into her eyes. "You know what I am."

"But not with me," she whispered, desperately hanging on to that hope. "I . . . I was sure you had genuine feelings."

"Harriet, Harriet, Harriet," he murmured. "Why would it be any different with you?"

Words failed her. How could she hold on to her belief that he was merely hiding behind his rakish nature in the face of such denial? "I see," she finally managed to say.

Harriet pulled the tattered remains of her pride around her and walked from the room.

The soft click of the door closing caused Steven to flinch. Hell, he'd almost have preferred if she'd slammed it shut. He'd hurt her, he knew, but it was far better this way, he assured himself. Being cruel was the kindest way to save her from any fanciful imaginings. If only he'd never kissed her.

Yet that would mean having missed out on knowing just how sweet her lips were, how soft she felt beneath his hands, how perfectly she fit against . . .

Steven forced himself to thrust those thoughts from his head. She'd read more into their kiss than she should have, he reminded himself.

Just because he'd felt more with Harriet than ever before only meant that he'd been too long without female companionship. Yes, that's all there was to it.

He needed to keep his eye on obtaining an heiress and forget his attraction toward Harriet. An easy objective.

As Steven headed for the door, a small voice inside of him mocked him with one simple statement—

Not bloody likely.

Praying Laurel would still be awake despite the lateness of the hour, Harriet descended from her carriage and headed up the stoop. She'd pleaded illness with her aunts and parents, insisting that they stay and enjoy the musicale. She'd assured them that she'd be perfectly safe with her footmen and driver to see her home, and that she'd send the carriage back for them.

Of course, she'd made no mention of making a stop at Laurel's town house, because if she had, her aunts and parents might have realized that something was wrong and needled her into revealing what troubled her.

The Van Cleef butler gave Harriet entrance and escorted her to the salon to await the arrival of Lady Tewksbury. Harriet paced back and forth, unwilling to sit down as she clung to her badly damaged confidence.

"Harriet?" asked Laurel as she entered the room wearing an embroidered robe. "What brings you about at this hour?"

At the sight of her dear friend, the tight rein she'd been holding upon her emotions snapped. "Oh, Laurel, it was so distressing, I simply had to come."

Concern traced deep lines upon Laurel's face. "Harriet, what's happened?"

"It's Steven," she admitted, keeping her voice steady. "Everything was going so well. We shared the most incredible kiss, but when I saw him tonight, he was flirting with that snooty Lady Camilla and . . ."

"Please, Harriet, slow down," urged Laurel. "I can't make heads or tails of what you're trying to tell me." She gestured toward a chair. "Why don't you take a seat and start from the beginning?"

Following her friend's advice, Harriet sat down and began telling Laurel about what had transpired with Steven in his stables, then how he'd behaved toward Lady Camilla and finally their scene in the library. ". . . so as you can see I'm uncertain if I'm correct in my idea that he was hiding behind his roguish facade."

"Of course you are," Laurel replied immediately. "Whenever men feel threatened, they act their worst."

"Threatened?" Harriet leaned forward. "Why on earth would I threaten him?"

"Because he's attracted to you," she countered.

"Being attracted to me isn't threatening."

"It is for Steven because you're the marrying type." Grinning, Laurel tucked her robe around her. "I don't believe our Steven is ready to settle down into marriage yet, so he's fighting his attraction for you."

Harriet latched on to Laurel's encouragement. "Do you really think so?"

"Absolutely," she pronounced. "Remember, I've lived with a reformed rake for a number of years now. I know how the breed thinks."

Harriet couldn't help but laugh. "You make them sound like dogs."

"One could argue that there are similarities between the two."

Warming to Laurel's analogy, Harriet said, "I suppose that's true. Take Steven for example. He returns to town and begins hunting for ladies like an incorrigible hound, bent on sniffing out the . . ." She gasped loudly. "That's it!"

Obviously confused, Laurel shook her head. "What's what?"

"That's what I've been doing wrong," Harriet exclaimed as her thoughts continued to take shape. "I tried to apply Royce's theory in precisely the wrong manner!"

Laurel shook her head. "I'm afraid I still don't understand."

"It's simple," Harriet continued, not really hearing Laurel's remark. "I don't know why I didn't figure it out before."

"Please, Harriet!" exclaimed Laurel with a laugh.

"Tell me what's going on before you drive me mad."

"When I applied Royce's fox hunt theory, I considered myself the hunter and Steven the hunted or, in accordance with the theory, the fox." She grinned broadly. "But that's where I went wrong. You see, in Royce's theory, the ladies were the clever vixen that would make the men the . . ." Harriet paused, eagerly waiting for Laurel to insert the missing word.

"Hunters?" she offered, obviously still confused.

"Close, but not quite." Leaning forward, Harriet ignored the fact that she was hopelessly wrinkling her skirt. "The hunters sit back and allow their dogs to chase down the clever fox."

Laughter broke from Laurel. "Are you trying to say that if you're to apply Royce's theory to Steven, then you need to consider him a . . ."

". . . dog."

As Laurel doubled over with laughter, Harriet elaborated on her personal twist on the infamous fox hunt theory. "If you consider everything, it fits perfectly. There is Steven sniffing around all these ladies, trying to run one to the ground and why? Because it's a pleasurable game to him."

"That makes sense," Laurel conceded.

Harriet nodded eagerly. "Of course it does. So now all we need to figure out is how to reverse Royce's theory. If Steven is the hound, then what do I need to do in order to make him want to give chase?" Harriet tapped her fingers upon the arm of her chair.

"You first need to think about what all dogs want."

Realizing Laurel had a valid point, Harriet began to list the points. "They want to be fed regularly, to be warm and dry in a suitable shelter, and to receive regular displays of affection." She snapped her fingers. "I can do that!"

Laurel's brows drew together slightly. "I don't know if it will be that easy."

"Of course it will," Harriet assured her blithely. "Men are very basic creatures, bearing many canine traits if truth be told. Since I already know Steven finds himself attracted to me, it makes this entire situation much easier. However, if I'm going to make this work, I'll need to induce him to avoid chasing other ladies until he realizes that I can meet all of his needs."

"And how do you propose to do that?"

"Easy." Harriet smiled brightly at her dear friend. "I'll simply have to become a fox in sheep's clothing."

Chapter Seven

I've heard Miss Kendall has a splendid voice."

"Hmmmm," Lady Camilla murmured, nodding vaguely.

Feeling awkward, Steven tried another attempt at conversation. "The Lansdownes have a lovely home, don't they?"

"Quite." She shifted away from him. "Please excuse me, my lord. I just spied Lady Jersey, and I need to discuss a most important matter with her."

Like what? How boring she found him? Squelching his wayward thoughts, Steven bowed to Lady Camilla. "It has been a pleasure conversing with you this evening."

She gave him a vague smile before gracefully walking away. Lord, he was off his mark tonight, Steven realized. He was finding it hard to come up with the easy phrases and glib replies that charmed the ladies. And he could lay his odd mood squarely upon Harriet's shoulders.

How could he concentrate on charming a lady when he

was still wondering how Harriet had seen beneath his remarks? It amazed him that she'd known he was still attracted to her despite his assurances to the contrary. Harriet was either the cleverest girl he'd ever met or the most naive.

Or perhaps she was both.

Unwilling to admit to himself just how intriguing he found that thought, Steven watched as Lady Camilla began to converse with Lady Jersey, noting her elegance, her ladylike manner, her perfect blonde beauty. Odd, though, how he suddenly preferred lively brunettes. Mentally kicking himself, Steven forced himself to focus upon his heiress. Stay the course, he reminded himself.

Before he could approach Lady Camilla once more, his mother appeared at his side. "Steven," she said, her overly bright tone alerting him to her nervousness. "Are you enjoying yourself this evening?"

"Mother," he said coolly, wondering how long it would be before he stopped being angry with her.

"Wasn't Miss Kendall wonderful?" she trilled, darting a glance over her shoulder.

Obviously something was bothering his mother. "Is everything all right?" he finally asked.

"Yes," she said with a shake of her head. "Everything's fine."

The blatant lie didn't sit well upon her, but before he could find out what was bothering her, three men joined them.

"Caroline," said the first man, who looked remarkably like a troll.

"This is where you got off to." The second man, who had the width of a maypole and the sour expression of a harpy, lifted his hand, offering her the glass of lemonade he held. "I fetched your refreshment like you wanted."

"Thank you, Percy," his mother murmured softly. "I didn't mean to run off on you like that; my son wished to speak with me." She turned an imploring gaze up at him. "Isn't that right, Steven?"

"Absolutely," he replied, with no litte confusion.

The third man stepped forward, patting his massive girth. "You must be Steven, then," he said jovially. "Edward Longley here."

Who the devil are these three misfits?

"I should introduce you all to my son," his mother said, filling the awkward gap. Placing her hand upon his arm, she pointed to the troll first. "Steven, this is Mr. Robert Connor and Mr. Percy Windvale," she finished, gesturing toward the maypole. "Gentlemen, my son, Steven Morris, Earl of Heath."

Stiffly, Steven bowed to them, wishing he hadn't allowed himself to become cornered like this.

"I became acquainted with these gentlemen on my year-long tour," his mother explained, filling the awkward silence that had fallen over their group.

"We were introduced in France." Connor's expression softened as he looked at Steven's mother. "And Caroline was so friendly, so wonderful; I do so enjoy her company."

"Indeed she is," interjected Longley.

Windvale pressed a hand to his chest. "A true angel."

Ignoring the fawning trio, Steven turned toward his mother. "What is going on here? Who are these men?"

Her hands fluttered. "I told you, Steven, I met these men while on my travels. As we have many of the same friends, we spent quite a bit of time together and became quite friendly during the last six months."

"There have been no improprieties," Connor hurried to reassure Steven.

Longley nodded vigorously. "We are simply taken with your mother's charm and beauty."

"And since each one of us has rescued Caroline, it's only natural that we feel protective of . . ."

But Steven latched on to that one word. "Rescued?" He fixed his gaze upon Windvale.

Nodding his balding head, the maypole offered more details. "The first time I met Caroline was at Lord Seagrove's hunt, where the horse she'd borrowed from Seagrove suddenly went mad, bucking and racing about, leaving her unable to control the poor animal."

"Is this true, mother?" Why hadn't she told him of this?

"I wasn't hurt," his mother said swiftly. "Luckily, Percy was in the vicinity and helped me back to Lord Seagrove's manor. I fared far better than my poor horse. Unfortunately, the horse broke his foreleg and had to be put down. Naturally, I felt responsible, as I was the one who lost control of the poor horse, so I purchased it."

Steven couldn't believe his ears. "You bought a dead horse?"

"What else could I do?" his mother asked.

"At least it cost less to replace the horse than it did to replace the boat," Longley offered helpfully.

Steven's head began to pound. "What boat?"

"The one Caroline rented for an afternoon jaunt that sank." Longley tucked his hands into the pockets of his waistcoat and rocked back on his heels. "Fortunately, I was attending the party and helped your mother reach shore."

Dear Lord, his mother needed a keeper! Steven pointed toward the troll. "What did you do, Connor?"

"Pulled her from the Tibaults' gazebo when it caught on fire," he replied.

"And you undoubtedly paid to rebuild the gazebo as well." Good God, what else had she been up to on the continent?

Spreading her hands, his mother shrugged lightly. "Naturally. What else could I do?"

"Were these the only accidents that occurred?"

His mother shook her head dismally.

"Oh, no," Connor interrupted, stepping forward. "Dear Caroline seemed plagued by mishaps."

Windvale sighed deeply. "Sadly, it's true."

"The unfair tragedy of Caroline's situation made me vow to protect her," Longley announced. "I offered to marry her in order to see to her safety."

"As did I," Windvale said, shooting an angry glare at Longley. "Not only would I keep your mother safe, I would also cherish and honor her."

Connor placed his hand on his heart. "I asked . . ."

"Enough!" Steven burst out. "I'd like you gentlemen to excuse us. Clearly I need to hear more about these matters."

Though Longley opened his mouth, Steven halted his protest with a fierce scowl. "Good night, gentlemen."

Waiting until they bade his mother farewell and moved away, Steven turned toward his mother. "I believe your explanation the other night was sadly lacking a few important details," he said evenly. "Would you care to elaborate now?"

"There's not much else to say." Tears glistened in his mother's eyes. "It was dreadful, Steven. It seemed as if horrid things kept on happening to me no matter how careful I was."

Steven stared down at his mother. Had she always been this helpless? Obviously his mother needed guidance and protection. Sighing, he patted his mother on her shoulder as he stared after the three men.

"Where did you say you met Longley, Windvale, and Connor?"

"I first met them in France at various parties and after they helped me, we began to tour together." She gave Steven a wavering smile. "Their companionship proved to be necessary."

Steven had little liking for the thought that these three men were traveling with his mother. "Who are they?"

His mother shook her head in confusion. "I introduced you."

"What I meant was what are their backgrounds? What do you really know about them?"

"Goodness, Steven, I didn't interrogate them," his mother returned.

"Yet you felt safe jaunting about Europe with them?" He didn't wait for her to reply. "Tell me this, Mother. Did you pay their way on these excursions?"

Shifting on her feet, his mother hesitated before finally saying, "Not all the time."

And with that, Steven had yet another explanation for the dire situation of their accounts. Three leeches could drain funds quicker than his mother could imagine. Steven made a mental note to investigate the backgrounds of Longley, Windvale, and Connor.

"Steven? Are you terribly mad at me?" his mother asked in a small voice.

The childish question only underscored how gullible and naive his mother truly was. How could he remain angry with her when she didn't understand the consequences of her actions?

"No, Mother, I'm not," he finally said.

In an uncharacteristic move, she lifted her chin. "I don't wish to be a burden to you, Steven, so I'd appreciate if you would teach me how to manage my finances."

If she'd asked him to strip naked and run about the salon in the buff, she couldn't have surprised him more. "Are you serious?"

"Absolutely," she said firmly. "I'm not stupid, you know."

Looking at his mother, he saw a determination in her expression that he'd never seen before. "No, Mother, you're not stupid." He nodded once. "We'll start tomorrow."

His mother smiled brilliantly at him, and for the first time since her return, he smiled back.

Bright and early the next day, Harriet stepped briskly up the front stoop and knocked upon Steven's door. Only the bold accomplished their goals, she told herself for the hundredth time. After leaving Laurel's, she'd spent the entire evening plotting out her next move in her revised strategy to catch Steven. Having struck upon the perfect plan, all that was required of her now was the determination to see the bold idea through.

As Steven's butler bade her enter, she hoped her cheeks weren't aflame with the embarrassment she felt.

Imagine what his butler must be thinking about her calling upon him, a single gentleman, at this hour . . . and alone! She flushed just thinking about it. Still, being a 'proper miss' had never gotten her anywhere, so it was definitely time to try a new approach to life. As the butler disappeared down the corridor, Harriet took a moment to gather her thoughts. Inhaling deeply, she prayed for the courage to pull off her grand scheme.

"If you would follow me, miss," the butler bade her at his return.

Let the games begin, Harriet thought as she followed him down the hallway. She stepped inside Steven's library and saw him rising from behind his desk. The papers strewn across the top of the large wooden desk told a tale.

"I'm interrupting you," she said, even more embarrassed by her boldness.

"Nonsense." Rising from his chair, he rounded his desk. "If truth be told, I welcome the distraction. Trying to balance my ledgers is not an enjoyable pastime." He stopped a few feet in front of her. "Though I have to admit that I am surprised to see you."

"After our last discussion?" At his nod, she continued, "I'm glad you mentioned last night, Steven, for that is the precise reason I am calling."

Crossing his arms, Steven leaned back against his desk. "Really?"

The sensual tilt of his lips made her swallow, but she maintained a hold on her senses. "Yes, really," she said briskly. "If anything, I appreciate your candor more than I can say. It is amazingly refreshing to find a gentleman who is so forthcoming and honest." She tugged off her gloves and set them aside, before removing her bonnet. "In fact, it is that very quality that I so admire that inspired me."

His brows arched upward. "Inspired you?"

"Most certainly." Smoothing her hands over her hair, she forged onward, maintaining her confident air when inside she felt frazzled. "I thought about our personal situations, and I realized that we could be of great assistance to one another."

Wariness darkened his gaze. "Oh? How's that?"

"I couldn't help but notice that you are spending quite a bit of time at more proper affairs."

Steven frowned at her. "What of it?"

She ignored the taunting question and forged onward. "I've also noticed that you are somewhat . . . shunned by the elite members of the ton."

"Preposterous," he announced loudly. "I speak with some of the finest members of society at my clubs. Trust me when I say that I'd notice if I was being ostracized."

"I'm speaking of the ladies, my lord," Harriet informed him tartly. "While the gentlemen accept you easily, it is obvious that the finest matrons of society will want to keep their daughters away from you."

His brows drew together.

"Your lack of response is most telling, Steven," Harriet said, pitching her voice to just the right tone. "I can help you become more acceptable to the premier hostesses."

Steven laughed briefly, cutting the tension in the room. "Really," he drawled. "And how precisely do you propose to do that?"

"By championing you," she said easily. "If you haven't noticed, I'm very well acquainted with the elderly matrons of society. Also, my reputation is impeccable, so if I pronounce you reformed, others will be swayed by my support."

"You think it could be that easy?" he asked, a corner of his mouth tipping upward.

"No, I'm positive it will be." She removed her gloves, tossing them on the table. "If there's one thing I understand, it is how the matrons of society react to gossip—both good and bad. Given enough time I could have them believing that you're considering joining the church!"

His eyes gleamed. "Not even on my deathbed."

"On your deathbed, my lord, I'm not even certain if Heaven would want you."

"Which is precisely why I'm so bent on enjoying myself while on earth."

"Is that the reason? I merely assumed that you were trying for some sort of record for debauchery."

Tossing his head back, Steven laughed heartily. "I do enjoy sparring with you, Harriet."

"I do appreciate the sentiment, Steven, but I'd rather hear your reply to my proposal."

His smile still in place, he asked, "Why do you want to help me?"

"Because I believe you can help me as well," she admitted, hitting closer to the truth than she had since she'd first thought up her scheme.

"How?"

Gesturing toward herself, she explained the final portion of her plan. "Look at me; I'm hardly the sort of lady that inspires desire in a man. I'm 'the best friend,' not the beautiful lady who captures the attention of every man she meets. I'm polite to the point of being boring, so proper that some people are afraid even to approach me for fear of a misstep, and hardly a stunning beauty." She sighed loudly. "Even my name is dull."

"I think Harriet is a perfectly nice name," Steven protested.

"Which is exactly my point. It is perfectly nice." Harriet rounded on him fiercely. "But I'm tired of being nice, tired of being overlooked, tired of being unremarkable in every way."

"But you're not . . ."

"Please, Steven!" she exclaimed, cutting off his protest. "At least be honest with me. I deserve that much."

Though he looked like he wanted to argue the point, he finally nodded slowly. "While I don't agree with much of your assertions, I can see that you believe them whole-heartedly. What can I do to help you?"

"You can help me hone my feminine wiles, so to speak," she said, hoping her face wasn't too red.

His brows shot upward. "You wish to have an affair with me?"

"Absolutely not," she replied, even though the idea sent a burst of heat through her. "I simply want someone with whom I can practice flirting." She gripped the back of a chair to steady herself. "You said last night you are no longer attracted to me, which works perfectly for this plan."

"And how's that?" he asked doubtfully.

"You'll be immune to my charms as I practice flirting," she countered, praying that he wasn't immune at all. "Besides, as a rake you've perfected the art of flirtatious remarks and have had enough women use feminine wiles on you to recognize if I'm hitting the mark or not."

"Helping you learn how to flirt?"

"While I help you rebuild your reputation with the society matrons."

Thrusting both hands through his hair, he exhaled sharply. "Isn't this plan a bit . . . well, crazy?"

"Not if I want to marry." Harriet stepped closer, placing a hand upon his arm. "I don't want to end up an old maid or trapped in a marriage with someone I can barely tolerate. I wish to marry for love, but the only way I can find that love is to meet an eligible gentleman." She gazed up at Steven. "Please. Won't you help me?"

Chapter Eight

It was sheer and utter madness.

Steven knew that as well as he knew his own name, but somehow he found himself listening. Like forbidden fruit dangling from the hand of the devil, the offer tempted him in the worst way.

She didn't believe in herself, didn't see her allure, didn't understand that he found her so attractive he felt as if he were wrestling with Hercules himself to overcome the urge to pull her into his arms and experience her mind-stunning kisses. It would be folly for him even to consider spending time with her, given his craving for her.

Still, what if he was to take her up on her offer?

There was no denying that her help with the dragons of society would aid his search for an heiress. Royce himself had mentioned that there were several heiresses he'd not met yet, would never meet because of his reputation. And since time was of the essence; it only made sense to become more respectable. That way, if he needed to move on to a new crop of ladies, the overprotective papas would find him acceptable.

But in return for her help, he would need to become the target for her flirtations. Lord Almighty! Just the thought of it heated his blood. Could he resist that temptation?

Of course, he reassured himself. After all, he'd been the object of feminine allure for years; he could certainly resist one innocent miss. As she said, it would prove to be beneficial to both of them.

Besides, he wanted to spend more time with her. And as long as they both understood that nothing could come of it in the end, there was nothing wrong with Harriet's plan.

Glancing back over his shoulder at the open ledgers that read like a death toll, Steven realized that he deserved this last opportunity to do what he wanted to do, rather than what his obligations had forced upon him. He could accept Harriet's offer, indulge himself in harmless flirtation, before settling down into the life his responsibilities dictated. At the same time, he would be helping Harriet become more self-assured, more confident.

Though he'd initially considered her plan madness, now that he'd had a chance to thoroughly examine it, he saw the logic behind it. "I think it's a marvelous plan, Harriet."

She released her pent-up breath. "I'm so glad you agree. It will be a wonderful opportunity for both of us."

"Indeed," he replied.

A happy laugh escaped her. "This will be so wonderful," she said again, as if she couldn't say it enough.

"So . . . where shall we start? Should we begin now? Or should we . . ."

"Not now." Grasping her hand, he held on to it gently. "Not only could you have been seen entering my house, but my mother resides here as well. As the whole purpose of this is to have me be seen as something other than a rake, it hardly behooves us to be caught alone together."

"We certainly can't have our lessons at my house, not with my aunts and parents there."

"True," he agreed readily. "What we need is somewhere private, somewhere we wouldn't be seen." As the words left his mouth, the perfect place popped into his head. "I do have this little . . . No," he muttered, embarrassed for even having considered the cottage.

"Where?" she asked, prodding him into continuing.

He shook his head. "It's not important as it's completely inappropriate."

A brilliant grin split her face. "I don't mind if you don't."

Lord, he loved her retorts! The location of the cottage was just outside the fashionable district, not far enough to be in a dangerous section of town, but not yet close enough to be in an area where they would be spotted. "My father purchased a small cottage near your town house that he used for his liaisons before he married my mother, that is. While I know it sounds wrong to suggest we . . ."

"It sounds perfect," Harriet countered, interrupting him again. "I could easily sneak out the rear garden door unnoticed and meet you there."

Her easy acceptance of his suggestion made him believe it hadn't been so insane to offer it in the first place.

"That's true," he agreed. "No one knows the cottage belongs to my family as it hasn't been used in years. As long as we were discreet, I doubt anyone would even see us meeting there." He cleared his throat. "I wish to reassure you, Harriet, that even though we will be alone, I will not take advantage of you."

"That's a shame."

Her remark sent a rush of heat through him, straight downward to pool in his groin.

A dimple appeared at the side of her mouth. "How was that?" she asked brightly. "Is that the sort of teasing remark gentlemen find appealing?"

When he could actually swallow again, he managed a reply. "I think that was a bit over the top, Harriet."

Her brows drew downward. "You didn't like it?"

No, he liked it too damn much! Clearing his throat again, Steven struggled to regain his composure. "It wasn't that I didn't like it, but rather that it was a bit too suggestive."

"Even for the type of woman who wishes to attract a rake?"

"It's too suggestive for a lady who wishes to attract a rake."

She bit the side of her lip. "There's a difference between what a woman can do and what a lady can do?"

"A world of difference," Steven assured her firmly. "After all, your end goal as a lady is to marry the gentleman, not become his mistress."

Tilting her head to the side, Harriet rolled her eyes. "It certainly seems as if it would be more entertaining if I didn't need to worry overmuch about this lady business."

"Perhaps, but if you play life fast and loose, there's always a high price to pay in the end." As he uttered the sentiment, he realized it applied to their very situation. Lord, he knew he should resist the temptation. It wasn't too late to tell Harriet it was a poor decision, to refuse her suggestion, but even as he thought about that possibility, he rejected it.

There was a great distinction between being a man and being a gentleman.

Steven wondered which one he would prove to be in the end.

Harriet's feet barely touched the ground as she ran into her house, ecstatic over the success of her plan. When she'd dreamed up this scheme, she'd imagined them meeting at his town house where they'd be surrounded by servants and family. The thought of being alone with him in a secluded cottage made her shiver with excitement. It would also provide her with a perfect opportunity to show Steven just how wonderful she could make his life.

Utilizing her 'dog theory,' she would ensure that the cottage was warm and welcoming, thereby providing him with comfortable surroundings that every dog she'd ever known wanted. In the privacy of the cottage, she could also cook for him, demonstrating her culinary skills, and proving that he would be well fed. In addition, the private house would enable her to offer him frequent displays of affection that he would find irresistible.

Her plan couldn't fail!

Tossing her bonnet and gloves upon the hallway table, she headed toward the salon, where she heard her parents.

"There you are, dear," exclaimed Harriet's mother. Waving at the tea set on the table, she offered, "Would you care for a bit of refreshment?"

Smiling at her mother, Harriet accepted. "That would be delightful." She glanced at her father. "And how are you two this fine day?"

"We're just as well as we were a few hours ago when we dined together," her mother remarked as she passed her a cup of tea. Her gray curls bobbed as she nodded toward Harriet. "But it would appear that something happened to lift our little girl's spirits, wouldn't it, Lionel?"

Tilting down a corner of his paper, Harriet's father peered over at her. "Indeed it would." With a snap, he closed the newspaper. "Tell us what caused this smittlish mood."

"I do hope it is an infectious mood, Father," Harriet replied, smiling at her dear papa. With his flyaway gray hair and blunt features, he looked every inch the comfortable country gentleman.

"Perhaps it would be if you shared the reason behind your grin," her mother interjected with a laugh.

Glancing at her mother, Harriet was swamped by her love for these two kind people. While she would like nothing more than to share the reason behind her elation, she highly doubted if her old-fashioned parents would approve of her plan to catch her lord. Instead, Harriet offered her parents a more palatable version of the truth. "As I mentioned before, I've met a gentleman whom I find most interesting."

A bright twinkle sparked in her mother's gaze as she leaned forward eagerly. "Are you finally ready to reveal his identity?"

Uncertain if she should give them a name, Harriet quickly realized that her mother would continue to ask for the gentleman's identity over and over until Harriet relented. "Lord Heath," she finally admitted.

"Heath . . . Heath . . ." her father muttered as if trying to place the name with a face. "Have we met this fellow yet?"

"No, but both Aunt Agatha and Aunt Hilda have . . . and they find him charming," she assured her father. "He even prefers the country to town."

From her father's expression of approval, Harriet knew she'd said just the right think to elevate Steven in her father's eyes. "Intelligent fellow then, eh?"

"Most definitely."

Her father snapped his fingers. "I'll wager he'd be interested in this new fertilizer old Mr. McKenny created. It works better than any I've ever seen. In fact, it nearly doubles the output of produce. If McKenny could find an investor to back him, I'm positive he'd make a fortune selling the stuff." Leaning forward, her father warmed to the subject. "He uses a mix of peat, manure, and . . ."

"Lionel, please," interrupted Mother, lifting a hand in protest. "You know how this talk upsets Harriet."

Normally, her mother would have been right; Harriet positively detested discussing fertilizers, but this time her father had added a word into his manure discussion that he'd never before added.

Fortune.

A frugal man, her father never tossed about a phrase like 'make a fortune' unless he was confident a person actually could. "It's fine, Mother," Harriet assured her before turning toward her father. "Do you really believe Mr. McKenny's fertilizer is special?"

"I've never seen the like, and I've been farming all my life." He fixed a gaze upon her. "You seem awfully interested in this, Harriet."

"I am," she admitted, setting down her teacup. "If what you say is true, then anyone who backs Mr. McKenny could, as you predicted, make a fortune."

"Very true. If I weren't a man of such modest means, I would invest myself." Her father reached out to pat her mother's arm. "I'd take your mother here on a whirlwind tour of the Continent with the money."

"Maybe you'll be able to."

At her comment, her father shot her a confused look. "How's that, Harriet? I don't have the funds to invest."

"But I do."

Stunned silence descended upon the room until her mother found her voice first. "Harriet," she murmured, pressing a hand to her chest. "Surely you aren't referring to your portion from your aunt Agatha?"

"I am indeed," Harriet stated, ignoring her mother's gasp.

"But without it, you'll find it difficult to wed one of these fine town folk you're so determined to marry," her father pointed out.

"I'm finding it difficult now, Papa. My portion isn't large enough to entice someone to marry me for my money, so I'm no worse off if I lose it, am I?" Harriet thought of all the possibilities. "But what I stand to gain if the investment goes well is beyond belief. As an heiress, the gentlemen of the ton will be able to overlook my other failings."

"Overlook what?" blustered her father. "You have no failings."

She smiled at him. "Thank you, Papa, but it makes no difference to my decision to invest my portion."

For a moment, her father stared at her, before finally nodding once. "Very well then, Harriet, if you're determined to see this through, I'll not be standing in your way. I'll send out a courier to McKenny and have him come to town with a sample and his proof of his results. When he gets here, I'll figure out the best way to market the fertilizer."

Jumping up from her chair, Harriet leaned to hug her father. "Thank you, Papa. I know everything will work out perfectly." She glanced at her mother and gave her a quick wink. "You'd best get busy planning for that tour."

Trying to teach his mother how to manage her finances was a far more difficult task than he'd ever imagined, Steven thought as he stepped into White's for a much-needed drink. To make matters even worse, he'd been distracted with thoughts of his bargain. The very idea of spending time with Harriet sent a desire rolling through him. Luckily he was confident his control would prove strong.

"Join me, Steven," offered Lord Hampton from the corner table.

Just the perfect person to ask about these men hanging around his mother, Steven thought as he joined the elderly gentleman with a smile. "You're looking well, Hampton."

Lord Hampton thumped a hand upon his chest. "Fitter

than ever." He gestured toward his ale. "Would you care for a drink?"

"Of course," Steven replied before turning to order a brandy. Shifting around in his chair, he settled back. "I'm glad I ran into you, Hampton. I thought you might be able to give me some information on a few contemporaries of yours."

"Not familiar with your elders?" he jested.

"Only with the gentlemen of importance," he replied easily.

Lord Hampton laughed out loud. "You should begin attending the House of Lords. I vow that glib tongue of yours would serve you well."

"I'm uncertain if that was a compliment or an insult."

"That's what I'm speaking of!" Lord Hampton slapped the arm of his chair. "Those pompous poppy-cocks could use those sort of remarks." He waved his hand. "But I'm interrupting your question. Who is it you wanted to know about?"

"My mother recently returned from a year-long tour with three men in tow. Naturally, I'd like to check them out a bit to ensure my mother's well-being," Steven said, phrasing his statement very carefully to protect his family name. "What do you know of Percy Windvale, Edward Longley, and Robert Connor?"

"Know of the first one," Lord Hampton began, rubbing at his chin. "Somewhat of a dour fellow and quite tight-fisted from what I can recall, but I've never heard of the other two."

As the servant returned with his drink, Steven masked his disappointment. "Would you mind making a few discreet inquiries with some of your friends? Perhaps they might know of the other two and have more detailed information on Windvale."

"Be delighted to," Lord Hampton announced, lifting his ale in a toast. "Here's to family and fortune."

Since he had blasted little of both, it was certainly a toast he could second. Reaching forward, he tipped his glass against Lord Hampton's. "To family and fortune."

Chapter Nine

As soon as her mother and aunts headed out for the literary meeting, Harriet hurried into the garden. Her aunts had urged her to attend the meeting, but Harriet had declined, claiming a megrim. She must be a fine actress to have hidden the brimming excitement soaring through her! Perhaps she should feel a little guilty at her white lie, but she was far too eager for her first visit to the cottage, for her first lesson with Steven, for her adventure of a lifetime to begin.

Pausing to pick an armful of flowers, Harriet slipped out the rear gate and onto the street. She tugged up the hood of her cape, pulling it down low to hide her face as she made her way to the cottage. A few short blocks later, she came upon a beautiful, doll-like cottage that sat surrounded by overgrown gardens and a peeling fence. Still, the sad air of neglect did little to detract from the cottage's loveliness.

The gate creaked from lack of use as she slipped into

the yard, making her way down the front path. Using the key Steven had given her, she let herself inside. The musty smell lay testament to the fact no one had used the place in a long time. Yet, if she looked beneath the sheets covering the furniture and the layer of dust and cobwebs, she could easily see the charm of the small house.

Pleased she'd arrived two full hours earlier than Steven's note had requested, Harriet went to work, setting the house to rights. Opening the windows, she allowed the fresh air to sweep in as she removed the dusty sheets from the furniture in the front salon first. Attacking one room at a time, she made her way from the front salon, back into the small foyer, then on to the dining room that lay off to the right of the foyer, and into the kitchen, where she set down all the dusty sheets.

Her plans to prepare a wonderful meal for Steven would need to wait until another day. Today she had her hands full simply trying to make certain they had a reasonably clean place to sit. After she dusted the tables off, Harriet wandered upstairs.

In the center of the large bedroom sat a huge bed, complete with tassels and gold angels atop four large posts. Her cheeks burned as she gazed around the room, wondering at the overlarge chair in the corner and the silken ropes dangling from the chair's legs and arms. She couldn't even make a guess as to the purpose of those ropes. Mirrors were everywhere, ensuring that no matter where you stood or sat in the room that you could see yourself from at least three different angles.

Curiosity drove her to open one of the two doors that led off the bedroom. The first led to a small room that was filled with robes. Stepping into the room, she ran her hand along the different materials; some of them silk, some fur, some finely woven tapestry. She guessed that the larger sizes on the right were once Steven's father's robes while the smaller ones of the left must have been for his lovers.

Lovers.

A delicious shiver ran through Harriet as she repeated the word in her head.

Leaving the robes behind, she opened the last door . . . to a room unlike any she'd ever seen before. Up on a two-tiered platform sat a huge, claw-footed tub, obviously made for two. To the right of the tub stood a marble pedestal that created a home for an assortment of lotions, oils, and bath scents. Behind the platform lay an extra-large divan, covered with a curious assortment of feathers.

What was one supposed to do with those? Use the feathers to dry off? The notion was utterly ridiculous, she knew, but couldn't fathom any other possible reason for them. It was obvious that she was woefully innocent.

Hopefully, Steven would alleviate that problem.

"Harriet?"

At Steven's call, Harriet spun on her heel and hurried from the bedroom. Pausing at the top of the stairs, she caught her first glimpse of Steven where he stood in the foyer.

He must have heard her approach for he glanced upward, giving her a smile that made her breath catch. "Harriet," he murmured, the tone in his voice touching her softly.

For a long moment, they stood still, gazing at each other in spellbound silence, until finally Steven looked away. The spell broken, Harriet descended the stairs as Steven wandered into the front salon. "You've been busy."

She shrugged, dismissing the hours of backbreaking work. "I arrived early, so I decided to clean up a bit."

"It looks wonderful." Removing his outer coat, he laid it over the back of a chair. "I was going to send a maid to clean, but I didn't want anyone to know I'd opened this house."

"I understand." A side of her mouth quirked upward. "And I think the upstairs would have shocked any of your maids."

"Really?" Steven glanced upward. "I've never been up there myself. From what I understand, my father used this place quite a bit before he married my mother. He even let a few mistresses live here . . . until he tired of them."

"At which point he gave them diamonds and sent them on their way," Harriet concluded.

"Emeralds," Steven corrected her with a grin. "And a lovely nest egg if they'd been with him long enough." Lifting one shoulder, he dismissed the behavior. "My father was quite advanced in his years when he married my mother and once he said his vows, this cottage was never used again."

"So he was truly a reformed rake."

Steven nodded once. "Just like Royce."

"And you'll be next." Harriet clasped her hands together. "Shall we begin?"

"In a moment." Glancing upward once more, he headed for the stairs. "First I have to see what all the fuss is about upstairs."

Not wanting to miss his reaction, Harriet followed him

up the stairs, watching him closely. As it turned out, she didn't need to watch closely at all.

"Good God!" Steven exclaimed, his jaw practically hitting the floor. "Would you look at this place?"

Harriet grinned broadly. "A mirror at every conceivable angle."

"Indeed." Steven slanted a look at her.

"Quite shocking," she retorted, her smile belying her words.

"You think so?" Rocking back on his heels, Steven captured her gaze in one of the mirrors. "I find it rather inventive."

"It is precisely that sort of remark that will not garner the favor of the matrons," she said reprovingly.

A laugh burst from him. "Perhaps not . . . though from the looks of this place I'd say I have a long way to go before I even come close to achieving the roguish behavior of my father."

"That's undoubtedly true, but perhaps all the time you'll be spending here in his hideaway, you'll be inspired to surpass his record."

"I don't know if I have enough energy for that feat," he muttered as he made his way to the small room containing the robes. For a moment, he peered inside before shutting the door again. "Apparently my father saw little need for any sort of clothing other than robes."

"Ah, but what elegant robes they are," Harriet teased. "A sensualist would revel in the feel of silk against his skin."

Steven froze in his tracks as he eyed Harriet, the intensity in his eyes making her tingle. Slowly, he slid his gaze along the length of her body, lingering at the swell of her breasts, the curve of her hips, before traveling back again. "Everything in due time," he murmured softly.

How she wished it was due time now!

Steven shook his head as if clearing his thoughts, before grinning at her. "I know," he murmured. "You're going to tell me that I can't make those sorts of remarks anymore."

Not exactly. She'd been too caught up in desire for sensible thought.

"Precisely," she returned when she found her voice again.

"You know," he began, "behaving in a staid manner is harder than it seems."

Harriet pressed her hands to her stomach, trying to calm the desire simmering inside of her. "I'm confident you're up to the challenge."

When Steven opened the second door to the bathing room, he stood for a long while, silent, as he gazed into the room.

"Almost beyond description, isn't it?" Harriet murmured as she moved to his side, peering over his shoulder into the decadent room. "I imagine your father spent quite a bit of time in here."

"Who could blame the man?" Steven shook his head slowly. "I had no idea."

"Of course not," Harriet replied. "By the time you were born, your father was reformed and had given up these . . . activities."

"Seems a bloody shame."

Harriet gave him a sharp look. "Really, Steven," she said in reprimand. "Your father is most commendable to have given up these . . ." She waved her hand toward the bath, unable even to name the events that must have taken place in the room.

"I know that," Steven conceded. "But still, once a man's had peacock feathers, I don't know how he could go without."

His remark sparked her curiosity. "What exactly is done with those feathers? I couldn't discern their purpose."

Slowly, Steven turned his head, until he was mere inches from her mouth. "Maybe I'll have to give you a demonstration someday."

Please, please, please, she wanted to shout, only managing to restrain herself by sheer will. Finally, she murmured, "Promise?"

The flare in his gaze created a mirror flame inside of her, making her wonder what he would do if she leaned forward and touched her lips to his. Before she could act upon her thought, he shifted, moving away from her and breaking the moment.

"Perhaps it's time we got started, don't you think?"

"Indeed," she said, using the same light tone he'd employed. "I wish I'd thought to bring some tea."

He grasped the conversational gambit like a drowning man. "I brought some lemonade and scones if you'd care for some refreshments."

"Yes, please. That would be delightful," she replied politely, as if they weren't standing in the midst of a well-used, carnal pleasure palace.

Without another word between them, Harriet made her way downstairs, aware of Steven behind her. She went into the salon, taking a seat on the settee as Steven retrieved his basket before joining her. Gratefully, she accepted a glass of cool lemonade. Whenever she was around Steven, she seemed to be overheated.

"As I said before, you must curb your remarks if you are ever going to have the ladies believe you're reformed," she said, as he set out the scones. "One sensual remark can undo weeks' worth of work."

"I realize that, but restraint is far harder than I thought," he admitted before taking a sip of lemonade. "Bold statements just seem to come naturally to me."

Harriet had to smile at that one. "Perhaps you are your father's son after all."

"After seeing my father's hideaway, I certainly hope so."

In the midst of taking another sip of lemonade, Harriet swallowed quickly before she choked on the refreshment. "Oh, my," she said, pressing a hand to her throat. "You shouldn't say things like that when I'm drinking."

"Sorry." But from the unabashed tone in the single word, he seemed anything but sorry.

Setting down her glass, she ran her hands along her skirt, smoothing it out, before moving into the next phase of her plan. "Now, Steven, you also need to alter your behavior around Lady Camilla and the other ladies of the ton."

"Alter it how?"

"First, you should ignore them."

"What?"

She arched a brow at him. "You heard me perfectly well. Trust me on this, Steven. Ladies like Camilla and her ilk aren't easily impressed; gentlemen are always chasing them . . . and their fortunes. If you ignore her, you will fascinate her," she finished, hoping Steven would forgive her for lying to him. Harriet knew perfectly well Camilla loved when gentlemen fawned all over her; she would dismiss Steven out of hand for ignoring her.

An expression of doubt creased Steven's features. "Are you certain?"

"Absolutely." Harriet crossed her feet at her ankles. "Just remember how many ladies found Royce utterly fascinating when he ignored them and treated them like chattel."

She knew she had Steven on that point as he nodded in agreement. "I'll try it," he agreed finally.

Hiding the elation she felt, Harriet simply smiled at Steven. "Perfect. Once the matrons see you ignoring ladies like Camilla, they'll begin to realize how much you've changed. Naturally, I will be right next to them, pointing out your amazing restraint. In no time at all, we'll have you regarded as a perfect gentleman whom anyone would find acceptable."

Raising his glass, Steven toasted her prediction. "From your lips to God's ears."

Offering him a weak smile, she lifted her glass half-heartedly, then lowered it again without taking a sip. She wasn't about to toast his success with another woman.

"Now we need to focus on you for a while."

Her head jerked upward. "Me?" she squeaked.

"Naturally. You don't think I'm going to renege on my part of our bargain, do you?"

Mutely, she shook her head, praying silently that he meant to kiss her.

"There is more to flirting than words," he began easily. "First, let's study your posture."

If he'd said he was going to examine her teeth like she

was a racing horse he was considering buying, she wouldn't have been more surprised. "My what?"

"Posture." He waved a hand at her. "You are sitting like a perfect lady with your feet crossed politely at the ankles and your hands folded upon your lap."

She frowned at him. "And what's wrong with that?"

"Nothing . . . if you're looking to attract a nice, perfectly respectable gentleman. However, if you wish to attract a rake, you'll need to show him you're willing to be more . . . adventurous."

Intrigued, she uncrossed her legs, leaving her feet placed firmly on the floor, side by side. "Like this?"

Shaking his head, Steven shifted until he sat next to her on the settee. "No; you still look like the proper young lady you are." He reached for her knees, freezing an inch away from touching her. "May I?"

She gave him a pointed look. "Rakes don't ask."

"I'm not a rake anymore, remember?" he said with a chagrined laugh. Through her skirt, he curved his hand under her knee, lifting it upward until it rested on the settee. Instinctively, she shifted her entire body, angling herself until she almost faced him. Feeling her arm crushed against the backrest of the seat, she lifted it, laying it along the top of the settee.

For a moment, Steven gazed at her, looking her up and down, before returning to her face. "Perfect," he murmured, his voice lower and huskier than before. "Now you look . . ."

"Wanton?" she supplied hopefully, feeling wonderfully free in the new position. With her leg lifted, her skirt gaped, showing a shocking amount of the leg that remained on the floor, and with her arm along the back of the settee, her bodice strained against her breasts, showing off her curves with stunning clarity. At his nod, she gave him a smile that made him swallow. Hard. "Wonderful," she practically purred. Overjoyed at the effect she seemed to be having on Steven, she decided to nudge him a bit further to see how he'd react. "I'm attending Lady Hammersmith's dinner party this evening. Should I sit like this at dinner?" she asked innocently, as if she didn't already know the answer.

His response didn't disappoint her. "Good God!" he exploded, reaching out to set her angled leg back on the floor. "Are you mad? Of course not! This position is only in an intimate setting, when no one else is around to witness your boldness."

"Then what am I supposed to do at this dinner party to capture the attention of the gentlemen?" she asked in earnest.

"You need to be more subtle when in public." He picked up her hand and stroked it down his forearm. "Touch the gentleman next to you in soft, stroking motions like this."

Tugging free of his grip, she tried to mimic his motions, sweeping her hand along his forearm, allowing the tips of her fingers to touch the bare skin at the back of his hand. "How is this?"

"Perfect," he remarked, his voice low and tight. Suddenly, he reached out to grab her hand, stopping her caress. Clearing his throat, he released her, allowing her hand to fall back onto her lap. "Not too much," he cautioned. "Just enough to intrigue, to catch his interest, to make him notice you."

Pleased with the instruction, she gave him a wide smile. "I shall try it this very evening."

Before she could say anything else, Steven thrust to his feet. "It is getting late, Harriet. If you're going to attend the Hammersmith party, you should be off."

"Very well." Rising as well, she retrieved her cloak. "Are you going to be there tonight?"

"Y-y-yes," he stammered. "Yes, I am."

Perfect, Harriet thought, as she pulled her hood up over her face. With a well-placed suggestion in Lady Hammersmith's ear, she could sit next to Steven and stroke his arm all evening. This plan of hers was progressing along quite nicely.

Leaning forward, she allowed her entire body to press against Steven as she rose up on her tiptoes to kiss his cheek. She shifted her head backward until she was inches from his mouth, before whispering, "Thank you, Steven."

If his clenched hands were any indication, she'd say their afternoon lessons had been a rousing success. "Same time tomorrow."

Instead of replying, he simply nodded tersely.

More pleased than she would have been with a cheery reply, Harriet waved farewell before slipping from the charming cottage. When she'd devised this bargain, she'd never dared hope for such immediate success. If anything, Steven's reaction today proved his attraction to her, making her feel as if she were filled with feminine power. Tonight, she'd see Steven again and, hopefully, be afforded the chance to entice him even more and tomorrow, she could lead him on a merry chase again.

Life was looking up.

Chapter Ten

~✦~

Steven watched Harriet wave at him, twitching her fingers, teasing him, tempting him to chase after her, pull her into his arms, and give free rein to the desire thundering through him. My God, she had no idea how close she'd come to being kissed senseless again when she'd leaned against him, pressing her sweet, curvaceous body into his eager, hard one as she kissed his cheek. He'd yearned to reach up, bury his fingers in her hair, angle her head to the side, and taste those lush lips once more.

Instead, he'd stood like a gentleman, holding in his base urgings, ignoring the pure, unadulterated lust pounding through him. If he'd acted in his true nature, he would have given in to his desire . . . and he wouldn't be standing here, throbbing and hard, needing relief from the passion thundering in him.

Perhaps there was something to be said for being a rake after all. He sent a rueful glance around the room, doubted very much if these four walls had seen such frustrating restraint. Not if those damn feathers upstairs were any indication.

Suddenly, an image of Harriet reclining in lush glory upon the divan, her silky hair streaming along her body, the strands catching upon her straining nipples, as he slowly teased her to passion with the subtle strokes of the feathers.

Christ! If he didn't want to remain hard as a pike for the remainder of the evening, he needed to stop those thoughts immediately. Wincing at the tightness in his britches, he stepped out into the lane and made his way briskly down the street.

After all, he needed to wrangle an invitation to the Hammersmith dinner party.

In her excitement at the approaching dinner party, Harriet had forgotten one minor detail—her parents and aunts were going to be there as well. If past experience had taught her one thing, it was that her aunts kept an eagle eye upon her. They would be certain to note every time she touched Steven or tried to flirt with him, and while Harriet was confident that Aunt Agatha would do everything she could to further the romance, she knew that Aunt Hilda would be applying just as much energy to destroying her chances with Steven. Harriet could only guess at her parents' reaction, but given her father's propensity to make loud observations, Harriet highly doubted it would be a quiet one.

Trying to rally her dampening spirits, Harriet accepted the footman's hand as she descended from the carriage and entered the elegant Hammersmith town house. The low murmur of conversation swept into the foyer as the

Hammersmith butler took their wraps. As Harriet entered the room, she searched for Steven, finding him almost immediately, standing with an arrogant flair near the fireplace. Since no lady stood nearby, Harriet could only assume that he'd taken her advice and ignored the beautiful Lady Camilla.

Harriet paused when she spied Lady Camilla gazing at Steven with a perplexed expression. Surely the haughty Lady Camilla would never stoop to chasing a man who ignored her. Dismissing the very notion as ridiculous, Harriet searched out her hostess.

When Lady Hammersmith broke away from her companions, Harriet took advantage of the opportunity to approach her. "Excuse me, Lady Hammersmith, I wonder if I might have a moment of your time."

Lady Hammersmith, a longtime friend of her aunt Agatha, reached out to clasp Harriet's hands with an affectionate squeeze. "For Agatha's sweet niece, most certainly."

Hoping Lady Hammersmith's generosity was as large as her heart, Harriet boldly made her request. "I hope you don't find me overly forward, but I wondered if you might seat me next to a certain gentleman during dinner."

A delighted gleam lit Lady Hammersmith's still-beautiful blue eyes. "Ohhh, an affaire du coeur," she whispered. "Has some gentleman finally captured your interest, dear Harriet? I vow your aunt had nearly given up hope that you would settle upon someone." Leaning forward, she turned her ear toward Harriet. "Whisper his name to me, and I'll make certain you're seated next to the gentleman."

"Lord Heath," Harriet murmured softly.

Straightening, Lady Hammersmith gazed solemnly at Harriet. "Lord Heath? But he's a . . ."

". . . changed man," Harriet pronounced, setting her part of the bargain into motion. "He's become most honorable and utterly charming."

A knowing look brightened Lady Hammersmith's eyes. "He always was charming, my dear. That's part of the problem I have with an innocent, sweet child like you spending time with him."

"You've known me for a long time," Harriet said softly. "I'm far too sensible to be taken in with smooth phrases."

"I've seen men like your Lord Heath scramble the senses of the most reasonable ladies." Pressing her hands to her heart, she sighed deeply. "Even as I urge you to use caution, I shall grant your request."

"I thank you, my lady."

"Save your thanks, but I do expect an invitation to your nuptials," Lady Hammersmith finished with a wag of her finger. With another gasp of pleasure and one last sigh with her hands pressed against her chest, Lady Hammersmith hurried off to arrange for the seating change.

With her mission accomplished, Harriet wandered toward Steven. As she approached, he broke off his conversation with Lord Hammersmith to greet her. "Good evening, Miss Nash," he said as he bent down to kiss the back of her glove-encased hand.

"Good evening, Lord Heath," she returned with not a hint of the intimacies they'd exchanged mere hours ago. The sparkle in Steven's eyes made her feel all warm inside; they shared a secret. A delicious, lovely secret that bound them together.

It wasn't until Lord Hammersmith cleared his throat in a pointed fashion that Harriet realized they'd been staring at each other. Tugging at his vest, Steven gestured toward their host. "Miss Nash, may I present . . ."

"No need for the formality," Lord Hammersmith boomed as he pulled Harriet in for a hug and kiss upon the cheek. "How have you been, Harriet? I haven't seen you in far too long."

"I'm glad that I can correct that this evening."

"As am I." Reaching out, he clucked her under her chin. "Before you know it, you'll be married and raising a passel of little ones and will never have time to visit an old codger like me."

"Never," she denied immediately. "I'll simply bring along my entire passel of children to visit you as well."

Laughter boomed out of Lord Hammersmith as he patted Harriet on the arm. "I'll hold you to that, Harriet."

"There will never be a need for that as I'll hold myself to it."

Her declaration brought a grin to Lord Hammersmith's face. "You always were a sweet one." His gaze shifted as he looked over her shoulder. "If you'll both excuse me, I see my lady wife is gesturing for me."

Harriet bid him farewell before turning her attention onto Steven.

"You seem to have an admirer," he remarked.

Harriet made a face. "Oh, yes, elderly people and young children adore me." She tapped her chest with her index finger. "And, as I told you before, I make a splendid best friend as well."

Steven reached out to tug on one of the tendrils dangling from her temple. "I think it's sweet."

"As does everyone else," she said, playfully batting his hand away. "The problem is very few gentlemen wish to marry for 'sweetness.'"

"Fools, the lot of them," Steven pronounced before striking a pose against the mantel. "Then again, perhaps it is only us rakish types that have more discerning tastes."

She was hoping that was true.

"Dinner is served."

The announcement saved Harriet from a reply. Accepting Steven's arm, she walked with him into Lady Hammersmith's large, formal dining room, eager to see what his response was going to be when he found out they were seated next to one another.

When he noted the place cards, his brows lifted. "You are sitting at my right," he murmured, glancing down at her. "How fortunate."

"Indeed," she returned with a smile as he dropped his arm and pulled out her chair. "Thank you, my lord."

As soon as she was seated, he slid into his chair. Her enthusiasm for the next few hours dimmed a bit as Lady Camilla sat down on Steven's left. Balsack, she thought, borrowing one of her father's lost words. No matter, she tried to reassure herself. After all, she had an advantage over the elegant Lady Camilla; she knew the perfect way to tease Steven right beneath everyone's noses . . . because he had shown her himself.

Feeling undaunted by Lady Camilla's arrival, Harriet turned toward the gentleman on her right, offering a greeting to Lord Conover, before glancing across the table . . . and right at her father. It was all she could do to hold in a groan as Harriet realized Lady Hammersmith had sat her directly across from her father. For heaven's sake, how was she supposed to flirt outrageously with Steven under her father's watchful eye?

It would appear that for all her love of affaires du coeur, Lady Hammersmith had a lot to learn about arranging for them.

Unfolding her linen napkin upon her lap, she waited until the pottages were served. When the table practically groaned from the weight of the various dishes ranging from a pottage of crayfish with carps and eels to Palestine soup, she accepted a cup of pease soup, taking a flavorful spoonful before turning to look . . .

. . . at the back of Steven's head.

Apparently the normally reserved Lady Camilla had overcome her shyness and was boldly conversing with Steven. As she watched, Lady Camilla placed a hand upon Steven's sleeve, lightly stroking her fingers over the cloth of his jacket. Indignant, Harriet set down her spoon. That was her move!

"Is something amiss, Harriet?"

Her father's loudly voiced question caused Harriet's cheeks to flush. Hopes for a wonderful evening dwindled by the moment. First Lady Camilla used the arm-stroking tactics to capture Steven's interest, and now her father sent unwanted attention her way, causing everyone within earshot to turn and send curious glances at her. With the direction the evening was taking, she would undoubtedly end up with some portion of her meal in her lap.

"I'm fine, Father," she replied, adding in a smile for good measure.

Her wish that it was the end of his inquiry died a sudden death. "You don't look fine," he countered, waving his spoon toward her.

And how lovely of her father to point it out to everyone at the table.

Before Harriet could reply, Lady Hammersmith called out from her position at the end of the table. "You are looking a bit peaked, dear."

What she wanted to say to Lady Hammersmith was that she wouldn't be pale at all if the seating arrangement hadn't been so abominable. Imagine seating her rival next to her love interest and her father across from her to watch the interplay. Silence descended upon the room as everyone paused in their enjoyment of the first course to await her answer . . . an answer she herself was searching for.

Then, like a knight on a white horse, Steven charged forth and rescued her from the embarrassing situation. "I fear I am to blame for Miss Nash's pallor."

"You, my lord?" Lady Hammersmith asked, obviously eager to savor an interesting tidbit of gossip. "What on earth did you say to poor Harriet to bring about such a reaction?"

Steven's mouth slowly curved upward into a deliciously wicked grin. "It wasn't my words, but rather my actions. In my enjoyment of your delicious pottage, I found myself so overcome with pleasure that I mistakenly laid my foot against Miss Nash's . . . no doubt causing her to believe I was making untoward advances."

Harriet's father slammed down his spoon. "Do you mean to tell me, sir, that you've been treating my daughter like a laced-mutton?"

Oh, dear heaven, Steven had done it now. "Of course not, Papa," Harriet interjected. "Poor Lord Heath was merely shifting in his seat, not making any improper advances."

Scowling, Harriet's father leaned back in his chair. "Likely story. I still say the action well suits a libidinist."

"A what?" asked Lord Hammersmith from the head of the table. "What the deuce does that mean, Nash?"

"Mr. Nash has just referred to me as a man who embraces lewdness," Steven clarified before Harriet's father could reply. "My dilemma lay in whether or not I should consider it an insult or a well-earned fact."

Laughter broke through the tension that had been steadily building in the room.

"I say, Nash, you should stop using all those ridiculous words that no one knows the meaning to . . . like that first one, laced-mutton. What the devil does that mean?" grumbled Lord Hammersmith.

"As for the definition of laced-mutton, it is not something to be shared in mixed company," Steven began before her father could reply. "And as for his usage of such unusual words, I find it rather astounding."

"You do?" Harriet asked softly, overwhelmed by Steven's generosity toward her father, especially after Papa had just attacked his character.

Turning his gaze upon her, he looked deeply into her eyes. "Indeed I do."

They gazed at each other for what seemed like an eternity, but in reality was only a few moments. "Consider this, my fellow guests; if we continue to lose words and their meanings from our English language, then a hundred years from now, we will have to resort to grunts and gestures to make our preferences known."

"That is precisely my concern!" exclaimed her father.

He paused to give Steven a long, hard look. "Perhaps I was a bit hasty in my judgment of you, my lord, and for that I can only offer my apology."

"Accepted, and I assure you I shall keep my feet firmly placed beneath my chair."

Another round of laughter filled the room before the guests returned to their soup. Harriet ate in stunned silence. Sweet heaven above, she had certainly taken her time in choosing a potential husband, but Steven was worth the wait.

As Steven sipped at his Palestine soup, he continued the discussion with her father.

". . . and I'm building a collection of these words. In fact, I hope someday to publish my words as a dictionary of sorts," her father finished.

Lifting his napkin, Steven swiped at his mouth before replying, "If you do, I assure you I will be the first in line to purchase a copy."

Steven's kindness to her father made Harriet's breath catch in a manner oddly similar to how he'd made her feel this afternoon when he'd almost kissed her . . . yet different in a deeper, stronger way. It was as if that afternoon he'd touched her desire; but tonight, with his kindness, he'd touched her heart.

After the servants cleared the bowls and set down plates of roasted pheasant with celery sauce, Harriet turned to converse with Steven only to be greeted by the back of his head . . . again. Her blood began to boil when she heard Lady Camilla ask Steven to slice her roast pheasant. Harriet knew what she'd like to roast and slice!

As Steven leaned over to fulfill Lady Camilla's request, the little witch shifted forward until her breasts pressed against his arm. Harriet fought off the urge to reach across Steven and shove the harlot off him. Imagine the nerve!

It was quickly becoming evident to Harriet that Lady Camilla was far more skilled at these games of enticement than she was, leaving Harriet with only one avenue to pursue—

To remind her "hound" of his warm, comfortable home.

Sometimes a dog might wander, sniffing everywhere, but he always returned to his home to settle in for the night. When Steven finished slicing the helpless Lady Camilla's fowl and leaned back in his chair, Harriet launched into her plan. "I read the most fascinating bit of news today," she said brightly, pitching her voice so she would be overheard. "It was an article about the many uses for feathers."

Beside her, Steven began to choke on a bite of pheasant.

The very picture of innocent concern, Harriet reached over to pat him on the back. "Are you all right, my lord?"

His face red, he nodded as he pressed his napkin against his lips.

Lifting her hands, she turned to face the other dining companions. "I promise my feet have been politely tucked beneath my chair."

Her jest drew an appreciative laugh from the other diners.

"Harriet," Steven began in a low voice, obviously not wishing to be overheard. "I don't think this is the place . . ."

"To what?" she asked, cutting him off. "I am merely discussing the varied uses of feathers."

From the look in his eye, she knew he was thinking of the assortment lying on the divan in the cottage's bathing room at this very moment. Their shared secret sent a delicious shiver along her spine.

Harriet could have jumped up and kissed Lady Hammersmith for taking up the gambit. "Feathers? How peculiar. I know that they're used for dusting and adorning hats, but what other use could they have?"

She hadn't the foggiest idea, but she could certainly use her imagination. Perhaps they are used to dry oneself, Harriet thought, imagining the soft, silky slide of feathers along dampened skin. Still, she could hardly toss out that idea without shocking everyone in attendance. "Well, floral arrangements were mentioned."

"Mixing feathers and flowers?" Lady Hammersmith shook her head. "What a ridiculous notion."

"No more than the original suggestion to place a pineapple in the middle of an arrangement must have been," Harriet countered, pointing to Lady Hammersmith's own centerpiece. "And just look at how beautiful it looks there."

"Why, thank you, Harriet," Lady Hammersmith said, obviously pleased with the compliment. "Perhaps I shall request a few feathers be added to an arrangement tomorrow, and we can see how they look."

Harriet nodded happily. She didn't care how silly this conversation was because it had accomplished her goal—to focus Steven's attention solely upon her. Take that, Lady Camilla!

Apparently, Lady Camilla wasn't one to "take" anything, for the next minute she leaned toward Steven, whispering to him so softly that no matter how hard Harriet tried to overhear them, she failed. Miserably. Double drat! What was it going to take to make that miserable woman disappear?

As Steven shifted toward Lady Camilla with a smile upon his face, Harriet decided she needed a stronger approach. It would appear that a verbal reminder just wasn't enough to make him forget about the unbelievably forward Lady Camilla. Harriet didn't know why the other woman had decided this evening of all evenings to be overly bold, and she didn't care. All she knew was that it was time to use heavy artillery.

Like what?

Before today she hadn't even known about the stroke-a-gentleman's-arm trick . . . and she couldn't use a tactic if she didn't know it existed. Where had she been when they were giving out lessons on feminine wiles? Undoubtedly in the sweet-to-the-elderly, best-friend-to-all lessons.

When God chose to hand out graces, He certainly didn't seem to spread them out evenly.

At least her father was busy conversing about his collection of archaic words to Lord Conover at her right, leaving Harriet free to converse with Steven . . . if she could get his attention away from Lady Camilla. As the servants cleared the pheasant and served a fine dish of poached herring in sherry sauce, Harriet struggled to devise a way of capturing Steven's attention.

Selecting a stalk of asparagus, she swirled it around in the sauce before lifting it to her mouth. As she took her bite of the vegetable, she glanced at Steven and found him watching her with an intensity that reminded her of the way he'd looked at her that afternoon. But why? She wasn't about to complain, but if she didn't understand why she'd seemed to arouse his interest, she couldn't repeat the action. Slowly, she pulled the fork from her mouth, startled to find Steven's gaze shift downward onto her lips.

Surely it wasn't that he found watching her eat sensual, Harriet thought. Testing out the silly notion, she cut off another piece of the tender stalk and slowly pulled it along her plate, catching the sauce upon the asparagus. She watched Steven carefully as she tested her theory. Sitting motionless, only his gaze shifted as he followed the ascent of her fork toward her mouth.

This time, she licked at the sauce first and was rewarded by the sight of his body jerking as if he'd been prodded with a sharp implement. When she slipped the piece of vegetable into her mouth, she moaned very, very softly as her lips closed around the fork. A few beads of perspiration dotted his upper lip as his gaze followed her every move.

Oh, my, she thought, fighting the urge to grin like a bawdy mistress who'd just found out how to turn silver into gold. Isn't this going to be fun!

Chapter Eleven

~~~

All through dinner, Harriet teased Steven relentlessly. If he so much as glanced at Lady Camilla, she licked at her spiced beef in red wine sauce, nibbled at her beetroot pancakes, or swirled her tongue around her potted mushrooms. She'd always known that gentlemen loved to eat, but who would have ever thought that they also enjoyed to watch ladies eat?

Fascinating stuff.

When they served the syllabub and macaroons, Harriet was well pleased with the rousing success of her evening. Picking up one of the delicate cookies, she snapped off a piece . . . but sent a few crumbs showering down onto Steven's lap. Not wanting the oil from the almonds in the cookie to stain his breeches, Harriet reached out to wipe them off.

The moment her hand touched his lap, Steven yelped as he jumped beneath her touch, obviously startled.

"What ever is the matter, Lord Heath?" inquired Lady

Hammersmith, eyeing Steven closely. "You're jumpier this evening than a rabbit cornered by a fox."

A dog cornered by a clever fox, Harriet mentally corrected their hostess.

"Again, I offer my apologies," Steven said smoothly even as he reached beneath the tablecloth and firmly removed her hand from his lap. "Conversation had begun to wane, so I thought I'd liven it up a bit."

Lady Hammersmith arched her brows. "By shouting out loud? A most interesting choice of techniques, my lord."

"It worked, didn't it?"

Everyone at the table joined Lady Hammersmith in laughter. "Yes, Lord Heath. It worked indeed." she finally replied. "Perhaps you might like to offer a topic of conversation that would entertain."

"There are a number of conversations we might explore," Steven began with an easy smile. "We could discuss how spectacular your jewels are this evening, Lady Hammersmith . . ." His lips curved upward, deepening the smile into a wicked grin. "Or we could discuss how deeply Lord Hammersmith had to reach into his pocket to purchase those sparkling pretties."

His shocking gambit brought gasps from the ladies and mutterings from the gentlemen. Harriet watched in amazement as everyone fell into private discussions: the gentlemen complaining about their wives' expensive tastes and the ladies agreeing that Steven's comment was in poor taste.

Steven took the opportunity to bend closer, and whisper, "Why the devil did you touch my leg?"

Surreptitiously, she gazed at him. "I think we'd be

better served discussing your outrageous comment."

"What was so outrageous about it?"

"You know perfectly well that a gentleman does not remark upon the cost of a lady's jewels," she murmured.

Steven frowned slightly. "Do you think I undid all my effort this evening?"

"Probably not," she said, dismissing his concern. "Lady Camilla seemed much friendlier this evening."

His expression lightened as he considered the matter. "She did, didn't she?"

Harriet nodded firmly. "It seems our arrangement is proving to be most beneficial."

In an instant, Steven's frown returned. "Did you touch Lord Conover's arm?"

"With stunning success," she lied smoothly. Though handsome and quite charming, Lord Conover wasn't the gentleman she'd wanted to practice her feminine wiles upon. However, in every hunt, timing was essential, so Harriet knew now was not the time for ardent declarations.

His frown darkened into a fierce scowl. "If I'd known you were going to use my suggestion upon that dastardly rake, I never would have taught it to you."

Lifting both of her brows, she drew back her shoulders. "I believe our agreement was an exchange of knowledge. You have no say in whom I choose to entice."

Steven opened his mouth to argue, but before he could utter a syllable, Lady Hammersmith stood and announced it was time for the ladies to retire to the salon, leaving the men to their port and cigar. Thanking God and Lady Hammersmith for perfect timing, Harriet offered a smile to Steven before rising and walking from the room. She could feel Steven's gaze boring into her as she left.

All in all, things were progressing better than to be expected.

"I must say, Agatha, your niece and Lord Heath were the rage at my party last night," Lady Hammersmith said as she stirred her tea. "They make a fine match."

After glancing around Lady Armour's drawing room to make certain that old poop Hilda wasn't nearby, Agatha nodded in agreement. "I've waited a long time for Harriet to settle upon a gentleman, and I easily admit I'm well pleased with her choice."

Lady Hammersmith tapped her spoon once against the side of her teacup before placing it upon her saucer. "I'm confident Lady Heath is pleased with the match as well."

"I do hope so," Agatha said, not wanting anything to stand in the way of Harriet's happiness. "Since I've yet to meet her, I'm unable even to hazard a guess at Lady Heath's reaction."

"You've never met?" Lady Hammersmith's brows arched upward in surprise. "Though I don't know why that surprises me as she's been touring the Continent for quite a while and before that, she seldom came to town."

"That's a shame," Agatha admitted as she picked up a sweetmeat. "I really would have enjoyed meeting her."

"We can accommodate your wish today."

"How can we do that? I thought you said Lady Heath was touring the Continent."

"She was, but she recently returned to London . . . and is seated across the room at this very moment," Lady Hammersmith said with relished satisfaction. "Lady Heath is to the right of Lady Armour."

Immediately, Agatha's gaze fell upon the beautiful woman conversing with their hostess. "That's Lady Heath?" she asked, astonished. "But she hardly looks old enough to have children, much less a full-grown son."

"She married quite young," Lady Hammersmith informed Agatha. "And while the former Lord Heath was a good deal older than his bride, it was said to be a love match. Their union produced one son a scant nine months after the wedding." Leaning closer, Lady Hammersmith delivered the juiciest piece of gossip. "I've heard from a very reliable source that Lady Heath often lamented her inability to bear more children. The lady herself assured my confidant that it wasn't for lack of trying."

Agatha laughed at the bold statement. "Good for her. I admire a lady who can speak her mind."

"Would you like an introduction?"

"Very much so." Setting down her treat, Agatha rose and followed her friend across the room, coming to a stop in front of the elegant Lady Heath.

"Caroline!" exclaimed Lady Hammersmith, reaching out to clasp both of Lady Heath's hands. "When I saw you sitting over here, I simply had to come over and see how your tour went. I've heard now isn't the best time to travel."

"Quite the contrary," Lady Heath countered as she rose to her feet. "I found it a delightful time for my tour; everywhere I went seemed far less crowded than usual." She seemed to glow when she smiled. "Though I did miss my friends," she admitted softly. "How have you been, Penelope?"

"Smashing," Lady Hammersmith pronounced as she released Lady Heath's hands. "Though there are times when I vow Lord Hammersmith will drive me stark, raving mad with all of his collections."

Apparently Lady Heath was well acquainted with Lady Hammersmith for she knew Penelope was merely jesting about her husband. For all her grousing, Lady Hammersmith adored her husband . . . though you'd have to threaten her with bodily injury to get her to admit it.

Agatha's thoughts were interrupted as her friend tugged her forward. "May I introduce one of my dearest friends of all time, Lady Agatha Dalrymple?"

The soft light in Lady Heath's eyes told of her kind nature. "A pleasure," she murmured.

"The pleasure is mine." Unable to hold in her curiosity one moment longer, Agatha launched into the heart of the matter. "I've already been afforded the pleasure of meeting your son."

Lady Heath smiled widely. "I hope he made a favorable impression upon you."

"How could he do otherwise?"

Lady Heath's smile broadened even more at Agatha's reply. "Very true . . . but I'm always uncertain of how much of that is motherly approval and how much is deserved."

"I understand precisely what you mean, for I often boast of my niece's many accomplishments," Agatha said. "In fact, it was Harriet who introduced me to your son."

"Really?" Lady Heath's eyes lit with interest. "May I inquire as to the name of your niece?"

"Miss Harriet Nash," Agatha readily supplied.

Unwilling to be left out of any conversation, Lady Hammersmith added, "I'm uncertain if you would have ever met her, Caroline. Harriet has only been living in town with her aunts for a few years."

"Before she came to reside with my sister and me, she lived with her parents in the country."

Lady Heath's expression darkened at Agatha's information. "Oh, dear me, did her parents pass away?"

"No, no," Agatha hurried to reassure her. "Harriet simply wasn't suited for country life, so she came to town with her friend, the Countess of Tewksbury."

"Your niece didn't enjoy living in the country?"

Hearing the note of concern in Lady Heath's voice, Agatha hurried to reassure her. "It wasn't that she didn't enjoy the country precisely as much as she didn't meet any gentlemen of interest there. I'm positive that Harriet would be delighted to settle in the country . . . with the right spouse, that is."

"Please forgive my boldness," Lady Heath began, "but I can't help wonder if you are implying that my son and your niece have formed a tendre for one another."

"I do so appreciate a woman who speaks her mind," Agatha reiterated.

Lady Heath tossed back her head with a laugh. "Then you and I are destined to become friends," she pronounced, before propping her hands on her hips. "Now, please cease prevaricating, Lady Dalrymple, and let me know if my son feels affection for your niece."

It was Agatha's turn to chuckle. "If their actions at Penelope's dinner last night were any indication, I would indeed say they are forming an attachment."

"I knew I should have gone last night," muttered Lady Heath with a slight scowl. "My stomach wasn't feeling quite right, so I decided not to attend the party. Foolish mistake, I can see now, for I might have had the chance to observe my son with your niece."

Homing in on Lady Heath's sentiments, Agatha asked bluntly, "Then you are not averse to a bit of matchmaking."

"Averse? Certainly not; I welcome the opportunity."

Agatha nodded in satisfaction at Lady Heath's reassurance. "In two days, Harriet will be attending the Thompsons' ball."

"I believe Steven is planning upon attending that affair as well." Lady Heath smoothed her hands down her skirt. "I'll arrive at the Thompsons' town house obscenely early . . . just to ensure I don't miss one moment of Steven's interaction with your niece."

"This sounds like wonderful fun," pronounced Lady Hammersmith. "I simply must help in these efforts."

Agatha accepted her offer eagerly. "Of course, Penelope. I shall put you in charge of keeping Hilda out of the way. I swear that woman gets more and more crotchety every day."

"She doesn't think my son and your niece would make a good match?"

"It's not Lord Heath that my sister opposes; no one would ever prove worthy of my niece if Hilda had her way." Memories assailed Agatha. "Unfortunately, Hilda had a love affair that went awry, forever scarring her heart."

"How tragic," sighed Lady Hammersmith, pressing her hands against her bosom. "Perhaps if we are successful in our matchmaking attempts between Lord Heath and Harriet, then Hilda will see love is possible and it will finally help heal her broken heart."

"I think you've been reading too many fairy tales lately," Agatha observed dryly. "I doubt if anything will be able to change Hilda's opinion, but, that's not my focus here. I want to concentrate on Harriet and securing her future."

"If I see Steven is truly interested in your niece at the Thompsons' ball, I shall join you in your efforts to unite them."

At Lady Heath's promise, Agatha clapped her hands in delight. "This has proved to be a most interesting and, I hope, fruitful afternoon."

"I'm positive it will be," asserted Lady Hammersmith. "Now why don't we settle down with a nice cup of tea, and I'll tell you about the entertainment Harriet and Lord Heath provided last night."

As the three women walked off, none of them noticed Hilda peer around the edge of the large wing-backed chair where she'd sat, hidden from sight, during their entire conversation.

Interfering old biddies, Hilda thought as she sank back down into her seat. And that Agatha! What nerve of her to be making light of her sister's heartache. Shameful. Utterly shameful.

If Agatha had her way, she'd manage to bungle everything and leave Harriet brokenhearted and betrayed. While that Steven might seem charming, those were the ones you had to watch out for. After all, who would know better than she?

When Conrad had first approached her, he'd swept her off her feet, making her seventeen-year-old heart skip every time he was near. She'd believed every word he'd uttered, ignoring the warnings that he was simply a fortune hunter and not truly in love with her. Oh, no, she knew better. She knew he loved her, adored her, desired her.

His proposal had made her feel complete. Overwhelmed by her feelings, she'd decided to ignore a lifetime of teachings and savor her passion one weekend while away at a country party. Feeling bold and daring, she'd snuck down the silent corridor toward Conrad's room. Afraid someone might see her, she'd slipped into the room without knocking, almost quivering with excitement, only to turn and find he wasn't alone.

Her sweet, honorable, upstanding gentleman was in bed with two of the housemaids!

A shiver raced through Hilda as she remembered standing there in frozen shock as the threesome romped on the bed in decadent carnality.

She'd left the room in disgust and horror, leaving as quietly as she'd come. In the morning, Conrad had been his charming self. He'd been so convincing that if she hadn't seen his debauchery for herself, she never would have believed it. Unable even to look at him, unwilling to touch him, she'd handed back his ring without a word of explanation, not wanting to foul her tongue by speaking of the debased scene she'd witnessed.

After a few attempts to contact her, Conrad finally ceased his efforts. It was only after she'd emerged from her room weeks later to rejoin society that she'd learned of his revenge. He'd informed all of society that he'd been the one to call off their engagement as she was too cold and far too haughty to wed. If he'd meant that she would never sink to frolicking upon the bed with an entire group of people, he'd been right.

Soon afterward, her father had lost his fortune through poor investments, and with no fortune, a sullied reputation, and modest looks, Hilda had found herself without a husband.

And, poor, dear Harriet suffered from two of her three problems; it was up to Hilda to ensure that nothing happened to sully Harriet's reputation as well. With a pristine reputation, Harriet would be able to make a fine match . . . to an honest, kindly gentleman from the country just as her sister Sally had done. Lionel Nash's steadfastness proved to Hilda that countrified gentlemen might not be as charming or as dashing as the gentlemen from town, but they more than made up for that failing with their steady, faithful nature.

As for Harriet's Lord Heath, he reminded Hilda just a bit too much of Conrad, with his glib tongue and dashing looks. From her sister's matchmaking ideas, it was apparent that she was the only one who possessed the wherewithal to protect Harriet from her own desires. Hilda wasn't going to let the Conrads of this world claim yet another victim.

Tomorrow, she'd start investigating this Lord Heath and see if he was all he claimed to be . . . or if he were another conniving, lying debaucher in a gentleman's clothes.

Two days.

Two whole bloody days since he'd seen Harriet. Since he'd seen anyone, Steven amended, as he rubbed his bleary eyes. He'd been trying to balance these ledgers, vowing he wouldn't attend any party or visit his clubs until he'd managed to deduce just how far into debt he'd fallen.

Without even so much as a knock, Royce strolled into Steven's study. "I informed your butler I'd let myself in," he said as he tossed his hat onto a side table. "Lord, Steven, you look half-dead." Walking over to the windows, he yanked back the curtains, allowing sunlight to stream into the room. "It even smells like someone died in here," he remarked as he cracked the window. "What the devil have you been doing, old man?"

"Praying I would die." Steven winced as he realized his attempt at a joke had fallen far short of the mark. "Sorry; that was in poor taste."

"I'd say . . . especially since it looks as if you've given trying to kill yourself a good attempt." Rounding the desk, Royce frowned down at the piles of papers and ledgers sitting before Steven. He leaned forward and pointed at the large number Steven had written on a scrap of foolscap. "Is this what you owe?"

"So far, yes."

Straightening, Royce took a step backward. "What do you mean by 'so far'?"

"I'm uncertain if all the vowels my mother signed while on tour have been sent to my solicitor," Steven explained, leaning back in his chair. "She didn't keep track of her debts." Sighing wearily, he tossed down his quill. "Not that it really matters. After all, the worst has already happened; my coffers are empty. I'm already in a huge hole; all that remains to be seen now is how deep it is."

Royce slammed his fist against the desk. "Dammit, Steven, stop being so bloody prideful and accept my help," he ground out fiercely. "Let me pay off your debts immediately and take the pressure off you." As Steven opened his mouth to protest, Royce held up both hands, cutting him off before he uttered a sound. "I know, I know. You don't want charity, but if you don't accept my help now, you'll destroy your chances of marrying an heiress."

Perhaps he was too tired to think straight, but Steven didn't understand what Royce was talking about. "I don't see what one has to do with the other."

"Heiresses are a skittish bunch and avoid fortune hunters like the plague. At the moment, no one knows about your financial difficulties, so all the heiresses welcome you with open arms."

"And if they find out I'm over my head in debt, they will go running in the opposite direction."

"Exactly." Crossing his arms, Royce leaned against the desk. "However, if I pay off your debts, no one will be the wiser. If you're so bloody stubborn that you insist on paying me back, then do so after you marry your heiress, but at least our arrangement will remain a private matter." With the skill of a master swordsman, Royce delivered the final thrust. "This solution will also save your family name and your honor."

As much as Steven loathed the idea of borrowing from his friend, he hated the idea of his disgrace being a matter of public scorn. He could call it pride, a sense of honor, or anything else he wanted, but it didn't change the fact that he felt compelled to hide his financial disaster from society.

"I would appreciate your help," Steven said, surprised he didn't choke on the words.

"After I badger you into accepting it," Royce countered as he straightened and rounded the desk. "I only make one provision for this loan—that we never mention it again. If you choose not to repay it, fine; if you are too pigheaded and insist on returning the money, then have your solicitor contact mine and make the arrangements through them." Bracing himself on the desk, Royce leaned into Steven. "But as far as you and I are concerned, this arrangement does not exist. Agreed?"

Steven couldn't help but laugh. "Ah, Royce, you know me far too well," he said, knowing that despite any promise he might make his friend, he'd feel beholden. Still, if the only thing Royce wanted in return for saving his sorry hide was a promise never to discuss the matter, Steven wasn't about to refuse him. "Agreed."

"Excellent." Retrieving his gloves and hat from the side table, Royce slapped them against his side. "I'll be off now to arrange for that thing we're never going to mention and as for you, my friend, I want you to close those blasted ledgers, put those depressing papers into a drawer, and get some fresh air." As he headed out the door, Royce tossed one last comment over his shoulder. "Why don't you try doing something you enjoy for a change?"

An hour after he'd departed, Royce's words echoed in Steven's head as he sat, alone, in his study. As if he possessed a magic wand, Royce had made his problems disappear. Not wholly, Steven acknowledged, but now at least his embarrassing fall from fortune would be his own personal, dark secret and not fodder for the gossips.

Taking Royce's advice, Steven opened his drawer and dropped in the stacks of papers and the ledgers, clearing his desk until no evidence of his two-day Hell remained. As he shut the drawer, Royce's parting shot echoed through his head once more.

Do something you enjoy.

Not giving himself a moment to change his mind, he dashed off a quick note, inviting Harriet to the cottage. After finding a servant to deliver the message, he gave the lad detailed instruction that the letter was to be placed in Miss Nash's hands directly or else brought back without delivery. He couldn't risk someone else opening the note. Once again the impropriety of the situation stung him, but his need to see Harriet, to escape from his world for a moment, overrode his caution. Besides, as long as they were careful, no one would get hurt. Steven leapt up the stairs, taking them two at a time.

Before he met Harriet, he needed to wash off the stench of red-lined ledgers.

Lord, he hoped she was home.

Chapter Twelve

✑

"Harriet?" At the lack of response, Hilda poked her head into Harriet's bedchamber. "Are you in here?"

Obviously not, she thought, as she stepped into the room. Slowly, she glanced around, noting the dress flung with disregard upon the bed, the open closet doors, the disarray on her dressing table. From the looks of it, Harriet had been in a hurry.

Hilda walked farther into the room to pick up one of Harriet's delicate shawls from the window seat. As she was folding the shawl, she caught a flash of blue out of the corner of her eye. Her hands clenched the soft lace as she turned to look out the window in time to see Harriet race through the garden and out the rear door.

It would appear that her sweet Harriet had a secret assignation.

Tossing down the shawl, Hilda began to look for the note that had arrived at the house less than half an hour ago. Normally, she wouldn't have even noticed the arrival of a missive, but their butler had sought her out because of the peculiar nature of this note. Apparently, the messenger was under strict orders that the message be placed in Harriet's hands directly.

Thankful that their butler had told her this information and not that flighty Agatha, Hilda immediately sought out Harriet to see who had sent the note. But, apparently, she'd been too late.

Looking out the window again, she realized it was futile to send a servant to follow Harriet at this point. Still, if she were of a gambling nature, she'd wager her stock of imported teas that Harriet was off to meet Lord Heath.

For two days, she'd made subtle inquiries about the fellow, but the gossip surrounding Lord Heath made her wince. If even half of the rumors were true, he was precisely the sort of man she feared would ruin Harriet. Worse still, she grew more and more convinced that she'd only begun to discover the worst of Lord Heath.

Tapping her fingers against the windowpane, Hilda realized it was time she stepped up her efforts to uncover information about Lord Heath. This situation was fast spiraling out of control. She would have approached Lionel and Sally with this matter, but they'd returned to the country last night. Since Hilda knew perfectly well that Agatha wouldn't be a stitch of help, she realized she was left with only one course of action.

It was time to bring in reinforcements.

Harriet's only regret as she hurried toward the cottage was that Steven's note hadn't arrived in time for her to arrange for a meal to serve Steven. Showing him that she could satisfy all of his appetites was part of her plan. Still, she wasn't about to let that minor disappointment spoil her day. She wasn't going to allow anything to steal even one instant of pleasure from the glorious, unexpectedly wonderful day, she decided firmly, as she pulled her blue cloak closer about her.

In her hurry to reach the cottage, she was running in a most unladylike manner . . . and she didn't care one whit if anyone saw her or not. Reaching Steven as soon as possible was the only thing that mattered to her at the moment.

The cottage greeted her in merry welcome as she hurried up the path and slipped into the foyer. "Steven?"

"In here," he called out from the small salon.

Draping her wrap over the banister, she smoothed her elegant rose dress, shifted the deep bodice downward until it revealed a goodly portion of her breasts, and arranged her curls to curve around her neck. Primped and ready, she stepped into the salon. "Good day, Steven. I was pleasantly surprised to receive your note." As he turned to face her, she was shocked by the drawn, paleness of his features. "Are you ill?" she asked, hurrying toward him.

Steven shook his head. "No, merely tired." Reaching out, he cupped her cheek in his hand. "I just needed to see you."

The admission sounded as if it had been torn from him, as if he hadn't wanted to reveal so much of his feelings, and it melted her. "Oh, Steven," she murmured, tilting her head into his hand. "I needed to see you as well."

"All the way over here I told myself I was going to ask you to make a list of matrons I should try to win over," he said as his gaze roamed over her face. "But I was lying to myself." His hand slid backward until his fingers were buried in her hair. "My entire life has been turned upside down, and the past two days have been unbearably hellacious. Then Royce suggested I do something I wanted to do, and only one thing came to mind." Slowly, he pulled her closer to him until she pressed against his chest. "To see you."

Oh, Lord, if she were dreaming, she prayed never to awake. All her life she'd dreamed of feeling this way, of having someone feel this way about her, and finally, finally it was coming true. "Steven," she whispered, leaning into him, tilting her head back, inviting his kiss.

A groan broke from him as he captured her lips in a feverish kiss. Desire, simmering for so long inside of her, burst to life. Harriet slid her hands up across his hard chest, along the strong lines of his neck, and into his beautiful, golden hair. Tightening his hold upon her, Steven tilted her head to gain deeper access to her mouth.

Over and over again his tongue dipped inward, caressing her, tasting her, inhaling her very essence. Mimicking his actions, she took delicious forays into his mouth, reveling in the splendor of his passion.

Suddenly, Steven broke off their kiss, pulling back to press his lips along the arch of her cheekbone, down the line of her nose, feathering against the curve of her lips. "Help me escape," he rasped, his breath whispering against her heated flesh. "Help me forget."

Moaning softly, Harriet arched into him, telling him with her body that she was willing to help him forget within the warmth of her desire. With eager acceptance, he pressed hot kisses along her neck, pausing to nibble at her nape. Tilting her head to the side, she gave Steven unhindered access to the tender spot.

His arm slid around her waist to secure her against him as he maneuvered her backward until slowly, he lowered her onto the soft cushions, never once breaking off his mind-shattering kisses.

"Steven," she gasped as he pressed against her aching core. Even through the layers of her gown and the thickness of his breeches, she felt open, vulnerable . . . yet so very eager for more.

At the sound of her voice, Steven froze, lifting his head from her neck, his passion-darkened eyes somber. "Harriet, I'm sorr . . ."

But she wouldn't let him say it. "No, don't be sorry," she interrupted, arching up into him, pressing herself against him. "I want this, Steven." Her hands clutched at his shoulders, pulling him down onto her. "Don't stop," she implored him. "Don't stop."

A groan rumbled from his chest as he answered her with a hungry kiss. Shivers rushed through Harriet when his hand slid along her shoulder, tugging her gown downward. Slowly, the tips of his fingers trailed along the edge of her draping bodice, tormenting her with teasing touches, heading steadily toward her aching breast.

Unable to bear his teasing one moment longer, Harriet arched upward, unconsciously rubbing herself against his leg. Her breath rushed from her when he curved his hand inward, beneath her bodice, to cup her breast. As he bent his head downward, a lock of hair fell forward, brushing against her tender nipple with a silky caress. The erotic feeling brought a soft moan to her lips.

A wicked grin slashed upon Steven's mouth as he watched her reaction when he repeated the motion. "Do you like that?" he asked, his warm breath rushing over her already heated flesh. "And how about this?"

She thought she might burst into flames when he licked at her turgid nipple before blowing upon the moistened tip. "Yes, oh, yes," she rasped, hoping he wouldn't stop his sensual torment.

"Then you're going to love this . . ." His mouth closed around her nipple, drawing it deeply inward as his tongue laved around the point.

"Steven!" she cried, her fingers clutching at him, pressing him closer. Desire clawed through her, raw, hungry, racing downward to pool between her legs.

As Steven showered her other breast with the same passionate attention, he shifted fully onto the settee, coming to rest between her legs. The feel of his body on top of hers intensified her yearnings. When he pressed fully against her, she thrilled at the knowledge that only a few layers of material separated her from his manly hardness.

This was Steven. Her handsome, dashing Steven.

Eagerly, she embraced him, rotating in counterpoint to his slow, sensual movements. A groan broke from him as he shifted upward to capture her lips in a voracious kiss. The new position brought him flush against her womanly desire, creating a swirling, rushing need within her.

His hips continued to move, the gentle rocking motion speeding up, giving way to a rhythmic thrusting that satisfied the growing hunger inside her. Harriet rose up to meet his thrusts. His burning kiss mirrored his body movements, driving her needs higher and higher. His pelvis moved faster, faster, pumping forward in frenetic thrusts. Yes, yes, she thought, eager to reach the satisfaction that shimmered just out of reach. Oh, how she wanted, needed . . .

Breaking off the kiss, Steven shifted his head backward, his face slack with desire. His body shook with the effort as he controlled himself, stilling his tantalizing movements. "Harriet, we need to stop," he ground out.

Every fiber of her being protested his words. "No, Steven, no." She held on to him tightly and pressed up against him. "Please, I need more, more," she whispered, her body calling for him. "I need you."

Her admission broke his restraint, sending him against her with a sensual thrust. His lips recaptured hers as he pounded against her, satisfying the unbearable cravings within her, pushing her ever closer, closer to that wonderful sensation that she knew was . . . just . . . out . . . of . . .

A moan burst from her, reverberating against his mouth as golden sensations poured through her, making her quiver with satisfaction. Every muscle in her body tightened for one beautiful, perfect moment, before melting beneath the heat of Steven's passion.

Twice more, Steven thrust against her, before pulling back, his jaw clenched, perspiration dotting his forehead. His eyes closed as he shook his head. "No," he groaned, every muscle taut as he held himself still.

His breath rasped from him as if he'd run up and down the stairs three times. Taking deep breaths, he seemed to regain control, before finally opening his eyes to smile down at her. For a long while, they lay there, entwined, connected in a way Harriet had never before experienced.

Finally, Steven lifted his head. "Harriet, I . . ." He stumbled to a halt, then lifted a shoulder, and murmured, "Thank you."

Emotion reverberated in the words. Touched, Harriet reached up to stroke his hair. "For what?"

Trailing a finger along her eyebrow, down over the curve of her cheek, Steven gazed into her eyes. "For being here for me."

"Then I should thank you right back," she murmured, blinking at the tears gathering. "I never imagined anything could feel this perfect."

"It was perfect," he said earnestly. "And I've never felt anything like this either."

"Really?" With his past, it was more than she'd hoped.

"Really."

The firmness of his tone made her smile. "But you didn't . . ."

A gleam brightened his gaze. "No, I didn't," he repeated, before levering himself up off her, pausing to adjust her skirts. "But this was more than just physical pleasure." Resting his elbows on his knees, he glanced over at her. "There are things happening in my life right now that make it difficult for me to breathe sometimes, but being here with you." He paused, shaking his head. "Somehow it eases the burden, and I can move forward." He smiled ruefully. "I know you probably don't understand a word I'm saying, but you need to believe me when I say I've never felt like this with any other woman."

The vulnerability she glimpsed in his eyes touched her more deeply than she'd ever known she could feel.

And like that . . . she fell.

When had it happened? she thought with a sense of wonder. With all of her plans, all of her flirtations, she'd never imagined that falling in love would seize her so swiftly. Her lips trembled as she sat up to kiss him gently. "Oh, Steven," she murmured, her voice breaking.

The look of vulnerability deepened, before he shifted, visibly pulling back from her as he rose. Harriet tried not to allow his withdrawal to hurt her now-open heart; just as before when he'd hid behind his rakish attitude, he pulled back whenever his emotions got too intense. She could see it, even if he couldn't.

Raking a hand through his hair, he shifted on his feet for a moment before offering her a hand. "I think it might be time for you to return home," he said, his voice still tinged with passion.

Accepting his proffered hand, she rose, brushing out her skirts. "You're undoubtedly right," she murmured. "However, I could delay my return if you'd like to show me how a sophisticate flirts with a gentleman while dancing so I can use the knowledge at the Thompsons' ball this evening."

A side of his mouth quirked upward. "Be gone with you."

"Oh, ho, and isn't that a fine thanks indeed," she teased, unbelievably happy. Stepping closer once more, Harriet pressed a kiss upon Steven's mouth, lingering for a moment, before moving away to retrieve her cloak. "'Til this evening," she whispered.

"'Til tonight." Reaching out he placed her wrap around her shoulder and adjusted the hood to hide her face. With one last wave, Harriet let herself out.

The moment she left, the cottage seemed to cool as if the only source of warmth had left with her. It felt that way inside of him as well. Shifting, Steven eased the tightness in his breeches, remembering how his control had almost broken. Good Lord, his actions this afternoon were inexcusable . . . yet undeniably needed.

Somehow, some way, he'd grown to need Harriet. When he'd pulled her into his arms, all the sorrow he'd felt, the humiliation he'd suffered at having to borrow from his friend, the worry he'd gnawed upon since learning of his financial ruin faded away, leaving him feeling clean and whole for the first time in weeks.

He couldn't imagine trying to live the remainder of his life without her.

Peace flowed over him at that realization. By having swallowed his pride, he'd freed himself from having to marry an heiress. He could marry Harriet, invest her modest portion wisely, and slowly rebuild his coffers. In time he could even pay back Royce.

Steven savored the calming thought. As soon as the monies had been transferred and his debts paid off, he would offer for Harriet, convince her she'd be happy in the country, then return to his estate. Everything would be perfect, he decided, feeling lighter than he had in longer than he cared to remember.

Smiling to himself, he locked up the cottage and headed home to dress for a ball. Perhaps he'd teach Harriet how to flirt with a gentleman while dancing after all.

"Where have you been, young lady?"

Harriet started guiltily as she turned to face her aunt Hilda. "Walking the gardens."

"First you sneak off, and now you lie to me?" Crossing her arms over her chest, Aunt Hilda scowled at her. "I don't know what's happening to you, Harriet, but I can assure you the changes are not positive ones."

"But they are, Aunt Hilda," she hurried to reassure her. "I've never been happier."

"A moment of happiness can cause a lifetime of regret." As Aunt Hilda stepped farther into her bedchamber, she eyed Harriet's rumpled appearance. "From the look of you, I'd say you were up to no good."

Ah, but it had been good, so very, very good. Wisely, Harriet kept that thought to herself. "You need to trust me, Aunt Hilda."

The stiff lines upon her aunt's face softened. "It's not that I don't trust you; it's simply that you're too young and inexperienced to understand the nature of men."

"Are you spouting nonsense again?" demanded Aunt Agatha from the open doorway. "For heaven's sake, Hildy, leave the poor girl alone!"

In an instant, Aunt Hilda snapped rigid again. "I'm only trying to protect her. If it were up to you, she'd be given a free rein."

"To make her own choices, yes," Aunt Agatha agreed readily. "Our parents never interfered in our lives."

"And look what happened with us! I was duped and almost trapped into marriage by a fortune hunter, and you wed a spendthrift." Aunt Hilda shook her head firmly. "Harriet deserves better and I believe it is up to us to ensure that she gets it."

"Stop being an old fool, Hildy. If you'd fought back, told everyone the truth about Conrad instead of retreating into yourself, you would have healed and eventually found someone to love," Aunt Agatha said, her voice softening toward the end. "As for my Roland, perhaps he was a bit free with his monies, but he made me happy and left me comfortable." She smiled gently at her sister. "I could want nothing more for Harriet."

"I want a happy marriage for Harriet as well, but I also believe that she'd meet more upstanding, honorable gentlemen in the country, where they're less prone to artifice."

"It's a man's character not his place of residence that makes him worthy," Aunt Agatha pointed out.

"Please, Aunt Hilda, Aunt Agatha," Harriet interrupted. "I'd like to rest before this evening."

Immediately, Aunt Agatha clapped her hands to her chest. "And here we are prattling on like a couple of old hens." She stepped forward and pressed a kiss upon Harriet's cheek. "Rest well, my dear." As she headed for the door, she paused near the doorjamb. "Come along, Hilda."

Aunt Hilda stepped closer as well, but instead of giving her a kiss, she stared pointedly down at Harriet's dress, making her aware of her hopelessly wrinkled gown. Finally, she caught Harriet's gaze. "Be careful," she murmured softly, before kissing her cheek and heading from the room.

The minute the door closed behind them, Harriet breathed a sigh of relief and flopped back down on her bed. Her aunt Hilda guessed that she'd been with Steven. Had she guessed at what actually happened, Harriet realized she'd be packing at this very moment to return to her parents.

Still, Aunt Hilda's fears were ungrounded. Harriet flung her hands over her head as she relived every glorious moment with Steven. She was in love with a wonderful man who cared deeply for her as well. Undoubtedly, he would cease this foolishness of hiding his feelings and he would offer for her.

They'd use the profits she was going to make from her investment in the new type of fertilizer and continue his improvements on his country estate. Picturing her perfect future was easy. They'd spend the Season here in town, then retire to Steven's country home. They'd raise a family and live happily ever after . . . just like Laurel and Royce.

And after her taste of fulfillment today, Harriet couldn't wait to experience more passionate delights in her marriage bed.

For the first time in her life, plain Miss Harriet Nash had captured the heart of the handsome prince. But unlike someone like Lady Camilla, who would have taken Steven's affection as her due, Harriet understood what a gift it was and vowed to cherish the gift for the rest of her life.

Smiling up at the canopy on her bed, Harriet continued to weave lovely dreams of a golden future.

The pleasant mood that had accompanied him all the way home from the cottage evaporated when he found two of his mother's suitors waiting for him.

"Good evening, Lord Heath," said the trollish man as he rose from his chair.

"Connor, isn't it?" Steven asked as he strode into the salon.

"That's correct, my lord. Robert Connor." He gestured toward his companion. "And Mr. Percy Windvale."

Steven greeted him with a nod. "What can I do for you, gentlemen?"

"We wished to speak with you about our concerns with Longley," said Windvale. "He's gotten most . . . persistent in his pursuit of Lady Caroline."

"Persistent?" Steven lifted his brows. "It was my understanding that the three of you have been following her about Europe," he finished coolly.

A dull flush stained Windvale's cheeks. "We have been escorting her, my lord, not following her."

"With her footing the bill," Steven pointed out bluntly.

Taking a step forward, Connor shook his head. "You are incorrect, my lord," he said adamantly. "I am quite secure and have never accepted a farthing from Lady Caroline."

Windvale shifted his feet. "I never discuss my finances."

Nor did he, Steven realized. Uncomfortable with the thought, he focused on the matter at hand. "What has Longley been doing that bothers you?"

"As you know," Connor began, "we all admire your mother greatly, and the three of us have all asked for her hand in marriage."

Tugging on his slightly frayed sleeve, Windvale agreed. "It would be an honor if she accepted."

Not once Windvale discovered his mother wasn't wealthy, Steven surmised. "I still don't see what this has to do with Longley."

"Lately he's started becoming . . . distraught whenever Lady Caroline rejects his proposal." A solemn expression did little to ease the harsh lines of Connor's face. "I'm concerned he's becoming unstable."

Unsettled at the news, Steven began to pace. "Do you think he will harm my mother?"

Windvale shrugged. "I doubt it, but then again, I never would have thought Longley would behave in such an erratic fashion either."

"Thank you for bringing this to my attention, gentlemen," Steven said. "I shall speak to my mother about the situation."

"Will you look into the matter?" Connor asked, concern deepening his voice.

"Of course." Giving them a pointed look, Steven smiled coolly at both Windvale and Connor. "I'm already making inquiries about all three of you."

Shock widened Windvale's eyes. "You're what? I find that offensive, sir!"

"You may find it however you like; it won't change a thing," Steven replied calmly. "When it comes to my family, I shall do whatever it takes to protect it."

Drawing back his shoulders, Connor frowned at Steven. "While I commend your reasoning, my lord, I don't believe investigating innocent people is the action of a gentleman."

"Haven't you heard?" Steven asked lightly. "I'm not a gentleman." He grinned in satisfaction. "Just ask anyone."

Chapter Thirteen

"*I*'d forgotten your father purchased this carriage."
Smiling, Steven glanced around the opulent interior of
the gold, white, and red carriage. "He said he wanted you
to ride like a queen."

A bittersweet curve tilted his mother's mouth. "I always felt like I was in a harem on wheels," she said, dab-
bing delicately at the corner of her eye. "Not that I ever
let your father know."

"I remember the day he brought it home," Steven rem-
inisced. "You were speechless, and he stood there, so
proud of himself for having bought something worthy of
you."

"He spoiled me dreadfully." His mother sighed softly.
"I still miss him."

Reaching across the expanse of the carriage, Steven
clasped his mother's hand. "I didn't mean to make you
sad."

"I'll be fine in a moment," she assured him, wiping the corner of her eye again. "I'm such a ninny to carry on like this. Be a dear and give me a moment to collect myself."

Respecting her wishes, Steven fell silent. He'd finally come to terms with his situation. Every morning he spent an hour or so with his mother to help her understand her finances. She wasn't a ninny at all, but rather a woman completely unprepared to face the world on her own.

Luckily he'd never have to worry about that with Harriet. She was one of the most capable females he knew. Still, she deserved to be made to feel special. In fact, the very reason he'd ordered this carriage uncovered and made ready for this evening was because he'd devised a special rendezvous for Harriet.

Eagerly, he leapt from the carriage when it pulled to a stop, before turning back to help his mother descend. From her smile, Steven knew she'd recovered her composure. "I'm very much looking forward to this evening," he said as he escorted her up the front steps.

"As am I." His mother handed over her cape to the waiting footman and paused in the foyer to be announced. "I'm hoping it proves to be a most interesting evening indeed."

He'd arrived!

Harriet couldn't contain her broad grin of welcome. She didn't care if anyone noticed her staring at Steven; she wanted to shout out her feelings to the world.

"Harriet!" Aunt Hilda hissed beneath her breath as she

tugged on Harriet's sleeve. "You're making a spectacle of yourself. Young ladies do not gape at gentlemen like they are bright shiny baubles."

Reluctantly drawing her attention from Steven, Harriet turned toward her aunt just in time to catch her aunt Agatha elbow Lady Hammersmith sharply. For a woman of exceptional girth, Lady Hammersmith certainly could jump in stunned surprise.

"What . . . wha . . . Oh, yes," she stammered. Pulling back her shoulders, Lady Hammersmith smiled at Aunt Hilda. "Hilda, would you be a dear and accompany me to the library?"

Aunt Hilda frowned. "The library? Why on earth do you want to go there? That's where the gentlemen congregate."

"Precisely," Lady Hammersmith agreed. "I-I-I wish to speak with Lord Hammersmith."

Even Harriet saw through the fib; what she didn't understand was what Lady Hammersmith was up to.

"Please, Hilda, I don't often make requests of you."

Phrased that way, Aunt Hilda had no choice but to grant the request if she didn't wish to appear boorish.

"Very well," Aunt Hilda finally acquiesced. She gave Aunt Agatha a firm look. "I'm entrusting Harriet to your questionable care," she grumbled softly. "I know you don't believe me, but she did disappear this afternoon, and I don't want a repetition of that incident."

"No, we wouldn't want that," Aunt Agatha agreed solemnly. "I promise to keep an eye on her."

Apparently satisfied, Aunt Hilda nodded once, paused to give Harriet a stern, warning glance, then followed Lady Hammersmith from the room.

Though she still didn't understand why Lady Hammersmith had come to her rescue, Harriet wasn't about to question her good fortune. When Steven appeared in front of her, she gasped in pleasant surprise.

"A pleasure to see you again, Miss Nash," he murmured as he bent over her hand to press a kiss upon the back of her fingers. As his lips touched her skin, he glanced upward, reminding her with one look of all the delights his touch could invoke. Shivering once, she hoped her reaction wasn't evident to her aunt or the woman at Steven's side.

Straightening, he drew the woman beside him into their circle. "May I present my mother, Caroline Morris, Countess of Heath?"

After the women greeted each other, Steven smiled down at Harriet. "I wonder if I might have the honor of this dance, Miss Nash."

"Most certainly, Lord Heath," she replied saucily as she accepted his proffered arm.

When Steven led Harriet onto the dance floor, Agatha turned toward Lady Heath. "Are you convinced now?"

"Positively. Steven practically wrenched my arm out of my socket in his rush to drag me over here," she replied, rubbing at her shoulder.

"Penelope did a wonderful job misdirecting my sister this evening." Agatha watched her niece twirl around the room, a laughing, petite brunette squired by a tall, dashing blond. "They make a lovely couple, don't they?"

"Indeed they do," Lady Heath sighed. "I've wondered when Steven would fall."

"Even though he might have fallen, the ring isn't on her finger yet," Agatha said firmly. "It's up to us to ensure that nothing goes awry during their courtship."

"That seems highly unlikely," Lady Heath protested.

"Perhaps, but I don't want to leave anything to chance. One of Harriet's dearest friends was heartbroken when her fiancé cried off."

Stiffening, Lady Heath scowled for the first time. "My son would never do something so dishonorable."

"I wasn't implying he would," Agatha countered. "I was simply using that as an example of how things can go disastrously wrong." Noting Lady Heath's doubtful expression, Agatha tried another approach. "At least agree to help me during the courtship. A little nudge in the right direction never hurt anyone."

Thankfully, Lady Heath agreed. "I doubt it will take much nudging," she murmured dryly, her eyes following Steven and Harriet around the room.

"On that point, we agree perfectly." As the music stopped, Agatha watched Steven lead Harriet out into the garden. "I think a spring wedding would be wonderful, don't you?"

"Steven, where are we going?" Harriet asked, as he led her down the steps onto the Thompsons' rear lawn.

"You'll see."

His evasive answer didn't bother her. What did she care where he was taking her? Anywhere Steven went, she would eagerly follow.

Rounding the corner of the town house and heading for the street, Harriet couldn't help but wonder if he were running away with her. A quick trip to Gretna Green would be lovely. Oh, please, please, please let it be that, she thought, sending the quick prayer upward.

Steven came to a standstill in front of a beautiful confection of a carriage. With the plush red seats, golden scrollwork, and gleaming white exterior, the carriage looked as if it had been plucked from the pages of a fairy tale. It was precisely the sort of carriage that a newly married couple should ride off in.

That thought stuck, resonating within her, breathing life into her fragile hopes.

Clasping her hand, he turned her toward him. "This afternoon you helped me find peace, generously opening yourself to me, giving me more than you will ever fully realize." He traced the tips of his fingers along the curve of her jaw. "Tonight, I wish to return the favor and give you something you long for."

"You?" she asked, unable to hold back the question.

He smiled softly. "An adventure," he corrected. "You told me once that you were always second best, the 'best friend.' Tonight, you shall become an enchantress, a goddess among mere mortals."

A giggle broke from her at the thought. "Me?"

"Yes, you." He released her hand to cup her face between his fingers. "Step outside yourself, Harriet, just for this evening, for this moment. Become the woman you dream of being—bold, strong, beautiful."

His words tempted her, but she knew it was a fool's notion to believe even for a moment that she could ever be more than remarkably unremarkable. "I can't," she whispered finally.

"You can if you want to badly enough." His gaze roamed over her features. "I see that woman inside of you. You have such strength, Harriet, such inner beauty; all you need to do is allow it to blossom, to release it and believe in yourself." His thumbs slid over her lips, bringing forth bright memories of that very afternoon. "Just for tonight." He captured her gaze. "For me."

Magical words, for Harriet would do anything for him. But could she do this? Could she become bold, wild, and confident?

Like she had today at the cottage?

She had been all those things today, hadn't she? The realization stunned Harriet. Today she'd been an artful seductress who had taken her lover almost beyond his point of control, driving him mad with desire, and here stood that same man, asking for her to take another adventure with him.

Why on earth was she even hesitating?

"A goddess such as I should never be kept standing in the chill night air," she said, putting as much haughty emphasis into her words as she was able.

Steven's grin was her reward. Releasing her, he swept into a deep bow. "Please forgive me, oh divine one," he murmured.

As he handed her up into the carriage, Harriet lifted her chin, thrusting her nose into the air, mimicking a gesture she'd seen Laurel do more than once. "You may touch my hand, plebian."

The velvet cushions muffled Steven's laugh. "Now you're overdoing it a bit."

"Sorry, I got carried away by the heady rush of power."

"Perfectly understandable," he said as he settled into

the seat across from her. "You possess more power than most women."

"Goddesses, if you please."

"Forgive me." He grinned at her as the carriage started down the lane. "I meant to say than most goddesses."

"Much better." Twirling a curl around her index finger, she continued their silly banter. "I'm pleased you appreciate the fact that I am practically aquiver with power."

"How could I not when you make me quiver every time I'm near you?"

My, my, what a delicious thought! "Did you perchance make an off-color remark to my personage?"

"You have to ask?" Making a tsking sound, Steven shook his head. "If you can't even tell when I'm making a suggestive remark, I must make a poor rogue indeed."

"I beg to differ, my lord rake." Lifting her hand, she began to tick off her points. "First you kiss me until I'm quite senseless . . . and I assure you I'm usually quite sensible; second you sweep me out of the ballroom under the very eyes of my aunts and your mother; and third you lure me into this beautiful carriage to have your way with me." Pausing, she gave him a searching look. "You are going to have your way with me, aren't you?"

"I hadn't planned on it."

She sighed dramatically. "Now that would be a disappointment."

"Really?" Leaning back against his seat, he crossed his arms, his eyes lit with a wicked light. "Do you think it would be more fitting . . . given my rakish past, mind you . . . if I did have my way with you?"

"Most certainly," she pronounced with a firm nod. "In fact, I do believe if you don't seduce me, it will do irreparable harm to your reputation as a man about town."

"Hmmmm," he murmured, a corner of his mouth tilting upward. "That is a problem."

"Indeed it is." She slid her hands slowly down her skirt. "What shall we do about it?"

"I'm confident I can devise a solution." Uncrossing his arms, he bent forward, resting his elbows on his knees. "Do you suppose my reputation would be unscathed if I . . ."

His eyes darkened as he reached over and lifted her slippered foot onto his muscular leg. The unusual position caused Harriet to shift forward until her bottom rested at the edge of the seat. Bracing herself with her arms, she balanced precariously, but far too curious even to consider lowering her foot again.

With tender care, he slid the slipper off her foot, tossing it carelessly onto the seat beside him. Expertly, he reached under her skirts and rolled down her stocking, his fingers sliding along her flesh in a teasing pattern that made her gasp. "I can see your education in the sensual arts has been sadly neglected," Steven said as he began to knead the instep of her foot.

"Regretfully so," she murmured.

"Lucky for you, I am well versed in them." He rested the heel of her foot in one hand as he stroked along her calf. "I fancy myself somewhat of a connoisseur of women."

"Do you now?" she asked, torn between wanting him to concentrate on his caress and wanting to hear the rest of his story.

"Indeed I do. How else could I have learned about this?" he said. Lifting her foot to his mouth, he bit upon the fleshy part near her toe, the sharp twinges an erotic contrast to the sweep of his tongue. "I learned how to make love to a woman from the finest courtesans, skilled in the art of passion unimaginable to the average person."

When he began to suck upon her toes, she moaned softly as fingers of desire spread through her, stirring to life an urgent need. "I never knew feet were so sensitive," she whispered, her eyes closing as passion seduced her into a trance.

"Then you probably don't know how many delights can be found right here," he said as he ran one finger behind her knee.

"Knees?" she asked weakly.

Slipping off his seat, Steven knelt before her, carefully placing her foot upon the cushion he'd just abandoned. Slowly, he slid the palm of his hand along the bottom of her leg, over the curve of her calf, then upward until the tips of his fingers rested under the curve of her knee. "Many men neglect this part of a woman's body, yet I've found it to be a most sensitive area."

Finding herself caught between the urge to moan and the urge to laugh was something she'd never thought to experience. "I would have to concur with you, Lord Heath," she agreed, as his fingernails scraped along the back of her leg.

"Somehow I knew you would," he murmured, leaning forward to nip at the flesh just above her kneecap.

A gasp ripped from her, need beginning to strum through her with insistent demand. As he outlined her knee with kisses, pausing to lick at the hollow underneath, Harriet arched in delight. "You are quite the master rogue."

His chuckle caused his breath to rush over her moistened flesh, a cool contrast to her heated skin. "To be perfectly honest, I'd grown bored with all this."

"This?" she exclaimed, unable to imagine ever growing bored of Steven's lovemaking.

Pausing, he glanced up at her, capturing her gaze with his. "I'd never realized it would feel so different with the right person."

The right person.

Those three words etched into her heart, bringing tears to her eyes. "Oh, Steven," she murmured, love filling her.

The words of love that hovered on the tip of her tongue stilled when Steven returned his attention to their erotic game. "Now where was I?" he said, as he stroked his fingers along the side of her calf. "Here?" he asked absently as he scraped his nails around her knee. "Or was it here?" Dipping his head, he pressed a kiss upon the lower portion of her thigh, nudging her skirt up even higher.

"I like there," Harriet gasped. Her most private area lay open, vibrating with need, mere inches from his mouth, she realized, closing her eyes as hunger overtook her.

As Steven suckled, he curved his palm around her thigh, edging her skirt up farther. Suddenly, she reached down, holding her skirt pressed against her womanhood, shy at the idea of exposing herself to his gaze.

The heat blazing out of his eyes scorched her. "Trust me," he rasped, his voice raw with need.

Trust him. She did . . . implicitly, but this required more than trust.

"Harriet," he murmured, leaning down to stoke her thigh with his tongue, his gaze capturing hers. "I want to see you. All of you." The sight of him kneeling between her knees, his mouth upon her naked leg should have shocked her, but instead it created a swirling need inside of her to see more, to experience more.

Wherever Steven wanted to take her, she would go willingly.

Keeping her eyes firmly fixed upon him, she leaned back, releasing her grip upon her skirt, allowing her hands to fall to the side . . .

And let him take her.

Chapter Fourteen

✦

*H*eady with the scent of her, Steven reveled in Harriet. Her gaze remained fixed upon him as he slowly pushed up her skirt, baring her completely. Unable to resist the lure of her lushness, he trailed his fingers along her glistening cleft. Soft brown curls brushed against his hand as he stroked her into a writhing frenzy.

"Steven. Oh, Steven."

Her breathy moans drove him mad, but he controlled his ardor. Tilting her hips against his fingers, Harriet urged him onward with her body . . . and he answered her in kind.

Leaning forward, he kissed her moistness, slowly dipping inward to taste her essence, and lost himself in her. Steven applied every trick he'd learned at the hands of skilled courtesans, but this time the act was more intimate, more meaningful, more fulfilling. Hunger clawed at him as he slid his tongue deep into her, making her gasp in ecstasy as she peaked beneath his touch. Again, he thought, suckling at her, drawing her into his mouth until she arched up against him a second time.

Her fingers dived into his hair, holding onto him as if he were the only solid thing in her careening world. Exultation filled him at the knowledge that he'd given her this; he'd driven her beyond herself and into a world of sensual wonders.

Needing more, he lifted his head and reached for her, claiming her mouth in a hungry kiss. As her arms entwined around his neck, pulling him closer for a deeper kiss, Steven worked at the fastenings on the back of her dress until all that lay between them was a thin chemise.

Steven shifted backward, allowing her dress to fall forward. Slipping the sleeves of her gown free, he unlaced the chemise. "No corset," he murmured approvingly as he bared her beautiful bosom to his waiting hands.

Her head fell back as she curved her body into him. Bending his head, he kissed her breasts, teasing the luscious peaks, nibbling at the plump sides. Lord, he wanted to feel her against his skin. Reeling backward, he tore off his cravat, casting it carelessly aside along with his jacket and vest. When he went to unfasten his shirt, he found Harriet already there, working to free him from the confines of his clothes.

As soon as he cast aside the shirt, he gathered her into his arms, pressing her softness against his hardness in achingly perfect splendor. "Perfect," he whispered, pressing a kiss upon her shoulder.

"Absolutely," she replied, returning the caress. Slowly,

she shifted her body side to side, rubbing against him. "Please, Steven." Lifting her head, she gazed into his eyes. "Show me everything."

Her words slammed into him, sending pulsating need shooting through him as she gave voice to his dearest desire. "Harriet," he rasped, struggling to maintain a hold on his control. Nothing they'd done was irreparable. If he took her virginity, there would be no going back.

Who was he kidding? There was no going back now.

He'd already realized he didn't want to live without her, so why not complete the bond with their bodies?

His hand shook as he loosened his breeches, freeing his throbbing manhood from the confines of his clothing. With one hand curved around the back of her head, he kissed her gently, lovingly, as he guided himself toward her, bracing himself at her entrance. "Harriet," he rasped, his muscles quivering with the effort of holding back. "Are you certain?"

"Oh, yes," she whispered, giving him a tremulous smile.

The affirmation caused his blood to pound through his veins. Slowly, he eased forward into her warmth until he reached her maidenhood. He paused, giving her time to adjust to him. As she closed around him in heated perfection, Steven groaned at the unbearable sweetness of the moment. With a forward lunge, he claimed her for his own, thrusting past the barrier to lodge himself firmly in her welcoming embrace.

Gasping his name, Harriet wrapped her legs around him, holding him against her body as she grew accustomed to him inside of her. After a few moments, she moved her hips in small, experimental pulses. Her breath caught in erotic little gasps, playing havoc with his already strained control.

When she dug her nails into his bare shoulders and arched against him, Steven's grip upon his control finally snapped. A shout of joy burst from him as he grabbed hold of her hips and began to thrust into her. Again, he applied his knowledge, pulsing into her with varying strokes, before driving inward with deep, hard thrusts.

Harriet's sensuality amazed him, elated him as he celebrated within her embrace. Though his body clamored for release, Steven waited until Harriet cried out in ecstasy, before allowing himself to find his release within her warmth. Blood rushed through his veins as every muscle in him quivered, tightening with sheer pleasure.

Enfolding her close, Steven buried his face against her soft breasts as he savored the feeling of perfect satisfaction.

How ironic that he'd had to face losing everything he held dear . . . just to find his salvation in Harriet.

"Have they returned yet?" Lady Heath asked as she took the seat next to Agatha.

Fanning herself, Agatha tried not to let her strained nerves show. "No," she admitted.

Lady Heath snapped open her fan. "Oh, dear."

The simple phrase held a wealth of emotions. "Exactly my sentiments." Lifting her fan to cover her mouth, Agatha whispered, "They've been gone far too long. Their absences are certain to be noticed."

"Undoubtedly," Lady Heath agreed, moving her fan upward too. "But would that really be so dreadful? I know my son, Agatha, and if the gossips notice their absence, he will feel honor-bound to protect Harriet."

"I hadn't considered that," Agatha replied, as she turned the idea over in her head. While it wasn't the perfect plan, for she'd prefer not to have Harriet's name sullied, Agatha knew it could work . . . if Lord Heath were truly as honorable as his mother claimed.

Before Agatha could discuss the idea further with Lady Heath, she caught a glimpse of Hilda striding toward her like a ship under full sail. "Brace yourself," she muttered to her companion.

Following the direction of Agatha's gaze, Lady Heath watched Hilda as she stormed toward them. "Who is that?"

"One of the Furies."

"Excuse me?"

Snapping her fan shut, Agatha shook her head. "No doubt you'll understand what I mean the moment my sister Hilda arrives."

"Where is Harriet?" demanded Hilda as she came to a halt in front of Agatha.

"She's around somewhere." Waving her hand vaguely, Agatha peered around Hilda. "You seem to have lost Penelope."

"Escaped her is more like it," snapped Hilda. "That foolish woman kept me running around this house, searching for her husband, and when I'd finally grown weary of looking for him, I asked a gentleman if he'd seen Lord Hammersmith. Amazingly enough, the gentleman said that he'd just left Lord Hammersmith . . .

at White's." Hilda scowled down at her. "That's when Lady Hammersmith began to giggle like a madwoman, claiming a megrim had caused her to forget her husband hadn't even come this evening! Foolish old woman!"

Panting from her efforts, Lady Hammersmith charged toward them. "So this is where you've gotten off to, Hildy." She patted at her overheated face. "There was no need to get so upset over my little mistake."

"That was no mistake," Hilda announced, turning slowly to spear everyone with her sharp gaze. "Something is going on here and I want to know . . ." Breaking off, she turned to look around the room. "Where is Harriet?"

"Harriet?" Agatha repeated, trying for an air of nonchalance.

Lady Heath began to fan herself quickly. "Do you mean your niece, Harriet?"

"Yes," Hilda drawled, glancing between Agatha and Lady Heath. "Are you going to introduce us, Aggie, or have you forgotten all your manners?"

"If you continue to be so testy, Hilda, I rather doubt Lady Heath will wish to make your acquaintance." After a short pause, Agatha gestured toward Steven's mother. "May I present Lady Caroline Morris, the Dowager Countess of Heath." She glared at her sister. "Lady Heath, I apologize for my introduction to my sister, Miss Hilda Amherst."

"Most gracious," snapped Hilda. "Now would someone please tell me where Harriet is?"

Again, Agatha's eyes grew wide as she spread her hands. "Harriet?" she repeated.

Lifting an eyebrow, Hilda stared at her companion. "Well, Penelope, aren't you going to ask which Harriet I mean, just like your accomplices here?"

"Oh, for pity's sake, Hildy, I can't even keep track of my own husband, much less keep tabs on your niece," snapped Lady Hammersmith as she dabbed her handkerchief along her collarbone. "And I must say, Hilda, you've always had a tart tongue, but lately you're becoming downright unpleasant to be around."

Hilda drew back her shoulders. "Forgive me if I'm not on my best behavior, Penelope. I happen to be trying to protect my niece."

"From what?" Agatha countered. "A bad bit of beef?"

"A bad turn of fate. One misstep, and her reputation could be destroyed."

Instinctively, Agatha glanced at Lady Heath, who sent her a concerned look back. If Harriet didn't return soon, all of Hilda's dire predictions could come true. While Lady Heath assured her that Steven would protect Harriet, Agatha suddenly realized she was putting a lot of faith and trust in a woman she'd only just met.

Was the reward worth the risk?

She prayed so. Taking a deep breath, Agatha threw Hilda off the scent again. "I don't know why you're carrying on so, Hildy," she began easily. "Harriet wished to refresh her person. I believe she stepped into the ladies' salon for a few moments."

Ever the skeptic, Hilda glanced around the room again. "Then where is Lord Heath?"

Calling upon every ounce of acting ability she might possess, Agatha shook her head and shrugged lightly. "I couldn't say. It wasn't my turn to watch him," she said with a half smile.

"Nor mine," Lady Heath added brightly. "That's the lovely thing about having a full-grown son; there's very little care required."

Though she tried to read her sister's expression, Agatha couldn't tell if Hilda believed them or not. Finally, Hilda nodded firmly. "Very well then. I shall put your explanation to the test." Pointing her finger, Hilda glared at Agatha. "But if she's not precisely where you say she is, I'll be back looking for truthful answers."

All three ladies breathed a sigh of relief as Hilda marched away. "Is Harriet really refreshing her appearance?" Lady Hammersmith asked hopefully.

"Of course not," Agatha said, tapping her fan against her leg as she tried to devise a new plan to distract Hilda.

Lady Heath twisted to face Agatha. "What are we going to say when your sister comes back?"

"Nothing," Agatha pronounced firmly as she looked at her two compatriots. "We're going to hide."

By the time the carriage rocked to a stop in front of the Thompsons' town house, Steven and Harriet had redressed and were seated across from each other, a perfectly polite distance between them. If people overlooked the wrinkles in her skirt and his slightly lopsided cravat, no one would suspect the passion they'd explored within the confines of this dream of a carriage.

Steven descended before reaching back for her, assisting her from their private haven. "I wish we didn't have to leave," she murmured, lifting her eyes to meet his darkening gaze.

"Fortunately, I own this carriage, so we can take a . . . ride anytime you wish."

His wicked promise fanned the ember of desire still burning inside of her. "I believe I'm available later this evening."

Grinning broadly, Steven led her around the house toward the rear yard. "I fear I have thoroughly corrupted you, my dear Miss Nash."

"As a proper rake, it is your duty, is it not?"

"Quite true."

"And as for being corrupted," she began, pausing to trace the outline of his lips, "my only regret is that it didn't happen sooner."

Steven nipped her fingertip before shifting her away, nudging her toward the doors. "Off with you," he said with a laugh. "I'll wait a few minutes before following."

Waving once, she turned and headed for the house, a warm glow inside of her. She meant what she'd said; she had no regrets for the wonderful passion they'd explored this night. Imagine, she thought as she fought back the urge to skip into the house, she'd begun to believe she'd never find this type of love. And now she had Steven. With his magic hands, gifted mouth, and generous spirit, he had far exceeded any expectations she'd had of lovemaking.

The things he did to her, the way he made her feel, were the stuff of dreams. For the first time in her life, she'd felt beautiful, a wild, sensual creature who drove men to distraction . . . or at least one very special man.

Unconcerned that she was suspiciously rumpled, Harriet slipped back into the house with a smile on her face.

Steven's gut tightened as he watched Harriet walk away from him, her hips swaying gently beneath her full skirts. There was a new confidence about her, an air of sureness that had been absent before their carriage ride. A flicker of heat licked at him. He'd done that for her. He'd taken her, made her his, and changed her forever.

When he'd convinced her to take the carriage ride with him, he certainly hadn't intended upon making love to her. Without conscious direction, their teasing had escalated into an alluring dance of foreplay. Even then, he hadn't meant to complete the act. For God's sake, he'd just claimed her innocence in the back of a carriage!

Yet, though he might regret the place, he didn't regret the act.

For the first time in weeks, he looked toward the future with eager anticipation. He would clear his debts with the loan from Royce, then he would approach Harriet's father and offer for her.

Standing here in the garden with images of his perfect future and a well-sated body, Steven couldn't imagine a better place to be.

"Lord Heath!"

At the call, Steven spun around to see Lady Camilla approaching him. "My lady," he greeted, trying not to resent her intrusion. "Are you taking in some fresh air?"

A blonde curl bobbed as she nodded briskly. "This ball

is quite the crush." Her gaze sharpened upon him. "In fact it's so crowded that I saw you only for the briefest moment, then lost sight of you altogether." Stepping closer to him, she tapped his chest with her fan. "Where did you disappear to, my lord?"

Hoping she hadn't seen him return with Harriet, he forced what he prayed looked like a rakish smile onto his face. "A gentleman never tells, my lady."

"So you did have a private interlude with some lucky lady here in the garden." Her eyes widened as she leaned in even closer. "I probably shouldn't be alone with you, my lord. For all accounts, you are quite dangerous to a lady's reputation."

He almost laughed at that remark. Lord, had he actually found this sort of erotic banter arousing? His spirited exchanges with Harriet were what he considered exciting. As soon as he thought about Harriet, an image of her spread in abandon before him flashed into his mind. Well, he amended silently, perhaps he was dangerous to one special woman. But as for Lady Camilla, she had nothing to fear. It wasn't that she wasn't beautiful or charming or graceful; she just wasn't . . . Harriet.

Lost in his thoughts, Steven was caught unaware when Lady Camilla lunged toward him, throwing her arms around his neck, and leaning up to kiss him. Stunned, he simply stood there for a moment, unmoved by the feel of her pressed against him.

Oh, Lord, how was he going to get out of this one gracefully?

Having looked everywhere else for her niece, Hilda searched the garden for Harriet. Despite what Agatha claimed, Hilda knew good and well that Harriet had snuck off with Lord Heath. No, Hilda amended to herself, there hadn't been any sneaking involved. Undoubtedly Agatha had wished them well before sending the pair off into the gardens . . . alone.

Not that she could question her sister, Hilda thought with a shake of her head. She'd returned from the empty salon only to find that her sister, Lady Heath, and Lady Hammersmith were all missing from the room as well. No matter, Hilda decided as she checked the gazebo, for she would find Harriet and return her to the safety of the Thompsons' ballroom. Imagine that foolish Agatha allowing Harriet to wander off. Hilda could scarcely fathom what thoughts flew through her sister's head sometimes.

Rounding the corner, Hilda spotted a couple standing intimately close just across the lawn. It was Lord Heath, all right. She was about to charge forward when she shifted her gaze onto the lady . . . who was not Harriet. A small gasp broke from Hilda before she pressed the back of her hand to her mouth. As she watched, the blonde flew into Lord Heath's arms, and they began to kiss.

Having seen quite enough, Hilda turned her back on the lying scoundrel and his lady. She knew she'd been right not to trust that Lord Heath. All her suspicions had been proven true this evening. The only problem that remained was convincing Harriet of that fact.

Hilda knew her niece well enough to realize Harriet would never believe her, at least not without proof. What she needed to do, Hilda decided, was move forward with her plan to hire a Bow Street Runner, have him gather undeniable proof, and show everything to Harriet.

Until then, Hilda needed to keep her niece out of Lord Heath's clutches.

Grasping hold of Lady Camilla's arms, Steven broke free of her embrace. "My lady," he began, fighting back the urge to wipe his mouth. "You'll make me forget I'm a gentleman."

Apparently he was a far better actor than he gave himself credit for because Lady Camilla seemed to believe he actually wanted her. "You're not a gentleman," she murmured. "I'm tired of gentlemen. I want someone who isn't afraid to take risks, isn't too polite to reach out and kiss a lady."

All those factors applied to him . . . but only with Harriet now. When Lady Camilla had kissed him, the only urge that had overwhelmed him was one to push her away. If Harriet had thrown herself at him, Steven knew he wouldn't be trying to find a way out of the situation.

"I'm afraid I shall have to disappoint you, my lady," he said finally. "My honor as a gentleman requires I never take advantage of a lady." Except when you're mad about her, he added silently.

A small crease formed between Lady Camilla's brows. "But I thought you were somewhat of a . . ."

"Rogue?" he asked, supplying the word. With a laugh, he shook his head. "Indeed not. Haven't you heard?" He smiled down at her. "I'm reformed."

Her frown deepened. "What do you mean by that?"

"Nothing," he replied. "May I escort you back into the ballroom?"

Accepting his proffered arm, Lady Camilla looked up at him. "Are you quite certain you don't wish to be a bit adventurous tonight?"

"Lady Camilla," he began, knowing he was grinning like a fool, "I've had about all the adventure I can handle this evening."

With his grin still firmly in place, Steven entered the ballroom, feeling amazingly fine for a man whose finances read like the obituaries. Spying Harriet across the expanse of the room, he wove his way through the crush to ask for a dance.

"Heath!"

At Lord Hampton's call, Steven turned to face the elderly gentleman. "Good evening, sir."

"Indeed it is." Glancing around, Hampton leaned forward. "Normally I wouldn't consider discussing business at a social affair, but I've just heard a bit of news on that private matter you mentioned to me and I thought you might find it interesting."

His interest piqued, Steven urged Hampton to continue. "What have you heard?"

"Apparently this Longley fellow is involved with Laird MacWilliam."

Longley again. The fact that the man's name had been brought to his attention twice in one day didn't bode well. "Who's this MacWilliam chap?"

Lord Hampton's eyes widened. "You haven't heard of MacWilliam? Everyone's talking about him."

"Apparently not to me," Steven pointed out.

"Can't imagine why not. MacWilliam is creating quite a stir these days. He's been purchasing up vouchers by the handful." Clearing his throat, Hampton straightened his waistcoat. "He's also responsible for freezing investments like the Lockley mines up in Scotland that I've invested in." His expression grew angry. "He's dishonorable, I tell you, Heath."

"His actions hardly sound criminal," Steven remarked.

"They are when he doesn't allow fine, upstanding gentlemen to repay their vouchers!" blustered Hampton. "Just the other day, Conover tried to pay off his marker, but MacWilliam refused. Worse yet, he doesn't even have the honor to refuse repayment himself. Instead he sends his man of business to do the dirty work for him." Clicking his tongue, Hampton shook his head. "It's a dark day for us all when a gentleman's pride isn't honored."

While MacWilliam's actions weren't alarming, they certainly weren't those of an upstanding gentleman. And if Longley was associating with that sort, he might be tainted as well. When combined with the information he'd received from Windvale and Connor, it was apparent he wasn't the type of man he wanted around his mother. "I appreciate the information, Hampton," Steven said, patting him on the arm. "If you hear anything else, please let me know."

"I will indeed." A shimmer of excitement brightened Hampton's gaze. "I'll admit I've enjoyed trying to uncover information for you. Feel a bit like a Bow Street boy."

Which is precisely whom Steven would have hired if he'd had the funds. "As I said, I do appreciate your help."

As Hampton stepped away, Steven tucked the information into his memory. For now he had a dance to claim. In short time, Steven made his way to Harriet's side.

"Lord Heath," she murmured, her eyes sparkling with sensual memories. "How pleasant to see you again."

"The feeling is mutual," he replied with a smile. "And aren't we being polite?"

Tilting her head coquettishly, Harriet widened her eyes. "Naturally, my lord. After all, I am a proper young lady who would only be acquainted with a proper young gentleman."

Steven crossed his arms. "Then why are you acquainted with me?"

"You're reformed, remember?"

"Oh, yes. That's right." His smiled broadened into an appealing grin. "I'm always forgetting that."

Harriet's laugh warmed him and he didn't care if he was standing here looking like a lovesick swain. "When you're finished laughing at me, might I have the next dance?"

"I'm afraid not," announced Harriet's aunt Hilda as she joined them. The hand she wrapped around Harriet's arm was decidedly possessive. "We are departing. Come along, Harriet."

"But, Aunt Hilda, I . . ."

"Now, Harriet," she snapped in a tone that brooked no arguments.

Looking over her shoulder as her aunt proceeded to pull her from the room, Harriet apologized. "I'm sorry, my lord. Perhaps we will be able to converse again soon."

Before he had a chance to respond, the other aunt and Lady Hammersmith ran out from behind a curtained alcove and hurried after Harriet and her aunt Hilda. Only one thing he knew could send elderly ladies running like that—when their innocent charge began to spend time with a rake.

Apparently Harriet's plan to redeem his reputation wasn't working as well as they'd hoped.

Chapter Fifteen

As his solicitor, Mr. Tyler, entered the library, Steven rose from his desk to greet the man. "It's good to see you," he said, eager to hear news that his debts had all been paid off. Steven had already arranged a meeting with Harriet this afternoon at the cottage, where he planned to propose to her. "Please have a seat and tell me how you fared."

Instead of the pleasant expression Steven expected, Tyler wore an alarmingly gloomy one. "Not well, I'm afraid," Tyler said, confirming Steven's fears.

"Why not?"

"It might be easier if I simply start at the beginning."

Trying to ignore the sick feeling in his stomach, Steven waved his solicitor on. "Fine, fine, just tell me what happened."

Tyler worried the edge of his jacket between his fingers. "As soon as I received your note informing me that the Earl of Tewksbury would be covering all of your out-

standing vowels, I sent notice to the various creditors informing them that I would forward a bank draft for the
amount owed within a few days." He frowned slightly.
"Then I received word back from not just one, but all of
your creditors stating that they'd sold the promissory note
within the last few days. More unusual still is the fact that
all your vowels were sold to the same gentleman."

Steven struggled to make sense of the news. "Who
bought them?"

"Laird MacWilliam."

"My God."

Tyler stepped forward. "You know Laird MacWilliam."

"Not personally." Lord Hampton's tale about how
Conover was unable to repurchase his markers worried
Steven. Perhaps MacWilliam had a vendetta against
Conover or something of that nature. As for himself,
Steven didn't even know MacWilliam, so there was no reason MacWilliam wouldn't accept repayment. "While this
situation is quite peculiar, it doesn't really change anything. My debt remains, only the debtor has changed." The
logic calmed him. "I want you to continue to secure the
funds from Lord Tewksbury. Then I want you to approach
this Laird MacWilliam and make payment arrangements
with him."

"Very well, my lord," Tyler said, rising to take his
leave.

After seeing his solicitor out, Steven walked over to
the window, staring out onto his well-manicured lawn as
he considered this strange turn of events. Who was this
Laird MacWilliam that everyone was talking about and
why had the man purchased all of his vowels?

He'd have the answers soon enough, Steven decided,

thrusting the disturbing thoughts from his head. There was nothing he could do about the situation until he knew exactly what he was dealing with. So, for now, he would think about more pleasant things . . . such as his appointment with Harriet.

It had been two days since he'd seen her at the Thompsons' ball. He'd sent around a note asking that she meet him yesterday, but she'd returned word that she couldn't get away. However, she'd promised to meet him today.

Disappointment washed over him as he realized he still wasn't free to ask for her hand in marriage. The delay irritated him . . . especially now that he'd taken her innocence. How ironic that he, the seducer of young ladies, would feel guilt over having enjoyed pleasures without benefit of marriage. The entire matter was somewhat comical given his past.

Grinning widely, Steven checked his appearance in the mirror before heading out to meet the future Lady Heath.

Tuning out Lord Hammersmith's dreadful poem, Agatha looked around Lady Hampton's drawing room at the people gathered for her weekly literary group. She'd written Caroline a note requesting that she join the group today in order to speak with her about their next move.

A sharp elbow in her side snapped Agatha's attention to her sister who sat at her left. "What is it?" she whispered. She'd been putting up with Hilda's ill tempers for a while now, but Hilda had never resorted to physical attacks before.

"When you turned and started peering around the room, you stepped on my foot," Hilda explained.

Agatha smiled at her sister. "Then you had every reason to elbow me," she agreed brightly, as she joined the people clapping for Lord Hammersmith's poem. "I was searching for Lady Heath. Have you seen her?"

"No," Hilda said shortly. "And I don't know if I care to."

Hilda's remark surprised Agatha. "I understand that you're concerned about Lord Heath spending too much time with Harriet, but what do you have against his mother?"

"Absolutely nothing." Hilda's mouth tightened. "I'm fearful that if I see her, I won't be able to resist telling her what a conniving cheat her son is."

Agatha rolled her eyes. "Not again, Hildy," she protested.

"Don't 'not again' me. I'm telling you, Agatha, that young man is just like Conrad." Leaning closer, Hilda whispered, "Last night I saw him in the garden kissing Lady Camilla."

"You must be mistaken," Agatha said, dismissing the very notion of Lord Heath kissing another woman.

"I saw it clear as day, Agatha. Lord Heath was kissing Lady Camilla in the garden last night," Hilda said firmly.

For the first time since she'd begun this matchmaking scheme, Agatha felt a twinge of doubt. What if Hilda really had seen Steven kissing someone other than Harriet? Surely that wouldn't bode well for her plans.

And while Agatha knew Hilda had no love lost for Lord Heath, she'd never known her sister to lie. No, Agatha thought, dismissing the very notion, Hilda was many things—opinionated, obstinant, irritable—but she wasn't a liar.

"You must have been mistaken," Agatha insisted once

more, unable to even think about the possibility that Steven was the sort of man who toyed with ladies' hearts.

Sighing dramatically, Hilda leaned back in her chair. "Very well then, Agatha. Keep on your blinders, but I, for one, know that Lord Heath is a scoundrel . . . and I'll soon have the proof I need to convince Harriet."

"What do you mean by that?"

"You'll see." As Agatha opened her mouth to protest, Hilda wriggled her finger back and forth. "Ah, ah, ah. Patience, patience, now," she said in an annoyingly gloating tone. "As Mother used to say, all good things come to those who wait."

"I always found that to be an annoying phrase," Agatha retorted, wondering what Hilda was up to. Still, as long as she kept Hilda near, Agatha kept her out of Harriet's way.

A loud crash interrupted the poetry reading. Everyone's attention snapped toward the back of the room to see what had happened. Amidst a pile of broken china stood Lady Caroline Heath, looking for all the world like she prayed the earth would open and swallow her whole.

"Caroline!" exclaimed Agatha as she jumped to her feet. "Are you injured?"

"Other than my pride, no," she admitted with a painfully embarrassed smile. Three gentlemen rushed to Caroline's side before Agatha could reach her friend.

"Let me help you, Caroline," offered a tall, lanky man who looked as if he'd been sucking on sour bits.

The second gentleman, a short, homely fellow asked, "What happened?"

"I don't really know," she said with a helpless wave of

her hand as the third fellow, a portly gentleman, patted her shoulder. "One moment I was entering the room and the next, I felt something bump into me, causing me to shift off-balance and straight into the table holding the empty teacups."

Stepping forward, Hilda joined their group. "Who bumped into you?"

"I don't know," she repeated, tears welling in her eyes. "I'm just unbearably clumsy."

"Oh, dear!" exclaimed Lady Hampton as she rushed into the room. "My mother's china!"

"Don't worry, Eugenia. Lady Heath is fine," Hilda remarked dryly.

Agatha held back her smile. There were times when her sister's tart tongue was just what the situation required. "You really ought to have your servants be more careful in their placement of the trays."

A dull flush stained Lady Hampton's cheeks. "I am so very sorry, Caroline," she said, obviously embarrassed. "Naturally, my first thought was of your safety."

Doubtful, Agatha thought, but kept it to herself.

Hilda didn't show such restraint. "If that's true, Eugenia, then why did you lament the loss of your china rather than inquire after Lady Heath's well-being?"

Drawing herself up, Lady Hampton struggled for a response. "I . . . I . . ."

"It's quite all right," Caroline responded. "I understand perfectly. You were distressed over the loss of something you hold dear. In fact, it is I who should ask for your forgiveness." She shook her head. "While I know I can never fully repay you for my clumsiness, I will, of course, replace the china set with another."

"Allow me to replace it for you." The offer came from the short man standing just behind Caroline.

"Why you, Connor?" demanded the lanky fellow. "I can just as easily purchase new china."

Not to be outdone, the portly gentleman chimed in as well. "As can I."

"Thank you, gentlemen, but no," she insisted. "While you all have made lovely offers, I'm afraid I cannot allow any of you to purchase the china on my behalf."

"It's just that . . ."

Holding up both her hands, Caroline spoke firmly to the short gentleman who had protested. "No, Robert. Please." She gave the man a strained smile. "Would you mind fetching me a cup of tea? It would help brace my nerves." As the lanky fellow opened his mouth, Caroline asked, "Would you please see if you can find a scone for me, Percy?" Turning toward the last gentleman in her entourage, she placed a hand on his arm. "Please be a dear, Edward, and get me a nice cool cloth that I can place on my temples."

Like eager puppies ready to do their master's bidding, the trio hurried off. "Who are those odious men?" asked Lady Hampton.

Caroline stared coldly at their hostess. "Pardon me?" she asked, ice dripping off each syllable.

"What I meant to say was . . ." Lady Hampton's words trailed off as she looked around nervously. "Please excuse me while I see about cleaning up this mess."

"Most certainly," Caroline replied formally. "When you purchase your new china, please have the bill sent around to me." As their hostess hurried off, Caroline turned toward Agatha. "I apologize, but I simply couldn't stand by and allow Eugenia to make disparaging remarks about Mr. Connor, Mr. Longley, or Mr. Windvale."

"Of course not," Agatha agreed firmly. "She did, after all, invite them into her home."

"I'm uncertain if she did." A wry smile turned Caroline's lips upward. "All three gentlemen have been following me around for months now."

"Really?" Agatha murmured, overwhelmed by curiosity.

Caroline nodded. "They're all harmless, I assure you. In fact, they seem to take turns asking for my hand in marriage." She lifted a shoulder. "At times their . . . devotion can be vexing, but usually I simply view it as sweet."

Though Agatha found the entire situation rather odd, she refrained from further comment.

As servants appeared to sweep up the shards of china, Caroline rubbed at her temple. "I don't know how I'm going to explain this to Steven."

"Why do you need to explain anything to him?" Hilda asked as she stepped back to accommodate the cleaning process.

"Because he'll question the bill when it's sent around if I don't tell him about it." She sighed softly. "I can only pray that the china Eugenia decides upon isn't too expensive."

Hilda leapt upon that statement like a starving cat with a fat, juicy mouse. "Why would that be a problem? Are you having financial difficulties?"

"Hilda!" exclaimed Agatha, shocked at her sister's gall. "How crass to question a person's financial situation!"

"It's fine," Caroline said, cutting off Hilda's response. "I imagine whispers of gossip will soon make their way into the drawing rooms of London." Leaning in closer, she lowered her voice until only Hilda and Agatha could hear her. "I've been having the worst luck lately and have incurred some rather large debts. I'm afraid our financial status is a bit strained at the moment."

When Caroline had begun her explanation, Agatha had wanted to clamp her hand over Caroline's mouth. Hilda would simply use the possibility of Steven having financial difficulties to draw another correlation to Conrad. And that was the last thing she needed!

Hilda's eyes narrowed as she tried to glean more information. "So are you . . ."

"I'm parched as well!" Agatha announced, cutting off her sister's blunt question. "Why don't we all head over to the tea service, and you can introduce us to your gentlemen, Caroline."

"They're not my anything." Another rueful smile crossed her face. "Though with the weekly marriage proposals I receive from them, I'll wager each one would very much like to be."

"Perseverance is an admirable quality in a gentleman," Agatha pointed out.

"True." Caroline's eyes sparkled with good humor. "Though I'll admit that at times it is simply . . . well, downright annoying."

Agatha laughed out loud as she started toward the sideboard. "Now I can't wait to meet them. I have a fondness for annoying personalities." Glancing over her shoulder with a grin, Agatha looked at her sister. "Isn't that right, Hilda?"

Hilda rolled her eyes. "It's a good thing I feel such affection for you, Agatha."

"You know, I've often thought the very same thing." Enjoying their teasing, Agatha waved her sister forward. "Why don't you come with us and meet Caroline's gentlemen? Perhaps you will hit it off smashingly with one of them."

"Oh, yes, please do," Caroline urged. "Just the thought of that makes my day brighter. And who knows? If one of the gentlemen transfers his affection to you, I'll be down to two admirers . . . which would be just lovely."

Shaking her head, Agatha patted Caroline's hand. "Come now, dear. This is Hilda we're talking about. Don't get your hopes up," she said, tossing a teasing glance at her sister.

Royce waved his solicitor to a seat in his study. "This is an unexpected visit, Mr. Giles. Did you have questions about my note regarding the advancement to Lord Heath?"

"None, my lord." Clearing his throat, Mr. Giles shifted awkwardly in his chair. "The only trouble I'm having, my lord, is fulfilling your request."

"What the devil do you mean by that?" Royce frowned at his solicitor. "My fortune is quite sizable, easily able to withstand a withdrawal of that amount."

"Your fortune, true," Mr. Giles began, "but as for actual cash available for lending, I'm afraid that amount is more than you have available."

Knowing his solicitor was quite mistaken, Royce shook his head. "That's impossible."

"I assure you, my lord, I have checked your figures, and they are quite accurate." Mr. Giles retrieved a sheaf of papers. "You made a few sizable investments over the past few months that used the major portion of your accessible funds."

"Then sell enough stock in the shipyard to cover the amount due," Royce instructed with a wave of his hand. Helping Steven was far more important than holding on to a few stocks.

"Having anticipated that request, I ascertained the status of all your current investments." Pausing, Mr. Giles tugged at his cravat. "Unfortunately, that option is not available either."

Royce laughed at that remark. "I assure you it is, Mr. Giles. I can sell any portion of my investments as I see fit."

"Not if all your assets are frozen."

The somber expression upon Mr. Giles' face told Royce he wasn't jesting. "How can my assets be frozen?"

"Yesterday, one of the major stockholders in your carriage company accused you of financial improprieties in a petition filed with the courts. This stockholder claims you stole large profits from the company, thus stealing from all the other stockholders."

Knowing the law, Royce easily finished the thought. "So until the matter is cleared, all my assets will remain frozen."

"I'm confident the matter will be dismissed in the courts," Mr. Giles assured him. "I've kept an accurate accounting of every farthing, so I know this won't have any long-lasting effects upon your financial status."

"But in the short term, I am, in essence, without means to help Lord Heath," Royce concluded. "There has to be some way I can assist him."

"There is, my lord, though it is not without considerable risk," Mr. Giles informed him. "Your reputation remains intact, naturally, so you could easily obtain a loan from a financial institution and return the funds as soon as your assets are released." Replacing his papers in his satchel, the solicitor explained, "However, I consider it my duty as your man of business to warn you of the risks involved. If you choose to take a loan and give all the funds to Lord Heath, you will be leaving your own estate vulnerable. There is always the possibility that this matter with your company will be tied up in the courts for quite a while and you will be denied access to your wealth."

It was all too easy for Royce to follow the awful pattern. "With a large loan outstanding, it would be highly unlikely that I could obtain another if my own family required funds." What had begun as an easy matter of helping a friend could now lead to his own financial ruin.

"With any hope, Laird MacWilliam's claim will quickly be proven unsubstantiated."

"Laird MacWilliam?" Royce repeated. "Who is this bastard that is accusing me of pilfering funds?"

"As I mentioned, he is one of the major stockholders in your company. Apparently he recently purchased the stocks and was looking over the financial information I supplied him when he came across some anomalies." Mr. Giles scowled darkly. "His calculations are incorrect, my lord, for I assure you there are no irregularities in your accounts. I'm absolutely confident that the courts will discover this for themselves soon enough."

But in the meantime, he had an awful decision to make: leave his best friend to certain financial ruin or put his family at risk. Thrusting his hand through his hair, Royce decided upon the best course of action. "I want you to find out all the information you can about this Laird who accuses me of theft."

"Very well, my lord." Mr. Giles rose to his feet. "And what of the matter of Lord Heath?"

What was he going to do about Steven? Royce shook his head. "Await further instruction on how to proceed. Before I make any decision, I need to speak with the most intelligent person I know." Royce smiled at the curious expression on his solicitor's face. "My wife."

Chapter Sixteen

Harriet's Hodge-Podge simmered merrily on the stove, the meat and vegetables already tender. When she'd first arrived at the cottage, she'd put a few beef bones to boil, then added beef, lamb, and veal cubes as well as barley, diced onion, quartered turnips, and chopped carrots and celery. She'd carefully wrapped spices in a double layer of muslin before adding it to the pot as well. She wanted to impress Steven with the cooking skills she'd learned from her mother, who adored the hobby of preparing her own meals.

Even though Harriet knew he wanted her, it didn't hurt to continue applying her hound theory . . . and everyone knew food was one of the most important things to a loyal hound. As the Hodge-Podge had simmered slowly, Harriet had cleaned the upstairs, lingering over the more exotic items.

Now all that remained was waiting for Steven to arrive. Her hands smoothed down her remarkably flat skirt.

She'd forgone underclothes, having donned a thin, silk dress that clung to her in a most scandalous fashion. Her efforts, she was quite certain, would not go unappreciated by Steven.

Though her aunts would be absolutely aghast at her actions, Harriet reveled in them, feeling free and incredibly alive in Steven's embrace. How could something that felt so wonderful possibly be wrong?

When she heard the front door open, Harriet flew down the corridor to throw herself into Steven's arms. As she pressed excited kisses all over his grinning face, he maneuvered them backward and kicked the door shut behind him.

After claiming her mouth for a long, sensual kiss, he finally set her away from him. "Now that's what I call a welcome."

Laughing, she clasped his hand and led him into the dining room. "I couldn't help myself."

"And I wouldn't want you even to try." When Harriet pulled out a chair at the table, he looked first at the set table, then at her in confusion. "I forgot to bring a picnic basket this time."

"Don't worry; I took care of everything." Patting the seat, she gestured him into the chair. "Make yourself comfortable, and I'll be back in a moment."

She hurried into the kitchen, where she ladled the Hodge-Podge into a heated tureen.

"I don't know what you're doing in there, but something smells delicious," Steven called from the other room.

Ah, men really were such predictable creatures.

Smiling to herself, she proudly carried her stew into

the dining room. "I thought you might be hungry, so I made you some Hodge-Podge."

The look on Steven's face was worth every minute spent chopping and cubing. "You made this, Harriet?"

"With my own two hands." She ladled some of the savory stew into his bowl. "If you remember, I grew up in the country; my mother had a woman come in to cook during the week, but she gave her the Lord's day off. So on Sunday, my mother and I would head into the kitchen and prepare a meal. Mother considered it an amusing hobby." Warm memories caused her to pause. "We prepared some absolutely horrid dishes until we learned to follow recipes. Cooking is not as easy as one would think."

"I believe it," Steven said quickly, his gaze fixed on the steaming bowl she placed in front of him. "I am awe-struck that you can prepare a meal like this." He lifted his gaze to her. "It smells incredible, Harriet."

"Then why don't you taste it and see if it lives up to its scent?" she countered as she sank into her own chair.

Spooning up a small amount, he blew on it softly before eating the fragrant bite. Chewing slowly, Steven closed his eyes as a look of rapture spread across his handsome features. "Heaven," he finally said, his gaze lifting to capture hers. "Absolute Heaven."

The look upon his face reminded her of how he'd looked when he'd been inside of her. She shivered at the memory. "I'm so glad you like it," she murmured huskily. "One of the reasons I couldn't meet you yesterday is because I wanted to surprise you with this meal, so I needed to gather all the ingredients. I'm so glad you could meet me today."

"I rearranged my schedule." Steven toasted her with his full spoon. "A fact I am doubly grateful for now. Your efforts are very much appreciated."

"I can see that," she said, watching him eat half his bowl in the time she'd taken one bite.

"Sorry if my manners are a bit lacking at the moment, but the rules clearly state that any food prepared by the hand of a lady should be eaten quickly."

"A most convenient rule, my lord," Harriet remarked with a laugh. "It's surprising I've never heard it before."

"Naturally. Since it happens so infrequently, it's not a commonly known rule." His grin embodied his teasing as he spooned in more stew.

"I shall have to make a note of that one."

"You do that." He paused to wipe his mouth. "What else occupied your day yesterday? When you wrote back that you were unable to meet me, I wondered if your aunt Hilda had locked you in your room."

"Even if she tried, my aunt Agatha would let me out," Harriet replied. "No, I happened to have a meeting with my father's solicitor."

Steven's eyebrows lifted. "Really? Seems a bit odd that you would meet with your father's man of business."

"Not if it's my monies being invested."

From his slackened jaw and wide eyes, her response obviously shocked him. "You invested your portion?"

"Yes," she said hesitantly. "My father presented a wonderful opportunity to turn my modest funds into a solid inheritance."

"Or lose it all."

Harriet nodded slowly. "I'd considered that possibility,

but since my modest portion didn't seem to be attracting any husbands, I didn't see a large risk involved."

Setting down his spoon, he met her gaze. "Harriet," he began in an encouragingly serious tone, "I have so many things I wish to say to you, so many things I want to ask you. Unfortunately, I'm not free at the moment to discuss these matters with you."

What on earth did he mean by that? Harriet was about to push for answers, but something in his face stopped her. A shimmer of emotion that seemed far too raw, too intense, for her to demand answers. Still, she felt confident that what he meant was he planned on offering for her soon. Why else would he have said that to her?

"I can wait," she said, telling him with her gaze all the things in her heart. "Even I can be patient at times."

Her quip made him laugh. "I find that hard to believe." Leaning back in his chair, he pressed his hands to his stomach. "That was delicious, Harriet. I applaud your efforts."

"Thank you, my lord," she said as she rose to her feet. Stacking the dishes, she carried them into the kitchen along with the half-empty tureen. "While our meal was cooking, I took the opportunity to clean upstairs," she said as she left the room.

She set the plates in the sink and turned to retrieve the pot when she bumped into Steven. "Oh!" she exclaimed, her hands coming to rest upon his chest. "I didn't hear you come in."

"I wanted to see if you needed any help."

His husky murmur slid over her like the fine silk she

wore. "No, I . . ." she stammered, her thoughts falling away as his hands began to roam over her body.

"You're not wearing anything under this gown, are you?" he rasped in an incredulous tone.

Breathless, she shook her head.

His fingers tightened upon her hips, drawing her against his hardening body. "Since I admired your cooking so much, perhaps you should show me the upstairs . . . so I can admire your cleaning efforts."

Lifting her gaze, she met his heated one. "Cleanliness is important."

"Indeed it is." A corner of his mouth tilted upward in a sensual slant. "I imagine you got quite dirty while cleaning the cottage."

"Not really."

Slowly, he shook his head, nudging her in closer to him. "I don't see how you could clean the entire upstairs without getting dirty." Lowering his head, he nipped at her jawline. "I think you should bathe . . . just to make certain you're squeaky clean."

"Bathe?" she replied weakly, as images of the exotic bath she'd just cleaned that afternoon took hold of her very vivid imagination. "Perhaps you're right."

Shifting his head, he caught her mouth for a soul-wrenching, heart-stopping kiss. His tongue plunged inward to stroke, then withdraw, to trace her lips and claim them again, to tease her with feathery touches before satisfying her with long bold strokes. Finally, he lifted his head. "Oh, I'm definitely right," he whispered, reluctantly withdrawing his hold upon her hips.

Clasping her hand, he led her up the stairs.

Her pulse raced when he brought her around the tub platform to the divan. Carefully lifting the feathers and placing them off to the side, he gestured for her to sit.

Harriet glanced down at the feathers. "What are those for?"

The look in his eyes nearly singed her. "I'll be more than happy to demonstrate."

"That would be lovely," she murmured, as a shiver raced through her. "I'm always willing to learn."

"Yes, I've come to know that." Gesturing toward the settee, he said, "Please have a seat, Harriet."

Eager to experience his touch again, Harriet quickly did his bidding. Her eyes never left him as he shrugged out of his jacket, stripped off his cravat and vest, then rolled up his sleeves.

"Don't move," he commanded as he turned on his heel. "I'll be back in a moment."

Startled, Harriet sat bolt upright. She'd been expecting him to join her, and now he was leaving? "Where are you going?"

"To fetch some water," he tossed over his shoulder. "A bit hard to bathe without it."

Deciding to enjoy the rare treat of having him wait upon her, she settled back onto the divan. After a while, he returned carrying a bucket of steaming water. She watched him bring up bucket after bucket of water until the tub was filled. Tendrils of steam wafted upward in sensual spirals of mist. A light sheen on Steven's skin made him even more appealing as he stepped around the platform, holding out his hand. "My lady," he said with an inviting smile, "your bath awaits."

Her fingers trembled as she accepted his assistance

in rising to her feet. Grasping her shoulders, Steven turned her away from him and began to unfasten her gown. As each clasp fell open to his clever hands, cool air kissed her skin. "I've been thinking of this moment," he murmured, pausing to stroke a finger along the opening in her gown. "With every bucket I carried up those bloody stairs, I could think of nothing else but the moment I stripped this gown and finally saw your beauty."

"You've seen me before," she said, her voice shaking.

As he undid the last clasp, he slid both of his hands from the base of her spine upward. "Not like this. I haven't done a very good job of initiating you to lovemaking, Harriet." He moved closer as his hands slid around underneath her dress to cup her breasts. "But I promise that today I'll take my time and show you all the wonderful ways to make love."

All she could do was moan, arching her head back to rest it upon his shoulder, her breasts thrusting forward to fill his hands. Her unfastened dress fell forward, puddling at her hips. "Put your arms around my neck," Steven instructed.

Mindlessly, she obeyed, reaching up to clasp his neck. The new position arched her backward even farther, and Steven rewarded her efforts by molding her breasts into peaks. Slowly, he stroked his way down her body, pushing once at her gown and sending it falling to the ground.

His groan reverberated through his chest as he traced the tips of his fingers all over her in an erotic caress. "Open your eyes," he urged in a low rasp. "See how beautiful you are."

Lifting her lashes, she gazed across the room . . . into one of the full-length mirrors. The sight of her clinging to Steven as he stroked her all over sent a rush of desire through her. She'd never even thought of looking at herself naked, yet somehow in Steven's arms, she enjoyed watching herself arch beneath his touch. The brush of his clothes against her back evoked another shiver, weakening her knees.

Steven bent low, catching her beneath her legs, and lifted her into his arms. Laid before him in naked bounty, Harriet continued to cling to him, awash in desire, awaiting the ultimate pleasure. With a harsh groan, he caught her lips for another scorching kiss, his hand caressing her thigh as he pulled her against him.

Breaking off the kiss, he stared at her with a smoldering gaze. "Any more kisses like that, and we'll never make it to the bath."

"And this would be a problem?"

Her soft whisper caused him to grin down at her. "I've always admired your spirit, Miss Nash."

"Thank you, Lord Heath," she replied as if she weren't lying naked in his arms.

Laughing, he eased her down into the steaming water that lapped at her sensitized skin like a warm caress. With her arms lying along the sides of the bath, she awaited Steven's pleasure. To her surprise, he sat down next to the tub and began to remove his boots.

"Are you going to join me?" she asked hopefully.

The look he sent her promised passionate fulfillment. "How else can I properly demonstrate the many pleasures of bathing?"

Oh, my. She'd often enjoyed her baths, but she

couldn't even begin to imagine the pleasures Steven spoke of. If they were anything like the ones he'd shown her in the carriage, she couldn't wait for him to begin.

Rising, he stood and faced her as he unfastened his shirt. His gaze never left her face as he peeled the fabric off his shoulders, tossing it onto the floor with a careless flick of his hand. Her breath rasped out of her when his hands dropped to the fastenings on his breeches. Finally, she'd see the part of him she'd felt inside of her.

Unabashedly, she watched him, eagerly awaiting her first glimpse of his manhood. When his breeches lay open in an enticing vee, Steven hooked his thumbs into the waistband and pushed them downward. Bending over, he stepped free of his breeches, then stood, straight and proud, facing her in all his magnificent glory.

Desire exploded inside of her, making her core tingle at the beautiful sight Steven made. His manhood jutted outward, a long, alluring length that she knew fit perfectly inside of her. Whorls of dark blond hair emphasized his broad, sculptured chest, before trailing downward in a thin line that ended in the curls at the base of his manhood. A tapered waist, lean hips, and powerful, molded legs finished off the picture of manly perfection.

Breathless, she lifted her gaze to his face. "I can only assume from your expression that you approve of what you see."

"You're beautiful," she whispered softly.

A flush of pleasure stained his cheeks as he bent and retrieved a feather.

"What are you planning on doing with that?"

Her question made him smile. "All in good time, my dear."

Shaking her head, she watched him take the first step on the platform. "You do so love to tease me."

"That's half the pleasure, my dear Harriet." Reaching forward, he stroked the tip of the feather along the curve of her jawline. "Aren't you aquiver with anticipation, wondering what I plan on doing with this feather?"

Her reply was no more than a breathless sigh.

A corner of his mouth slanted upward as he set the feather down on the small pedestal that held various jars of lotion and oils. "Stand up for me, love," he bade her, offering his hand to assist.

Without hesitation, she accepted, rising to her feet as water dripped off her body. A muscle in his jaw began to pulse as his gaze swept over her, pausing upon her breasts, before lifting to her face again. "You're stunning," he finally said, his voice low and dark.

Beneath his heated gaze, that was precisely how she felt. Imagine her, plain, unassuming Harriet Nash, standing naked before a gloriously handsome, equally naked man . . . and loving it.

Steven stepped into the bath, so close that she could feel the heat from him radiating toward her chilling flesh. Without another word, he reached over to retrieve one of the bottles, unfastened the stopper, and poured a bit of the jasmine-scented liquid into his hand, before replacing it on the pedestal.

Rubbing his hands together, Steven seduced her with promised delights. "I'm warming the oil that I'm going to spread all over your body. The feel of it will drive you wild with desire."

"I'm already there," she informed him, needing his touch more than her next breath.

His husky laugh resonated within her. "Not nearly wild enough for me."

Wearing nothing but a wicked grin, Steven stroked his hands over her shoulders, along her collarbone, and downward to caress her breasts. He used his thumbs to spread the warmed oil over turgid peaks, bringing a soft moan from Harriet as she arched under his touch, using her body to beg for more.

With tormenting leisure, Steven moved his hands downward, feeling the curve of her waist, the flare of her hips, before sliding his hands around to cup her buttocks. The last hold brought her forward until his heated manhood pressed against her belly, making her gasp as desire lanced through her, forceful, hungry.

A sensual chuckle escaped him as he rubbed against her, the oil creating a slick friction between their skin. The hair on his chest teased her breasts, making her yearn to feel his mouth upon them again. As if he heard her thoughts, Steven bent forward to claim one tip, suckling it deep into his mouth, swirling it around with his tongue, nibbling gently at it to send erotic cravings pulsing through her.

Lifting his head, he claimed her mouth in a carnal kiss that stole her very breath. Undeniable need grabbed hold of her as she clung to him. With a groan, he broke off their kiss and twisted her around until her back faced him.

She'd opened her mouth to protest, but all that came out was a soft moan when he grasped her hips and pulled her back against him. His oiled manhood slid back and forth between the cleft in her buttocks, invoking dark desires that demanded to be fed. Capturing her breasts in his hands, holding her tightly against him, he rubbed in rhythmic thrusts against her softness until she sobbed for relief. "Please, Steven," Harriet whispered.

His teeth bit down on the flesh at her nape, before he bent her forward, guiding her hands to the edge of the tub. Shifting backward he positioned the tip of his manhood at her moist core . . . and thrust forward with one powerful lunge.

A scream of sheer pleasure erupted from Harriet as his body melded with hers, sending her over the edge into the glorious world he'd shown her. Before she had a chance to even catch her breath, he grasped her hips in his hands and began to move in her with strong strokes. In the carriage, his lovemaking had been sweeter, softer, but this time it was purely erotic, a carnal exchange of raw hungers.

Moaning once more, she moved back against him in perfect counterpoint, as he pushed her over the edge again and again until all she knew was the golden glow of satisfaction and unabated desire. His fingers tightened their hold upon her as he drove forward, faster, harder, hungrier, until at last, a shout of exultation broke from him and he froze inside of her. The feel of his manhood pulsating with completion sent Harriet spiraling over the edge again.

Her legs quivered, threatening to give out, and, as if in perfect tune with her needs, Steven wrapped an arm around her waist and lowered them both into the warm water without withdrawing from inside of her. A peaceful happiness settled over Harriet as she leaned back against her lover, savoring the perfect moment.

"Damn," Steven muttered, his voice rumbling from deep in his chest. "I forgot to use the feather."

A laugh of pure happiness burst from Harriet. "Perhaps you can show me later."

Shifting forward, Steven retrieved the feather, using the soft end to tease her nipples. "No time like the present."

"Indeed not," she returned as desire began to pulse within her again. "I've always loved the present."

Chapter Seventeen

"Where could Harriet be?"

While Hilda had her suspicions, she still had no proof. They'd arrived home from Lady Hampton's over three hours ago and discovered Harriet had once again snuck out of the house without escort. "Don't fret, Agatha."

Wringing her hands, Agatha paced to the window for the fortieth time that hour. "How can I not worry? It's growing dark, and she's roaming around town alone."

"No, she's not," Hilda informed her sister, deciding it was time to alleviate Agatha's worries. "A Bow Street Runner is following Harriet."

If she'd just announced she was eloping with a man half her age, Hilda didn't think she could have shocked her sister more.

"What?" exclaimed Agatha.

"You heard me clearly the first time," Hilda replied. "I hired a runner to follow Harriet because I'd caught her sneaking out before . . . though you wouldn't believe me that first time."

"I did believe you; I simply didn't concern myself because I thought she was meeting Lord Heath."

Hilda rolled her eyes. "Sometimes I wonder if you ever truly think things through, Agatha."

"I most certainly do," she protested as she stole another peek out the window. "Are you positive your runner will keep a close eye on Harriet?"

"Since he's paid handsomely to do that precise thing, I'm quite confident in his abilities." Hilda smiled at the success of her plan. With the report from the runner, Hilda would have the proof she needed to convince Agatha, Sally, and Lionel that it would be best if Harriet returned to the country. "Tomorrow morning, I should receive a report from the fellow who's following Harriet, with details of her activities this evening."

A shaky laugh escaped Agatha. "I find myself torn between wishing you'd never hired the runner because I want to protect Harriet's privacy and overjoyed because at least I know she's safe."

Hilda almost snorted at her sister. Agatha's description of her inner turmoil perfectly reflected how she felt about the entire situation. Torn between treating Harriet as an adult and fearing for her well-being. As Agatha had delighted in pointing out, she'd become downright ornery with the stress. "Welcome to my world."

Steven doubted if he could move a muscle.

Then again, why would he want to? Lying in this bed with a beautifully naked Harriet draped overtop of him, every ounce of his being filled with satisfaction, he couldn't imagine Heaven could get better than this. With one hand, he toyed with the long, silky strands of hair that streamed down her back.

After they'd made love a second time in the bath and the water had grown cold, he'd carried her into the bedroom, where they'd both rested for a while. Glancing to the side, he smiled at the picture they made in the mirror beside the bed: her legs entwined with his, her arms cradling him even in sleep. Not even the long shadows of impending night could dim the image of . . .

Panic shot through Steven as he jerked his gaze toward the window. Good Lord! The waning light told him of the lateness of the hour. They'd been here far too long; Harriet's presence was certainly going to be missed. "Harriet," he began softly, shaking her shoulder lightly. "Time to wake up, love."

Murmuring a protest, she snuggled in closer, her knee lifting to brush along his manhood. The traitorous part sprang to life despite Steven's attempts to keep it from stirring. Amazing, he thought with a rueful smile, even after having achieved release twice today, he still hungered for more.

Shifting her off his shoulder, he stroked the hair from her beloved face. He would never get enough of Harriet.

"Harriet," he said again, this time bending down to kiss her.

In an instant, her arms wrapped around his neck and she returned his kiss, changing it from a gentle caress of lips into a sensual exchange of passion. Drawing upon his last vestiges of control, Steven drew back his head. "Harriet, it's late," he explained, fighting his need to find himself within her once more.

"Hmmmm," she murmured, shifting her hips upward to brush against his now turgid manhood.

With a groan, Steven rolled from the bed and stumbled a few steps to the plush chair. "We need to leave before someone notices you're gone."

At his explanation, Harriet sat up, tossing her hair over her shoulder, leaving his view of her perfect breasts unobstructed. "I wish we didn't have to leave."

"As do I," he agreed wholeheartedly. "However, I fear we've tarried too long as it is."

"I don't believe we've tarried at all this afternoon," she retorted with a smile.

He grinned back at her.

"It's a shame it's so late," she began, easing her legs forward to dangle them over the side of the bed. "I was hoping you'd explain that chair to me."

"The chair?" Glancing down at his seat, he shook his head. "I don't understand your question; it's just a chair."

Rising, she walked toward him, her gliding steps more arousing than he'd ever imagined possible. "No, it's not," she said, reaching out to lift one of the long silk ribbons dangling from the arm. "What are these ribbons here for?"

Steven closed his eyes against the sight of her stroking the long silken strand as images of the precise reason behind them danced through his head. Despite all they'd shared this afternoon, he found himself strangely embarrassed to describe the exact purpose of the ties. "It's really getting late," he repeated, wondering if his protest sounded as weak to her ears as it did to his.

"You've said that before, Steven, and I . . ."

As her words trailed off, he opened eyes to see

what the problem was. The expression on her face told him he was the one in trouble.

"I just realized what these are for," she murmured as she gathered the other ribbon and tied it around his wrist, fastening him to the chair.

"Harriet, don't."

Ignoring his weak protest, she secured his other arm before dropping to her knees in front of him and repeating her actions with his legs. She settled back on her heels and surveyed him as he sat before her, open, vulnerable, at her mercy.

"Oh, my," she breathed, her gaze roaming over him with heated strokes. "This is quite a chair."

"It's too late, Harriet," he said, trying one last time to reason with her.

"We're late already. What will another half hour hurt?"

Sliding her hands along his calves, up to his thighs, and on to cup his manhood between her fingers, she inched forward until her mouth was mere inches from his aching hardness. That sight alone made him groan as he imagined just how it would feel to have her slide her sweet lips over . . .

Rational thought crashed to a halt as she pressed a kiss upon the tip of his pulsing tumescence. "Did you like that?" she asked, her warm breath rushing over him.

"God, yes."

Smiling seductively up at him, she shifted one of her hands to gently cup the sacs hanging beneath his shaft, squeezing them softly as she closed her mouth around him. A low growl rumbled from deep within him, his hips convulsing upward, instinctively seeking more of her warm caress. Over and over, she took him deep inside her mouth, brushing the tip of her tongue against the sensitive underside of his shaft, applying the perfect amount of pressure. Her fingertips traced erotic patterns along the base of his manhood, along the edges of his sacs, and down to that unbelievably sensitive skin below them.

She made love to him with all the skill of a trained courtesan, teasing him to the point of breaking. Moments from spilling his seed into her eager mouth, Steven tore his hands free of the silken bindings and reached for her, dragging her up his body until she rested atop him.

Curving his hands along the backside of her thighs, he spread her wide, draping her legs over the arms of the chair, and settled her onto his hardness. Matching moans of satisfaction echoed from them as her hot core enfolded him within her welcoming body.

He gripped her hips, driving upward, showing her how to ride him with the skill of a master seductress. Bracing her hands on the back of the chair, she tightened her legs for leverage, moving up and down. As her breathing increased, so did her movements until she rode him wildly.

Unable to hold back for much longer, Steven tucked a hand between them, his fingers playing with the sweet, sensitive nub hidden between her legs. Her gasp of pleasure told him he'd found the perfect spot. With circular motions, he toyed with her, driving her higher and higher until, finally, she clamped down onto him, squeezing him tightly, as her orgasm shook her. The increased tightness sent Steven over the edge to join her in ecstasy.

After a long moment, Harriet fell forward, her body resting against his in sated exhaustion. Turning her head, she pressed a kiss upon his neck. "I'll never be able to look at a chair in quite the same way again."

A laugh broke from him as he hugged her close. Only his Harriet. Here they'd played erotic games all afternoon and instead of shocking her, she jested about it.

His life would never be boring.

"You really didn't have to walk me home," Harriet said for the tenth time since they'd left the cottage.

Steven lifted a brow. "Did you think I'd allow you to walk home without escort in the evening?"

"The sun just set," she pointed out.

"Regardless, it is still evening. Besides, I'm leery enough of you traipsing over to the cottage during the day, much less after the sun's gone down."

"My hero," she murmured, going up on tiptoe to kiss him.

Clasping her shoulders between his hands, Steven gazed down at her. "How are you going to explain your absence to your aunts?" He glanced up at the garden door. "Perhaps I should come in and . . ."

"No, Steven." Pressing two fingers to his lips, she halted his words. While she appreciated his offer, she didn't want him to escort her home. For if he did, her aunts would demand he marry her, and while she wanted nothing more than that, she also wanted him to offer of his own free will. And she sensed he was close to asking for her hand.

But what if he didn't?

Pushing aside that doubting voice inside her head, Harriet focused on his remark about wishing he could say more to her. Surely he meant marriage. And if not, then she would retire to the country and marry a simple man who wouldn't mind that she was soiled goods.

But it wouldn't come to that! Harriet reassured herself firmly as she pressed against Steven's chest. "When will I see you again?"

"I'll call upon you tomorrow, and we can go for a carriage ride."

Her heart began to race. "Like last time?"

"Alas, I fear I've thoroughly corrupted you, my dear Harriet."

"It's true," she agreed in a cheerful voice. "And I shall be eternally grateful."

Laughing, he reached behind her to open the garden door. "Off with you before you tempt me further."

The notion gave her pause. "Could I?"

"Very easily," he replied, leaning down to kiss the tip of her nose, before gently nudging her through the door. "Good night, Harriet."

"Good night," she replied, smiling at him as he shut the door, leaving her standing alone in the dark garden. Wrapping her arms about her waist, Harriet whirled around twice in glee before finally coming to a stop and facing . . . her aunts. Wearing matching expressions of displeasure.

"Harriet," Aunt Hilda began sharply, "I believe you have some explaining to do."

"Where were you?" exclaimed Aunt Agatha. "I was worried sick."

Guilt assailed Harriet. She hadn't even considered that her aunts might be worried about her well-being. "I was off visiting Laurel," she said, hating that she was lying to them.

From Aunt Hilda's snort, Harriet could only conclude that she didn't believe her explanation. "When did Steven Morris, Earl of Heath, change his name?"

Her aunt's accurate guess startled Harriet. How could she reply to that question?

Luckily, Aunt Agatha saved her a response. "Never mind that now, Hildy," Aunt Agatha said, tucking her hand around Harriet's arm. "We have more pressing matters at the moment. We promised Lord and Lady Hammersmith that we would attend the theater with them this evening, so we must begin our ablutions immediately."

Breathing a sigh of relief, Harriet accompanied her aunt without a murmur. She was thankful the dark hid her lack of undergarments beneath her now-wrinkled gown. If she were quick enough, she could dart up the stairs and into her room without her aunts catching a glimpse of her scandalous appearance.

It was hard to behave in a decorous fashion when she felt like shouting for joy from the highest rooftop. Still, she didn't want to say anything until Steven declared himself. Hopefully he would soon ask for her hand. A thrill ran through her at the thought of being able to claim him for her very own, to shower him with warmth and care, to taste the delicious delights of passion.

Her revised fox hunt theory had worked beautifully.

The next morning, Harriet was up and out of the house before either of her aunts arose. She'd been awake half the night, too excited to sleep, and had been dressed since dawn's first light. She'd tried to calm herself by reading, walking, even drawing, but nothing had worked. She simply had to tell someone about her belief that Steven would soon offer for her.

Deciding Laurel was the absolutely perfect person to confide in, Harriet hurried over to her friend's house at an obscenely early hour. The Van Cleef's butler informed her that Lady Tewksbury had not come downstairs yet today, but he would inform the countess of Harriet's arrival.

Harriet was waiting in the library when she heard Royce enter his study. When she caught the sound of Steven's voice as well, she strode toward the open door, but Royce's first words stopped her.

"Steven, I have a serious problem that I need to discuss with you."

As Royce's voice drifted into the library, Harriet moved away from the connecting door, not wishing to eavesdrop, yet she could still hear their conversation.

"Yesterday, my solicitor informed me that all my funds are frozen."

There was a long silence. "So you are unable to cover my debts."

The deadened sound of Steven's voice alarmed Harriet. "Not exactly," Royce replied in a somber tone. "I could borrow the funds necessary, but it would leave me in a vulnerable position. After speaking with Laurel, we both believe your needs outweigh the potential risk and would like to go forth with the loan."

"I can't allow that, Royce." Steven's tone brooked no argument. "It is bad enough that I stand to lose everything; I can't ask you to risk the same." A harsh laugh echoed throughout the library. "To think that yesterday I thought I finally had the world set straight again. I was even going to propose to Harriet today."

"That's wonderful news . . ."

"No, it's not," Steven interrupted. "Not anymore. Oh, I'm still going to ask her to marry me, but I'll be asking her to step into poverty. In order to cover my mother's debts, I'll need to sell everything I own . . . and pray to God the sales will generate enough revenue to cover all the vowels." There was a loud crash as if he'd slammed his fist against the wall. "The name I'll give Harriet will be tainted. I would have been far better off if I'd stuck to my original plan and found an heiress."

"Steven, take my help," Royce ground out.

"And place your family at risk? I can't do that."

"What if we speak with your creditors and try to put them off for a bit," Royce suggested. "With any luck, the matter that froze my funds should be cleared up soon enough, and I'll easily be able to cover your debt."

"Luck doesn't seem to be on my side lately," Steven said, bitterness edging his tone. "I'm going to begin selling off my assets and pay off the debts on my own."

"Is the idea you had of marrying an heiress inconceivable now?"

"Definitely." Steven paused for a moment. "I've compromised Harriet," he admitted.

"Dear God, Steven, what were you thinking?"

"That I was going to offer for her anyway, so anticipating our wedding night wouldn't be a problem," he retorted. "Regardless, I'm committed now. If you'll excuse me, Royce, I need to see to this business."

"Are you going to tell Harriet about your situation?"

"Of course," Steven replied immediately. "I have to be honest with her."

"At least she has a modest portion that you can use," Royce pointed out.

"Had. As in past tense. Apparently Harriet invested her portion, so those funds are gone as well."

A soft curse escaped Royce. "Perhaps her investment will pay off."

"Not soon enough," Steven replied. A bitter laugh escaped him. "I won't get an heiress that easily."

As their boot steps faded, Harriet remained seated in the library, her dreams shattered around her. All her wonderful, beautiful plans for her future were destroyed by one realization.

She couldn't marry Steven now.

She's heard the bitterness in his voice, heard him speak of needing to marry an heiress; all that stood in his way was her. Lady Camilla would undoubtedly accept Steven's proposal in an instant and provide him with enough money to save his estates, his pride, his family.

What could she offer him? Nothing.

In time, she knew he'd grow to resent her, resent that he'd felt honor-bound to marry her, to sacrifice all he loved for her because she'd seduced him. Her eyes fluttered closed as she acknowledged her culpability. She'd purposely set out to snare him, not knowing of his debts. Having seen the success Royce had with Laurel, she'd known her theory would work beautifully.

And it had.

Only now, she wished she'd never revised Royce's fox hunt theory. If she hadn't purposely enticed Steven, he would undoubtedly be engaged to Lady Camilla at this very moment . . . and his financial situation would be secure.

It wasn't too late, she realized, ignoring the breaking of her heart. Indeed not. When Steven offered for her, she would simply turn him down, claim that she'd only wanted a wild fling before returning to the country with her parents. Once she'd convinced him, she could pack her bags and leave town . . . and her shattered dreams behind.

There was only one problem with her plan.

She didn't know if she was a good enough actress to pull it off.

Chapter Eighteen

⚊⟡⚊

*H*arriet lay upon her bed, unmoving, as she struggled to overcome the crushing blow she'd been dealt at Laurel's. It was said that nothing good ever came from eavesdropping, and now she could vouch for that statement. Still, wasn't it better to know? If she'd married Steven, ignorant as to how dire his situation was, would he have grown to resent her, to look at her and see his failure? The thought was intolerable. She loved him far too much to ask him to sacrifice everything for her. If pushed between a choice of honoring his commitment to her and salvaging his pride and his family, she knew he would be hard-pressed to betray her trust.

But could she allow him to make that choice?

The answer, much to her heart's despair, was a resounding no.

Unable to even face Laurel, Harriet had left the Tewksbury home before Laurel came down to greet her, hurrying home to hide in her room. She'd prayed for true love, for the type of deep love Laurel had found with Royce, and Harriet had indeed discovered it with Steven. And now, because of that love, she would have to walk away from him.

When she'd wished for it, Harriet hadn't realized true love could be a double-edged sword. Closing her eyes, she now wished she knew how to fall out of love.

The noon sun shone high in the sky when a knock came at the door. "Miss Harriet?" At her bidding, Harriet's maid poked her head in the door. "Lady Agatha and Lady Hilda request your presence in the study."

She wondered if Steven had come to offer for her. The very thought made her ache. She'd wanted him to ask her to marry him because he'd realized he loved her . . . not out of a sense of duty.

Thanking her maid, Harriet sat up on her bed, bracing herself for the scene that was to come. Because her aunts had requested she come to the study, Harriet knew it was a most serious discussion. The only times they ever met in the study was for extremely aggrievous offenses.

Pausing in front of the mirror to pinch her cheeks, she prayed for the strength to see this through. With a deep breath, she made her way down to the study, knocking once before entering. Only her aunts sat waiting for her.

"Where's Steven?" she asked before she could catch her remark.

Aunt Hilda raised a brow. "If you asked after him, then you must know what we wish to discuss with you."

Something about this situation felt odd. Warily, Harriet shook her head. "I'm not certain."

"Perhaps you're not, but your question was well placed," Aunt Hilda continued. "In fact, we sent your Lord Heath a note requesting his immediate presence."

So did her aunts know about his intention to ask for her hand or not? Treading carefully, Harriet tried to discern why she'd been asked to the study. "Is there a problem?"

"I'd say so," Aunt Hilda snapped, waving a sheaf of papers at her.

Aunt Agatha gestured toward a chair. "You'd best sit, Harriet, as we have quite a bit to say to you."

Looking at her Aunt Agatha, Harriet was confused by the mingling emotions of concern and excitement in her aunt's expression. "What's happened?"

"I hired a Bow Street Runner to follow you yesterday is what happened."

Harriet's stomach sank at Aunt Hilda's remark.

"Yes, you'd do well to look remorseful," her aunt stated. "While I believed you'd met Lord Heath without proper escort, I must say that this report shocked me to my core." Clicking her tongue, Aunt Hilda shook her head in disappointment. "I thought you'd been raised with more sense than to destroy your chances at a good marriage."

"She didn't destroy them," Aunt Agatha protested. "In fact, she secured them."

Alarm clutched at Harriet. "What do you mean by that?"

"I should think it quite obvious." Folding her hands, Aunt Agatha smiled softly at Harriet. "You will wed Lord Heath."

"Oh, no, I . . ."

Her protest was cut off by Aunt Agatha's sharp reply. "Oh, yes, you will, Harriet. You've made your choice, and now you must abide by it."

Dear Lord, this situation just kept getting worse and worse. "But I can't marry him."

"And why, pray tell, not?"

Unused to such firmness from her aunt Agatha, Harriet didn't know what to do. Usually it was her aunt Hilda who was strict, and she could look to her aunt Agatha for help, but in this situation, they were standing united.

Or so she thought.

"Let's not be so hasty," Aunt Hilda said slowly. "If Harriet has no desire to wed Lord Heath, perhaps it might be best if she doesn't."

"How can you say that, Hildy?" gasped Aunt Agatha. "She's ruined."

"But only we know it." She pointed to the report. "Luckily, we discovered her foolish behavior before someone else spotted them and it became fodder for the gossip mill."

"Even so, there's no getting around the fact that Harriet is no longer an innocent," Aunt Agatha pointed out firmly. "I can't understand why you, of all people, would suggest such a thing. Marrying Lord Heath is the only way to save Harriet."

"Not if he'll be a shabby husband to her," Aunt Hilda exclaimed.

"Why in heaven's name would you think that?"

"Because I saw him kissing Lady Camilla at the Thompsons' ball!"

Aunt Hilda's outburst shocked Harriet. "You saw what?"

"Never mind that," Aunt Agatha said, dismissing the topic with a wave of her hand. "Whether or not he kissed another woman is immaterial to this discussion."

"How can you say that?"

Aunt Agatha frowned at her sister. "Quite easily, Hildy." She pointed toward the runner's report. "If that is to be believed, then Lord Heath did far more than kiss our Harriet . . . which obliges him to marry her."

Harriet's head began to pound. "But I can't marry him!"

"Whatever your reasons, young lady, you should have thought of them before you agreed to rendezvous with him," Aunt Agatha retorted briskly.

Dropping her head into her hands, Harriet tried to think of how to respond to her aunt's logic . . . and the only plan she could devise was the truth. "Aunt Agatha . . ." she began slowly, only to be interrupted by a knock upon the door.

"Ahhh! I'll wager that's Lord Heath." Smiling with ill-concealed glee, Aunt Agatha bade their butler to enter, thanking him as Steven walked into the room.

Without hesitation, he stepped forward to bow politely to her aunts before lifting her hand to his lips to press a kiss upon the back of her fingers. "Good morning, ladies," he greeted them politely.

Harriet felt his gaze upon her, but she didn't meet it. She couldn't meet it, not if she were going to pull off her deception.

"That's quite enough of that, sir," pronounced Aunt Hilda, gesturing toward their clasped hands.

Steven froze. "Pardon me?"

"You should be asking for more than our pardon if half of this report is true," Aunt Hilda replied, retrieving the runner's report and waving it at him.

"What report is that?" Steven inquired warily as he sank into a chair.

Crossing her arms, Aunt Hilda gave him a stern look. "It is from the Bow Street Runners I hired to follow both you and Harriet."

Unable to resist seeing Steven's reaction, Harriet peeked a glance at him from under her lashes. It proved to be a mistake. One look and sweet memories of yesterday came tumbling over her. *This is hardly the place or time to remember yesterday!* she told herself, but the strength of her memories was hard to resist.

As hard as it would be to resist Steven himself.

Fortifying herself with the power of her love for him, Harriet strengthened her resolve to protect him from his noble nature. "My aunts have discovered our little hide-away, Steven."

The color drained from his face, but he didn't waver as he faced her aunts. "I can only apologize for my actions and assure you that my intentions toward your niece are honorable."

Aunt Agatha nodded. "I would expect nothing less, my lord."

But Aunt Hilda wasn't so easily swayed. "And what of your intentions toward Lady Camilla? Were they honorable as well?"

"Lady Camilla?" he asked, obviously confused by the question.

"Yes. You remember Lady Camilla, don't you?" Leaning forward, Aunt Hilda caught Steven in a piercing stare. "She was the one you were kissing in the gardens at the Thompsons' ball."

A dull flush stained Steven's cheeks as he glanced at Harriet. "Regardless of what you might think, I assure you that I did nothing to initiate that embrace and swiftly removed myself from her presence."

Realizing it was the perfect time to enter the conversation, Harriet adopted an attitude of nonchalance. "I still don't understand why I should be concerned even if Steven were kissing Lady Camilla," she said casually. She kept her eyes fixed upon her Aunt Hilda even when, out of the corner of her eye, she saw Steven's head jerk toward her. "I, for one, never considered our affair mutually exclusive."

Steven stiffened in his chair. "What the devil are you talking about?"

"You'll have to explain that remark, Harriet," demanded Aunt Hilda.

Aunt Agatha fanned herself. "Oh, good heavens!"

All three reactions were nothing less than she'd expected. "It's the truth," she said with a shrug. "Steven and I had an arrangement of sorts, but we never agreed to anything other than an exchange of information."

Both of her aunts began to protest her statement, but Harriet tuned them out, focusing instead on Steven's reaction.

Lurching to his feet, he turned toward her aunts. "Would you give us a moment alone?" As Aunt Hilda opened her mouth, he lifted his hand, silencing her. "I realize this request is poorly timed, especially given the report you now possess of our indiscretion. However, I would like a moment alone with Harriet to clear up this situation."

Without hesitation, Aunt Agatha rose, smoothing her skirts. "Come along, Hilda," she said briskly. "We can finish this conversation after Lord Heath has had an opportunity to talk some sense into our niece."

"I think we should stay here." Aunt Hilda crossed her arms. "After all, there's no telling what they could be up to the moment we leave the room."

"Oh, for heaven's sake, they're going to carry on a conversation, Hilda, not run into each other's arms." Pausing, Aunt Agatha gave Steven a questioning look. "Isn't that correct, Lord Heath?"

"Positively," he reassured her. "I give you my word."

"That and a farthing wouldn't get you a pot to . . ."

"Hilda!" Though slow to anger, Aunt Agatha was a force to be reckoned with when she reached her boiling point. "You and I are going to step into the salon and leave Harriet and her Lord Heath to sort through this mess."

Having heard the steel thread in her sister's voice, Aunt Hilda reluctantly stood as well. "We'll be right next door in the salon," she said to Harriet. "Call out if you need us."

What did Aunt Hilda think was going to happen? Harriet wondered. "I'll be perfectly fine," she reassured her aunt.

With one last warning glance to Steven, Aunt Hilda preceded Aunt Agatha out of the room. As the door clicked shut behind them, Harriet prayed fervently for the ability to see this through.

"Harriet," Steven began in a somber tone, "about Lady Camilla . . ."

She cut him off with a wave of her hand. "I don't need any explanation, Steven. What you choose to do with Lady Camilla is your affair."

He frowned at her reply. "How can you say that . . . especially after yesterday?"

"I'm afraid I don't see what one has to do with the other," she said in what she hoped was a blithe tone. "As I told my aunts, we never agreed to making our arrangement exclusive."

"Arrangement?" he exclaimed, twisting in his chair until he faced her fully. "I thought we had an understanding."

"Indeed, we did." She smiled pleasantly at him. "Our understanding was that I would help you rebuild your reputation and you would allow me to practice my flirting with you."

Steven's scowl deepened. "Perhaps that was our agreement in the beginning, but our relationship changed all of that."

"How?" she asked, adopting an air of confusion.

Exploding, he thrust to his feet. "We became intimate!"

"Oh that!" Deliberately, she leaned back in her chair and crossed her legs. "I considered that part of our original agreement. After all, what is lovemaking but the final culmination of flirtation?"

Steven looked as if she'd struck him. "You don't mean that," he rasped.

"Well, of course I do, silly," she said, smiling up at him even though her heart felt as if it were dying inside of her.

"I must commend you on being an excellent partner, Steven." Purposely, she dropped her eyes over his body, surveying him like a potential bedmate. "You were extremely inventive."

He swayed slightly. "You don't mean this," he ground out. "We had an understanding. You knew I was planning on offering for you."

"You were?" Pressing her hand to her mouth, Harriet widened her eyes in feigned shock. "I had no idea you'd gotten so serious. I thought we were simply enjoying the physical pleasures together."

Steven grew so rigid that Harriet wondered his spine didn't snap. "Then you do not wish to marry me?"

Yes, yes, a thousand times, yes! her heart shouted, but Harriet, squelching that inner voice, drew on her last vestiges of strength to laugh gaily. "Oh, goodness, no!" She slanted a seductive look at him out of the corner of her eye. "Though I wouldn't mind if we continued our arrangement. As I said, you are a wonderful instructor in the art of lovemaking."

Disgust transformed his features into a harsh mask as he gazed down at her. "Good day, madam," he said stiffly as he strode from the room like the hounds of Hell were nipping at his heels.

The moment the door shut behind him, she dissolved into tears.

Steven strode from the house, needing to put as much distance as possible between himself and Harriet. She'd been playing games with him all along.

Grabbing the reins off the post, Steven leapt onto his horse, kneeing the animal into a gallop as he tried to outrun his anger. Ignoring the surprised looks he received from the people he galloped past, Steven rode through Hyde Park like the devil himself was after him.

It was only fitting, he thought with a bitter laugh, for he'd been tossed into Hell.

When he'd called upon Harriet, he'd thought he'd lost everything there was to lose . . . only to find out he'd been horribly wrong. Losing Harriet had made losing his fortune seem like child's play. He hadn't realized how much he'd come to depend upon her over the past few days. Whenever his life had gotten overwhelming, he'd sought solace within Harriet's welcoming embrace and renewed his sense of purpose, regained his ability to face the world.

But she'd only used him.

Something about that thought struck at him, ringing over and over in his head with discord. Pulling back on the reins, Steven slowed his horse into a walk as he tried to look at the situation objectively. She'd used him. No. Not Harriet. Try as he might, he couldn't imagine her using anyone, much less deceiving them to that degree. She was the one adored by the elderly and young, he thought, remembering their conversation at the Hammersmith dinner party.

Her kind heart was evident in all of her actions. He knew her . . . and she wasn't the type of woman who would ever use someone. As his pain receded, logic took shape, forming an image of Harriet that didn't coincide with her claims of enjoying lovemaking as an extension of flirtation. She wasn't a woman who gave her affection easily . . . for if she had, she would have long ago found a willing suitor to provide physical companionship.

No, Harriet had more dignity, more self-respect, than the woman she'd claimed to be. Then why had she claimed she'd only wanted an affair? As thoughts swirled around inside his head, Steven grew positive of one thing.

Something wasn't right with this situation.

"Harriet?" Aunt Agatha called through the closed door. "Are you all right in there?"

Praying her aunt wouldn't come in and see her in tears, Harriet struggled to find her voice. "I'm f-f-fine."

"Well, you don't sound fine," Aunt Hilda pronounced as she stepped through the door. At the sight of Harriet's tear-streaked face, she melted. "Oh, my poor, dear girl," she murmured, rushing forward to gather Harriet in her arms. "I'd hoped to spare you this pain."

Tears welled in Aunt Agatha's eyes as she pressed her hands to her cheeks. "He didn't offer for you?"

"No, he did," Harriet said in between sobs.

Aunt Agatha shook her head in confusion. "Then are these tears of happiness?"

"Don't be idiotic," snapped Aunt Hilda. "It's perfectly obvious that the girl is distraught. She told us before Lord Heath arrived that she had no intention of marrying him."

Reaching out, Aunt Agatha rubbed Harriet's shoulder. "The question is why won't she marry him?"

"That is indeed the question."

All three women looked toward the door to find none other than Lord Heath filling the entryway. "I let myself in," he explained, strolling into the room, his eyes focused upon Harriet's tear-stained face. "My darling Harriet gave me a lovely song about how she simply wanted to have an affair. But something about her explanation didn't ring true." He gestured toward her tears. "And this display only proves me right." Propping a booted foot onto a chair, Steven leaned over, resting his elbow upon his knee. "So why don't you tell me the real reason behind your refusal of my offer of marriage?"

Chapter Nineteen

⁓

"I . . . I . . ." Harriet stammered, swiping at her tears as if she could hide the evidence of her distress.

Steven wasn't having any of it. "Why don't I help you start then?" He pinned her with a fierce stare. "How did you find out?"

Though she shook her head, he saw the truth in her gaze. "About what?"

"Come now, Harriet," he chided her, anger simmering inside of him with the remnants of his pain. "We've always been truthful with each other. Don't start being dishonest now."

He could almost smell her panic. "I don't know what you're talking about."

"Really, Lord Heath, this sort of badgering is . . ."

Steven held up his hands, halting Lady Hilda's protest. "Absolutely necessary," he finished for her. "Your niece purposely misled me when I asked for her hand, and I believe it is my right to inquire as to the real reason for her refusal." He shifted his gaze back onto Harriet. "It is my personal belief that your report contained information about my financial situation."

"As a matter of fact it did," Lady Agatha supplied helpfully. He could see by the gleam in her eyes that he had an ally in her.

"I suspected as much." Standing upright, Steven clasped his hands behind his back. "So, tell me, Harriet, did you decry because of my lack of fortune?"

"No . . . yes . . . Oh, I mean . . ."

Loosing her hold upon Harriet, Lady Hilda shifted backward to stare into her niece's face. "Did you realize he was a fortune hunter and refuse to marry him?"

"No!" Harriet pulled away. "The very idea is preposterous. What would a fortune hunter want with someone who lacks the very thing he seeks?"

Seeing that Harriet's aunt recognized the logic in the question, Steven returned to the matter at hand. "Did you refuse me, Harriet, because you only found me attractive before you realized I was without funds?"

"Of course not!" she exclaimed, shooting to her feet. Agitation colored her cheeks a pretty pink. "I find you overwhelmingly attractive, and I'd like nothing more than to . . ." She clamped her hands over her mouth as if she'd realized she'd said too much.

Pouncing on the words, Steven tried to uncover the truth. "Nothing more than to what?"

Stubbornly, she shook her head.

"Out with it, Harriet," he demanded, stepping forward to grasp her shoulders. "Tell me why you won't marry me."

"Because I love you too much!"

Her declaration brought gasps from both her aunts, one in delight, the other in distress, but Steven ignored them both. All he could do was repeat her words in his head, hanging onto them like a mantra of hope. "You love me too much to marry me?"

Twisting out of his arms, Harriet paced in front of him. "I was at the Van Cleef's this morning, waiting for Laurel in the library, and I overheard your conversation with Royce."

"Harriet," he began softly, "I promise you everything will work out."

"It certainly will . . . if you don't marry me."

He shook his head, unable to follow her logic. "What are you talking about?"

Finally, she stopped her infernal pacing and turned to face him. "If you don't marry me, you'll be free to wed Lady Camilla or some other heiress who can save your estates and your family honor." As he opened his mouth to protest, she pressed two fingers upon his lips. "I know you believe that because we were intimate you must marry me, but I release you from your bond." Unshed tears shimmered in the depths of her eyes. "I refuse to be another burden for you to carry."

Grasping her hand, he pressed a kiss upon the palm. "You're not a burden, Harriet. I lo . . ."

"Don't!" Her sharp exclamation stopped his avowal of love. "Please don't," she murmured, tugging her hand free of his clasp. "I know you'll do anything to convince me of your desire to marry me, but we both know the only reason you're saying those words is because you believe I need to hear them." A bittersweet smile twisted her lips. "And you're quite right, Steven. I do need to hear them . . . but not as a way to convince me it will be best if I marry you."

"Harriet," he began, flicking a quick glance at her aunts and wishing them out of the room. From their fascinated gazes, he knew that wish wasn't going to come true. "We must wed. Yesterday . . . "

". . . gave me a beautiful memory that I shall cherish forever." Reaching out, she trailed her fingertips over his cheek in a soft caress. "But I can't become a burden to you, Steven." Her hand dropped to her side as she drew back her shoulders. "I won't become a burden. So, I thank you for your proposal of marriage and regretfully decline."

Before he could say another word, she spun on her heel and raced from the room, leaving him alone with her aunts. Astounded at this turn of events, he looked to them for help. "What shall I do now?"

"Go after her!" Lady Agatha urged him.

But Lady Hilda shook her head. "She won't listen even if he did go after her," she pointed out firmly. "You heard her, Aggie. She meant every word she said, and when she makes up her mind it takes a minor miracle to change it." She lanced him with her stare. "Is what Harriet said true? Are you completely without means?"

Though embarrassment shifted through him, Steven stood firm. "At the moment, yes," he admitted.

Lady Hilda's gaze sharpened. "Did your mother incur much of this debt, perchance?"

Anger flooded him at the impertinent question. "The particulars are unimportant; the only thing that matters is that I have debt which needs to be covered, and it will very likely require liquidation of all my assets."

"You poor dear," Lady Agatha murmured in sympathy. "How noble of you."

Lady Hilda shot another question at him. "And what of Harriet's suggestion that you turn your attentions to Lady Camilla? Her monies would ease your situation and from all appearances, you would not be averse to the match."

Of all the luck that this sharp-eyed harpy saw him in the garden with Lady Camilla! The only bit of good fortune he'd had lately was finding Harriet. Taking a deep breath, Steven offered her an explanation. "While I find myself unable to fully explain the situation in the garden because of my honor as a gentleman, I can assure you, my lady, that the embrace you witnessed was not of my making, and I ended it a moment after it had begun." He fixed his own fierce gaze upon her. "And the idea of marrying anyone but Harriet is completely out of the question. You saw the reports," he reminded her. "It is my honor and duty to wed your niece."

"What of pleasure?" Lady Hilda retorted. "Is my niece to be your burden then as she worries?"

"Absolutely not!" His control slipped as he shouted, "Harriet will never be a burden to me. I need her, damn it!"

A gleam of satisfaction shimmered in Lady Hilda's eyes as she relaxed back onto her chair. "She claims to love you."

The knowledge calmed him. "I know," he murmured, smiling at the thought.

"But what are we going to do about it, Hilda?" asked Lady Agatha, moving around the settee to stand beside Steven. "You said yourself that Harriet wouldn't change her mind."

"Then we'll leave her no option." Lady Hilda's grin made him feel a twinge of pity for Harriet. "When we left her to her own devices, she made a muddle of things. Now it's time for us to step in and fix it."

Warily, he gazed at Lady Hilda. "Why would you want to do that? You've never approved of my relationship with Harriet."

"That's true," Lady Hilda agreed. "But knowing that Harriet loves you and that you return her affection makes me realize I might have been wrong about you."

"Might have been?" Lady Agatha asked pointedly.

Lady Hilda scowled. "Accept my wavering gracefully, Aggie."

Ignoring their exchange, Steven gazed at Lady Hilda as he returned to their conversation. "How do you propose we fix this situation?"

"We simply announce the engagement."

"Oh, Hildy," whispered Lady Agatha, her eyes wide. "Do you really think we should do that?"

"Absolutely. If we wait for Harriet to change her mind, I could be six feet under." Lady Hilda waggled a finger at her sister. "And, to my way of thinking, time is of the essence." She lifted her brow. "Have either one of you considered the possibility that Harriet might be enceinte?"

The idea struck him in the gut, causing Steven to sway on his feet. Harriet. Expecting. His baby. The words strung together filled him with delight . . . and horror at the same time. Lord, he might be bringing a son into this world, but instead of leaving him a thriving estate, he'd gift him with a mountain of debt.

Never! Strengthening his resolve to overcome his misfortune, Steven gritted his teeth and promised himself that he would do whatever it took to regain his family honor and fortune.

But first, he needed to claim Harriet for his own.

"Shall I make the announcement at the Hammersmith ball this evening?"

Tapping her fingers upon the arm of her chair, Aunt Hilda smiled at him. "I do believe I'm starting to like you after all, Lord Heath."

"God help me," he muttered before he could call back the words.

"I found the entire situation most distressing," Agatha admitted to her dear friend, Penelope Hammersmith. "It was perfectly clear that Harriet wishes to marry Lord Heath, but she decried. As I explained to you, that matter of his financial circumstances keeps her from her heart's desire." Snapping open her fan, Agatha fanned herself in agitation. "Now Hilda's devised this forced engagement and, to be perfectly honest, I'm uncertain of how Harriet will react to the announcement."

"At least it will ensure my party is a grand success," Lady Hammersmith said with a broad smile.

Agatha tapped her fan against her friend's arm. "My niece's welfare is at stake here, and all you're concerned about is your party? Really, Penelope."

"I was simply jesting," she replied as she reached out to pat Agatha's hand. "Don't fret, Agatha. I'm positive everything will work out for the best."

"I do hope you're right." At that moment, Agatha caught a glimpse of Steven as he made his way toward the orchestra. "Please excuse me, Penelope. I wish to be near Lord Heath when he makes his announcement."

As Penelope watched her friend hurry off, she sighed deeply, wishing there was something she could do to help. Unfortunately, her own financial situation, though comfortable, didn't allow for any excess expenditures.

"Why the gloomy expression, my lovely?"

Turning toward her husband, Penelope melted with love for him. Nearly twenty years later, and she still felt that way. What amazed her even more was that the dear man seemed to reciprocate her feelings, despite her greatly increased size. Either the man was blind or desperately in love, she decided, but she was far too happy to spend time questioning her good fortune.

If only there was a way to ensure Harriet the same happiness she'd found in marriage.

"I was merely upset by something Agatha told me." Launching into the full explanation of Lord Heath's financial circumstances, she finished by saying, "I only wish we could help out in some manner."

Lord Hammersmith shrugged lightly. "Perhaps I could sell off a few of my collections and give the profits to Harriet as a wedding present."

"You would do that?" Penelope asked, astounded by her husband's generosity. "I know how much those collections mean to you."

His plain features glowed as he smiled down at her. "True, but seeing a smile upon your face means far more."

Giggling like a schoolgirl, Penelope leaned over to whisper in her husband's ear. "I'll show my appreciation . . . later," she said, making certain he understood her sensual intent.

The way his eyes lit up she'd have thought she was one of the young, nubile beauties filling her ballroom. "I'll hold you to that, my love."

Laughing with pure joy, Penelope thanked God for striking her husband blind.

"Congratulations!"

Harriet's hands froze on her hair as she looked toward Lady Hampton in confusion. "Pardon me?"

"I was just offering you my best wishes," Lady Hampton said as she moved in front of a mirror and began patting her face with powder. "On your upcoming nuptials."

Dizzy, Harriet sank down into the chair, thoughts of securing her hair ribbons forgotten. "My nuptials?"

"Yes," Lady Hampton replied with a happy smile. "It's a shame you needed to refresh yourself just when Lord Heath made the announcement, but your aunts explained that you were too overcome with joy to be there at that moment." She sighed dramatically. "You would have loved seeing how proud your Lord Heath looked with your aunts standing beside him, one on each side."

An odd mix of emotions swirled inside of Harriet as she struggled to contain her outburst. How dare they make an announcement after she'd made herself perfectly clear that afternoon? She fumed silently. She'd tried to remain at home this evening, but her aunts had insisted she attend the ball. No wonder they wanted her present; they'd planned all along to announce her engagement . . . without her consent.

It was time she taught her hound that this fox had teeth.

The congratulatory calls that followed her as she made

her way toward Steven only fueled her fury. As soon as he caught sight of her, Steven grinned wickedly, his eyes sparkling with undisguised anticipation as if he knew she'd be furious and welcomed the challenge of overcoming her protests. Nothing he could say would change her mind!

Coming to a stop before him, she opened her mouth to announce she had no intention of marrying him, but the only sound that came out was a squeak of surprise. Grasping her shoulders, Steven bent his head and claimed her open mouth in a kiss. Not a sweet, innocent kiss, but a raw, hungry, bend-her-over-his-arm kind of kiss that was met with a cacophony of gasps, some in approval, others in shocked displeasure. None of which seemed to affect Steven for he continued to kiss her until her desire for him overrode her anger and she lifted her arms, holding him close.

As she sagged weakly against him, Steven lifted his head, his eyes glittering with success. "Consider our engagement officially announced."

Harriet didn't know if she should yell at him for his presumptuous attitude or pull him down for another kiss. Tucking her under his arm, Steven turned toward their audience, offering them a jaunty smile. "I apologize for this shameless display of affection, but it seems I've allowed my emotions to carry me away."

Mind-numbing kiss or no kiss, she wasn't about to let him get away with this stunt. "There is no . . ."

" . . . reason to explain further," Steven interrupted, cupping her cheek and pressing a thumb against her lips.

To everyone else, Harriet was quite certain the gesture looked romantic, but she understood the purpose behind his caress was to quiet her. She tried to tug away from him, but his seemingly casual hold was deceptively tight, locking her into place against him.

"If everyone will please excuse us, I shall escort my fiancée and her aunts home. The excitement of the evening has been overwhelming," he added, making her sound like even more of a mindless twit.

Twisting her head, she tried to contradict Steven's announcement, but this time her protests were cut short by her aunts.

"Come along, dear," Aunt Agatha said, tucking her elbow beneath Harriet's. "It's been an exhilarating evening and I vow I'm quite exhausted."

Harriet dug in her heels. "Aunt Agatha . . ."

"Wait until we're in the carriage. Please, Harriet."

Her aunt's plea reached Harriet's heart, and she fell silent, allowing herself to be led out to their carriage. The moment she sat in the darkened conveyance across from her aunts and beside Steven, she finally spoke again. "Why can't any of you understand that I'm doing what is best for all of us?"

"And what if you're carrying my child?" Steven asked quietly. "Is refusing to marry his father the best thing for him?"

Instinctively, her hands cupped her abdomen as she wondered if she might indeed be expecting a baby. Uncertain if she would be happy or alarmed at the prospect, Harriet struggled to remain calm. "Very well then. Until we know if I'm with child or not, we will forgo any discussions about our future and this engagement nonsense."

"Absolutely not," Steven said emphatically.

Lifting her hands, Aunt Agatha drew all eyes upon her. "I believe I have the perfect compromise. Why don't we allow the engagement to stand until we know for certain if Harriet is enceinte?"

"But, Aunt Agatha, I've already told you why I can't marry Steven," Harriet protested.

The carriage rocked beneath them as Aunt Hilda reached over to tap Harriet's knee. "If you are expecting, it changes everything, and for your child's sake, you will not have a choice as to whether or not you should marry Lord Heath."

"That's true," Aunt Agatha chimed in. "Which is precisely why the engagement must stay in place. If we discover you're enceinte and then announce an engagement, all of society will be able to do the math after that poor, innocent babe is born."

"But if you're already engaged, the early birthday might raise a few eyebrows, but no one will be aghast." Aunt Hilda gave Steven a pointed stare. "After that display this evening, I'd wager all of the ton expect you to enjoy the benefits of the marriage bed during your engagement."

There was no denying the logic of her aunt's argument. If she were expecting Steven's child, she would do whatever it took to protect the baby . . . including becoming a burden to the man she loved.

When Steven picked up her hand and cradled it between both of his, she accepted the touch without complaint. "Would it truly be so horrible to marry me?"

Blinking back tears, she looked at him, feeling a rush of love for this wonderful man. "Marrying me would be one of the worst things you could do," she murmured, pulling her hand free. "I'll agree to let the engagement stand on one condition. If we discover I'm not carrying your child, you agree to end the engagement without argument."

"Done."

The swiftness of his answer stunned her.

As if he could read her mind, Steven grinned at her. "We rogues are gambling men."

Chapter Twenty

"This material would look particularly lovely on you, Harriet," gushed her aunt Agatha as she fingered the rose muslin. "Don't you agree?"

Harriet knew she was probably staring at her aunt like she'd grown two heads, but she couldn't seem to restrain herself. How could her aunt Agatha think for one moment that she had any interest in shopping? The only reason she was here at all was to escape the sharp gaze of her aunt Hilda. Between the two of them, Harriet was quite certain she'd go mad before the fortnight had elapsed.

"It's lovely," Harriet murmured finally. "Would you excuse me a moment, Aunt Agatha? I'd like to look at the ribbons in the front room."

Caught up in perusing the pattern templates, Aunt Agatha waved her hand. "That's fine. Why don't you see if they have some silk ribbons that would go well with this rose?"

Eager to escape her aunt's presence for a few minutes,

Harriet hurried from the room, breathing a sigh of relief. For the past few days, she hadn't been able to step outside her bedchamber without one of her aunt's accompanying her. Worse still, all they seemed to want to do was point out how advantageous it would be to marry Steven. Harriet rubbed at her temple. Didn't they realize she wished she could marry him? But how could she grab her own happiness when she knew it would bring about his ruination? If she married the man she loved, she would destroy him.

Why couldn't her aunts understand that?

When the bell over the door of the dressmaker's shop rang, Harriet automatically glanced over at the entrance . . . and did a double take when she saw Lady Camilla and her maid enter. Of all the luck. Trying to duck behind a rack of cloth, Harriet prayed Camilla hadn't spotted her.

"Harriet!"

Groaning softly, Harriet straightened and turned to face Lady Camilla. Though she'd never been particularly fond of the blonde beauty, Harriet liked her even less now that she knew about the kiss Lady Camilla had given Steven. "Lady Camilla," she said with as much graciousness as she could manage. "What a surprise it is to run into you here." As nice a surprise as being run down by a carriage, Harriet added silently.

"I'm so glad you're here," Lady Camilla exclaimed.

Why? was all Harriet could think. Instead, she tried to be more polite. "Really?" Harriet winced at her question.

Luckily, Lady Camilla didn't seem to notice. "Indeed." Reaching out her hand, she clasped Harriet's fingers, ribbon and all. "I wanted to congratulate you on your engagement, you sly thing, you."

"Er . . . thank you?" Harriet finally said, hoping it was the correct response.

But for all the attention Lady Camilla paid her replies, Harriet wondered if Lady Camilla would even bat an eye if she said something utterly outrageous.

Before Harriet could test her new theory, Lady Camilla leaned in closer. "I must confess, Harriet, that when I first met Lord Heath I thought him a bore like all the other gentlemen, but the more I saw of him, the more I realized he's somewhat naughty, isn't he?"

An image of Steven tied to the chair, his eyes darkened with passion, his body hard and willing, rose unbidden into Harriet's head. Slowly, she nodded. "He's naughty all right."

A shiver shook Lady Camilla. "Oh, I do so envy you, Harriet. You've caught an exciting one."

Harriet stared at Lady Camilla, knowing she was the solution to all of Steven's problems. If she wasn't expecting Steven's child, their engagement would be over, leaving Steven free to pursue an heiress. If the avid gleam in Lady Camilla's eyes was any indication, Harriet knew Steven would find it easy to convince Lady Camilla to become his bride.

The thought of that pierced Harriet's heart, but she couldn't afford to waver. If she were selfish, she would destroy Steven.

Ignoring the pain inside, Harriet casually dropped the ribbon back onto the pile and began to shift through the twisting strands. "I noticed the very same thing myself," Harriet said in a conversational tone, "though I must admit that I don't find it appealing in the least." Leaning into Lady Camilla, she whispered, "Did you see him kiss me at the Hammersmith affair?" At Lady Camilla's nod, Harriet glanced around as if to ensure their privacy. "Well, he wants to kiss me like that all the time . . . and I won't even tell you where he wants to put his hands!" Seeing the jealous glitter in Lady Camilla's gaze, Harriet knew she'd hit upon the perfect plan. "I must admit that I find it most scandalous." She pressed the back of her hand against her forehead as if she were in danger of giving into vapors. "I truly don't know if I can wed Lord Heath. He's so overwhelming, so physical, so . . . much." Lowering her head, Harriet sighed dramatically. "I fear he's too much."

The shiver that ran through Lady Camilla disgusted Harriet. What was wrong with the woman that she couldn't appreciate the kindness inside of Steven, his charm, his love of his family, or any of the other admirable traits that made him a wonderful man? It seemed that all Lady Camilla found appealing was the idea that Steven was sensually dangerous.

Reaching out, Lady Camilla patted Harriet's arm. "I do hope everything works out for you," she said in a sweet voice.

"As do I." A thought struck Harriet, causing her to lean closer in earnest. "You won't say anything to anyone, will you?"

Lady Camilla twisted her fingers in front of her mouth, mimicking a locking motion. "Not a peep."

As Harriet watched Lady Camilla walk away, she blinked the tears from her eyes.

Trying to save his home and court a reluctant fiancée all at the same time was quite taxing on a man, Steven decided, as he rubbed at his eyes. For the past two days he'd been so busy with the first item that he'd fairly neglected the second.

Steven thrust aside exhaustion and concentrated on the work in front of him. He'd been making notes on the list of his assets his solicitor had provided him, deciding which items would be sold off first and which ones he hoped to retain.

A knock on the door interrupted his depressing thoughts. When his mother poked her head around, he rose from his desk to bid her welcome.

"If I'm intruding, I can come back later," she offered with a nervous smile.

The tone told him she didn't have good news. "What's the problem, mother?"

When she began to wring her hands, he grew more positive that he wouldn't like what she had to say. "I've been meaning to speak with you for a while, but with your engagement . . . which still thrills me . . . well, I didn't want to dampen your spirits with the bad news."

"What's happened?" he asked bluntly.

"You'll be getting a bill soon for a full set of china."

Damn, double damn, Steven thought. "A full set?" he asked, not even wanting to hazard a guess at how much that would cost. "What happened, Mother?"

"Another accident." Grabbing hold of his arm, she turned regret-filled eyes upon him. "I was at Lady Hampton's the other day when I knocked over an entire tray filled with her china. Naturally, I had to offer to pay for it."

"Naturally," he repeated, his voice sounding hollow.

"It was horribly embarrassing," she admitted softly. "I

don't know what happened. One minute I was entering the salon and the next I fell forward, knocking over the tray."

The explanation sounded . . . off. "Was anyone behind you?"

"Yes," she replied with a nod. "I was followed by . . ."

"Longley, Connor, and Windvale," he finished for her as suspicion grew in his mind. "What do you know of Longley, Mother?"

"Not much other than he's been most charming to me." A slight frown marred her face. "Recently, however, he's been less than cordial at times."

"In what manner?"

Her hands fluttered on her lap. "I'm probably making too much of it, but the last time I turned down his proposal, he got most upset and even knocked over an end table at Lady Hampton's home."

"I don't think you're making enough of it," Steven countered. "I want you to stay away from him, Mother. It's past time I paid a visit to our Mr. Longley." He tapped his fingers against his leg. "I'm beginning to wonder if all these accidents that have happened to you have truly been by chance."

His mother's eyes widened. "Do you believe Edward had something to do with my bad luck of late?"

"I don't know," Steven said, walking over to his desk. "But it should be considered."

"Why would he want to cause me such harm?"

Steven shook his head. "I believe that's another question for Longley."

Rising to her feet, his mother came to a halt on the opposite side of the desk. "While I know you'd like to find someone other than me to blame for our misfortune, I fear you shall be unable to do so, Steven." She pointed to the open ledgers. "Our situation is quite hopeless, isn't it?"

Steven glanced down at the red-lined books. "There has to be a way out of this, some way that I'm just not seeing right now," he murmured.

"There is." Drawing back her shoulders, his mother met his gaze squarely. "I shall accept Robert Connor's proposal of marriage."

"What?" he exclaimed, unable to believe he'd heard her correctly. "But you don't love him."

"Of course not, Steven," she said immediately. "Then again, how many marriages happen for love? Even your father and I weren't in love with each other when we wed, but it wasn't long before we couldn't live without one another." All the animation drained from her features. "What I should have said was that we couldn't live happily without one another."

Steven shook his head firmly. "You will not marry this man, Mother. You can't even speak of Father without growing sad."

"I'll always love your father," she said softly. "Even if I do marry Robert, that won't change. However, I know Robert is quite wealthy, and if I marry him, it will solve all of our troubles." A smile turned up the corners of her mouth. "Please understand, Steven, marrying Robert won't make me unhappy."

"But you don't wish to marry him." As his mother opened her mouth to protest, Steven raised his hands. "I don't wish to argue about this. I'm not having you marry to save the family . . . and that's final."

Apparently, his mother decided to listen to reason. Leaning against his desk, she picked at her skirt. "I'd rather live in a small cottage, tucked away in the woods somewhere, than marry anyone else," she admitted.

"Then you shall have it." Twisting the ledger, Steven studied the holdings listed in the first column. "We'll sell off the country estate, then the town house, our stable of horses, our . . ."

"Do you remember when your father built the stables?" His mother's face softened with memories. "He wanted to become a breeder of champion Thoroughbreds." Laughing, she shrugged lightly. "What amused me most of all was that your father didn't even ride very well, yet he thought he could pick out prime horseflesh. He always said he rode like a farmer, plodding along with an appalling lack of grace, but he was so proud of you, Steven. He used to say you had an excellent seat and could . . ."

"That's it!" Steven couldn't believe he hadn't thought of it before; the answer had been in front of him all along. "That's our way out of this mess."

Obviously confused, his mother shook her head. "I don't understand, Steven."

Yanking open a drawer, he began to rifle through the papers. "I received a note from the manager of Father's stables up in Northumberland saying he had a few horses he thought were champions."

"Really?"

For the first time since this disaster had begun, Steven wondered if he'd finally figured a way out that wouldn't require he give up all he held dear. "Here it is," he pronounced, retrieving the note from his stable manager. "Mr. Bingham says that he has four horses he considers prime runners. Apparently, these four have won all the local races he's entered and many of the local breeders have offered for them."

"Their sale will bring in enough to offset all of our debts?"

"No," Steven replied, hope and excitement mingling inside of him, "but if we race them here in town and they place first in a number of races, we might make enough on the winnings to repay our debt."

Laughing with joy, his mother rushed over to hug him. "And to think I used to tease your father over his ridiculous dream of becoming a premier horse breeder."

Steven hugged her tightly. "Father's dream might very well prove our salvation."

Chapter Twenty-One

The sun washed over Harriet as she lay upon the chaise. Having promised her aunts she wouldn't sneak out to see Steven, she'd been allowed to sit in the garden for a while, enjoying a moment of privacy. The sleepless nights had caught up with her, and the warm sunlight was making her sleepy.

Closing her eyes, she grew drowsy, slipping easily into a dream-filled rest. Steven came to her as he always did, his hand cupping her cheek, his lips pressing so sweetly against her own. Here in her fantasy, she claimed him, lifting her arms to deepen the kiss. Hunger devoured the sweetness as passion flared between them.

When the tips of his fingers began to trace the edge of her bodice, Harriet sighed in welcome, arching against his hold. Now he'd tug down the constricting material, free her to his touch, before sweeping his hand lower and . . .

"Wake up, Harriet."

Scowling, she resisted the call, not wishing to give up this vivid dream.

"Come on, love, open your eyes."

As Steven's voice penetrated her dream, Harriet allowed her lids to open slowly. "Steven," she whispered breathlessly.

"That's right," he murmured, kneeling beside her chair. "I needed to speak with you."

The realization that she wasn't dreaming anymore struck Harriet. Snapping her head backward, she broke away from his hand that cupped her cheek and adjusted her bodice. "Steven," she repeated briskly. "I thought you were a dream."

"I've always wanted to be someone's dream," he said with a smile.

Harriet struggled to regain her composure. "Why are you here, Steven?"

"Is it so unusual for a gentleman to spend time with his affianced?"

"When the engagement is a farce, it most certainly is," Harriet retorted.

His smile faded. "It's only a farce in your mind, Harriet."

At his comment, she slid even more deeply in love with him. Honor-bound to marry her, Steven had obviously decided to convince her he was in love with her. The gesture was so sweet, so . . . Steven, she couldn't help but melt. "You truly are a good man, Steven."

"Does that mean that you'll give up this foolishness and agree to marry me?"

"No," she countered. "It means that I appreciate your finer qualities."

Anger glimmered in his eyes. "I understand now. You like me, you desire me, but you don't want to marry me because of my financial situation." When she opened her mouth to protest, he laid two fingers upon her lips. "It's true. You've even said it yourself that you don't want to be another burden for me to carry." Leaning forward, he boxed her into the chair. "What you fail to understand, Harriet, is that I can make my own decisions about what burdens I wish to take on and those I want to avoid." He nudged her legs aside with his hip, taking a seat on the edge of her chair. "And for some reason I've yet to comprehend, I want to take you on, Miss Nash."

Pulling her close in an embrace, Steven held her tightly against him, the lashing of his tongue driving her further and further toward uncontrollable desire. There was no softness in his touch, no finesse to his caresses, only hunger and burning need. It spoke to her very core, calling upon the most elemental of her emotions, making her crave for more.

With a swiftness that made her gasp, Steven reached under her skirts, sliding his hand upward, until his fingers stroked against her moist womanhood. Swallowing her moan, Steven caressed the swollen nub until she arched against him, aching for him to finish what he'd started.

He broke off their kiss to stare down at her, his eyes ablaze with an odd mixture of raw desire and unabated anger. "Do you see what I do to you, Harriet? In an instant, I can make you burn for me, make you need me so badly you don't care that you're in the middle of your garden and anyone can walk along at any moment. All you want is for me to satisfy you like you know no one else can."

The next instant, he plunged two fingers into her, stretching her softness with delicious strokes, driving her over the edge. The incredible sensations he brought to life within her swept over her, making her arch backward and cry out in completion.

As her body shook with sensual tremors, Steven slowly withdrew his hand and straightened her skirts. "You're mine, Harriet," he said finally.

"I've never tried to deny that." She felt like weeping. "The only reason I won't marry you is because you'll be giving up everything if you take me as your wife."

The anger surged back into his expression. "You need to trust me, Harriet. I can provide for us, I promise you. In fact, I've come by here today to tell you that I'm heading off for my estate in Northumberland." Excitement lightened his voice. "I own Thoroughbreds that I could race here in town and, if they win, it could replenish my coffers."

"You plan to save your estate with gambling?" The moment the question was spoken, Harriet knew she'd made a mistake.

"Have you so little faith in me?" Rising to his feet, Steven stood before her, stiff and unyielding. "I've asked for your trust, Harriet, and you give me your scorn."

The quiet dignity in his softly spoken reprimand touched her deeply. "I'm sorry, Steven."

Inclining his head, he accepted her apology. "While I am gone, I'd very much appreciate if you could learn to believe in me. When you become my wife, I promise to provide and care for you." He drew back his shoulders. "You will never regret marrying me."

How could she ever regret her heart's greatest desire?

"Please, Harriet," he ground out. "I'm asking you to believe me, in my ability to overcome my current financial difficulties."

Thinking upon all of the humiliation Steven had been forced to stomach since his financial problems had started, Harriet needed to give in to his request. "I do have faith in you," she finally said softly, praying that he would indeed find a way to recover his fortune.

A huge breath rushed from his chest as a side of his mouth quirked upward. "You won't regret it," he promised, before bending down to kiss her mouth. "I'll be back in a few days."

As Steven walked from her garden, he took the sun with him, leaving her feeling cold and so very alone.

"Where's that girl of mine?"

At the sound of her father's booming voice, Harriet tossed down her book and ran to greet him. Wearing a smile, she returned his exuberant hug. "Papa!" she exclaimed, pressing a kiss upon his cheek. "What a surprise it is to see you!"

"When I received the note from Hilda and Agatha, I came back to town right away."

Apprehension caused Harriet to stiffen, drawing away from her father. Had her aunts sent a copy of the Bow

Street Runner's report to her father? "Note?" she asked nervously. "Why did they write to you?"

"My little girl gets engaged, and you don't expect they'll tell me about it?"

Her father's blustering made her smile. "Ohhh, that's all," she said in relief.

"Well, they did mention the other matter as well," her father admitted.

Her nerves couldn't take this! "What other matter?"

Clearing his throat, her father glanced away. "About Lord Heath's financial troubles."

"Yes, well . . ." She trailed off, unsure of what to say. How would her father react if he knew Steven might be riding north to collect some horses for racing and pinning all his hopes on them to rebuild his fortune? Somehow, she didn't think her solid, practical-minded father would think highly of the plan.

"Not to worry, Harriet." Father patted his pocket. "I'm here to help."

Hope warred with confusion inside of her. "Help, Papa?" she asked, knowing her parents had no extra funds. "How?"

"Because I took your young man's advice and approached a publisher about my book." A proud grin split her father's face. "He paid me handsomely for it too." Withdrawing the note of credit from the publisher, her father handed it over to her. "I don't know if it will be enough to cover the amount Lord Heath owes, but it should at least settle some of his accounts."

Tears filled her eyes as Harriet clutched the paper to

her chest. "Oh, Papa," she whispered. "I can't take this. You and Mama . . ."

"Are perfectly happy and content just as we are." He snorted loudly. "What would we do with money like that? No, Harriet," he said, patting her on the shoulder. "Your mother and I have all we need except one thing—seeing our only child settled and happy." He pointed toward the note. "If my book can help you achieve that, it would fulfill our greatest wish."

Holding the note to her chest, Harriet wondered if it would fulfill her greatest wish as well. "Thank you, Papa," she said, gratitude thickening her voice. "You don't know how much this means to me."

"I can hazard a guess. Now why don't you go find that young man of yours and tell him the good news?"

Hoping to reach Steven before he left, Harriet paused only to kiss her father on the cheek, before tucking the missive into her pocket. Calling for her maid, Harriet rushed off with a smile on her face.

"Guess you're still useful after all, old man," Lionel murmured to himself as he headed off in search of a good meal.

"Thank you so much for seeing me, Lady Heath," Harriet began awkwardly.

"Please call me Caroline." Steven's mother patted Harriet's hand. "We are going to be family, after all."

"Yes." With a bit of luck, Harriet added silently. She wanted more than anything to be part of Steven's family and the slip in her pocket might be her key to entrance. Still, Harriet hesitated, uncertain as to how much Steven's mother knew of his financial situation. "I'm sorry to bother you, my lady. I was hoping to catch Steven before he headed to Northumberland."

"You just missed him," his mother said as she poured a cup of tea. "He's off to look over his stables."

Caroline's remark surprised Harriet. "You know the reason behind his trip?"

"Indeed I do," she replied, her eyes darkening. "We spoke of the matter before he left." She set the teapot down heavily. "I feel so dreadful that he's been forced to this point."

Suspecting his mother knew all the details, Harriet cautiously picked her way through the conversation. "It was his decision."

"Not really," Caroline murmured, her eyes filling. "My carelessness forced him to pursue this option."

"The reason I called upon him was because I can help." Pulling the note of credit from her pocket, she handed it to Steven's mother. "My father gave this to me today in order to help pay off Steven's debts."

The hope that had illuminated his mother's eyes dimmed as she looked at the note. "I'm afraid it's not enough."

Disappointment threatened to overwhelm Harriet, but she wouldn't allow herself to become discouraged. "Perhaps not, but it's a goodly sum and should help decrease a portion of his debts."

"It will help," Caroline agreed.

Poor Steven, Harriet thought, understanding for perhaps the first time why he'd turned to her in the cottage, wanting to forget. The burden he'd been carrying was unbelievable. "Then it's a start," she announced, determined to find a way to overcome this obstacle. Her father had inspired her. "Do you know how much is owed?"

Caroline nodded eagerly. "Steven showed me the ledgers."

"Excellent." Accepting her cup of tea, Harriet looked at what she hoped was her future mother-in-law. "Are you willing to help me solve this problem?"

"I thought Steven's plan was to race his horses."

"It is," Harriet agreed, "but you must admit that trying to recoup one's fortune from something as mercurial as gaming is a difficult undertaking." She took a sip of tea. "I would like to help him in a more dependable fashion in case his gamble doesn't pay off." Especially since her future depended upon the outcome. She'd been a martyr for long enough. "I think I know of a way to solve this mess."

Caroline laced her fingers together. "Can I help?"

"Yes," Harriet replied without hesitation. Achieving a miracle took a lot of work. "First off, we need to make a list of people who would lend us money."

Caroline's brow drew downward. "I don't know if we should approach anyone about this," she said, caution coloring her voice. "I believe Steven wishes to keep it a private matter."

"That's true, but what I'm proposing isn't any different than when he tried to borrow funds from the Earl of Tewksbury." Using logic, Harriet appealed to Steven's mother. Without her help, Harriet knew she'd have little hope of success. "Surely you have a few close friends who might be willing to discreetly lend you some money." She warmed to her plan. "But the beauty of my solution is that no one knows how large an amount you owe."

"Won't the risk of gossip be higher?"

Harriet smiled at Steven's mother. "Not if you choose your friends wisely."

For a long time, Caroline fell silent as if she were considering the matter from all angles, before finally nodding firmly. "I'll write my notes this afternoon and have them delivered immediately."

"I'll do the same," Harriet replied. Praying this plan would work, she smiled at Steven's mother. "I think we're going to need another pot of tea."

"That stallion there is Windstar," Mr. Bingham said, pointing to an Arabian galloping around the pen. With a glorious white mane and the regal arch of his neck, the horse looked like a champion. "He's the fastest horse I've ever seen." Tugging on the bill of his cap, Mr. Bingham grinned cheekily. "A horse that fine, you'll make a bundle off stud fees after he's proven his worth on the track a few times."

"From your lips to God's ears, Mr. Bingham." Turning to his left, Steven gazed out at the pasture where a bunch of colts frolicked. "What of Windstar's offspring? Do they possess his speed?"

"That and then some." Patting his jacket pockets, Mr. Bingham muttered, "Where are my glasses?" Finally, he pulled a pair of spectacles and a folded piece of paper from the right pocket. "Here's a list I made of Windstar's racing times in the quarter-mile track and these three horses listed here," he said, pointing lower on the paper, "are his colts. As you can see, his blood runs true."

More pleased than he could say, Steven refolded the paper. "Do you mind if I keep this?"

"Not at all," Mr. Bingham replied. "Would you like me to put Windstar through his paces for you?"

Gazing around the prosperous farm, Steven grew confident that his coffers would soon be overflowing. "Nothing would please me more."

Chapter Twenty-Two

"When your aunt Agatha told me, in complete confidence, mind you, I simply had to help." Lady Hammersmith folded her bejeweled fingers over her stomach. "My dear husband sold a few of his moldy collections which, it turns out, earned more pounds than we'd hoped."

As she stared down at the pile of money in the box, Harriet shook her head, suddenly feeling self-conscious about taking money from friends. In all her planning, she'd failed to consider how it would feel to accept charity. "Lady Hammersmith, I don't know how to thank . . ."

"No thanks necessary," Lady Hammersmith said firmly. "Consider it a wedding present if you must, but you will accept it." She smiled fondly at Harriet. "Why, you're almost like my very own niece."

"I share the sentiment, my lady."

Lady Hammersmith nodded. "Then it's settled. Will

that be enough, or shall I have Lord Hammersmith sell another of his collections?"

"You can tell your husband that his collections are safe," announced Harriet's mother as she sailed into the room, waving a bag. "I have the rest we need right here."

"Mama!" Harriet jumped to her feet to give her mother a hug. "What are you doing here?"

"Do you think I'd allow your father to be the only one to charge forth and save you?" she asked, the indignant tone in her voice ruined by the sparkle in her eyes.

"It's so wonderful to see . . ."

"Yes, yes, yes, there'll be time for that later," Lady Hammersmith said, cutting Harriet off midsentence. "Have a seat, Sally, and tell me what you meant by you have the rest of it." She eyed the bag her mother carried. "Is that the jingle of coin I hear?"

Laughing, Harriet's mother gave the bag a good shake. The clanking of coins filled the room. "Indeed it is." Turning toward Harriet, her mother smiled brilliantly. "I've been saving a portion of the household funds your father gives to me for quite a while now. I'd wanted to have a second fireplace built into our kitchen, but I want to help you even more," she explained as she upended the bag, sending coins and pound notes scattering all over the table.

Her mother's love humbled Harriet. "I don't know what to say."

"You don't have to say anything, love. Don't you understand? You're my daughter." Her mother stroked a gentle hand down Harriet's hair. "I'd do anything for you."

As a tear slipped onto Harriet's cheek, Lady Hammersmith levered herself out of the chair. "Now look at what you've done, Sally. You've gone and made the girl cry." Picking up the box she'd brought, Lady Hammersmith opened it and began to add Mama's money to the contents. "Why don't we do something useful . . . like see how much we have here? And if it's not enough, we'll figure out who else we can call upon for a donation."

The night air blew into his bedchamber as Steven sat totaling the figures once more. He'd had no idea that charging stud fees could generate so much revenue. When Harriet had questioned the wisdom of trying to rebuild his fortune on the uncertain nature of horse racing, he'd been bothered by that comment more than he wanted to acknowledge.

Yesterday, when Mr. Bingham had given him a demonstration of Windstar's speed after having mentioned the stud fees, a wild idea had taken root in his head. This morning, he'd tested his idea, contacting a few of the neighboring gentry and inviting them over for a look at Windstar. Steven had received over ten offers for the handsome Arabian, but he'd refused them all.

After he'd shown the landowners how Windstar's colts looked, they'd immediately arranged for the horse to provide stud service to their mares. Still in disbelief, Steven studied the figures again, wondering if he'd somehow made a mistake. Three times he'd done the addition and three times, he'd come up with the same answer—this morning alone he'd earned almost half of what he owed.

Tossing aside his loosened cravat, Steven realized how easy it would be to earn the rest of the funds he needed. He'd host a weekend party, invite all of his wealthy friends from town, and show off Windstar. By the end of the weekend, he'd undoubtedly have earned enough money from Windstar's stud fees that he'd be able to pay off all his debts . . . and, perhaps, if he was very, very lucky, have something left over to start the long road toward rebuilding his coffers.

Inhaling deeply, Steven imagined how sweet success would smell after the smell of . . .

. . . fire?

Panic crashed through Steven as he raced to the window. Please, God, not the barn! Yet even as he prayed, one glance out into the dark night told him the far end of the barn, near the tack room, was on fire. Racing out his door, he bellowed for the servants, shouting at them about the fire as they stumbled from their rooms.

When he reached the barn, Steven joined Mr. Bingham and the few stableboys who had just arrived, running into the stable to lead the panicked horses into safety, while another group struggled to put out the swiftly spreading fire. As soon as all the horses were free of the barn, Steven's group joined the fight against the flames until all that remained was smoldering remnants of the tack room.

Breathing heavily, Steven looked at the soot-stained faces around him. "What happened here?"

A shower of soot sprinkled down as Mr. Bingham shook his head. "I don't know, my lord."

"It was the new fellow," chimed a young boy. "I saw him set the fire."

As one, all eyes turned toward one of the groomsman's sons. The lad's father placed a hand on his son's shoulder. "You're making a very serious accusation here, boy," he said solemnly. "Are you certain of what you saw?"

"Yes, Da." There was a ring of truth in the boy's voice. "When you were brushing down the horses for the night, I'd snuck in to watch you work and fell asleep on the hay bale over there. You must've left because it was dark when I woke up." He pointed toward the tack room. "I heard noises coming from over there, and I thought it must be you, Da, puttin' away your tools, but when I looked over, I saw the new fellow, Alain, come out of the tack room." He shuddered, the movement shaking his entire frame. "Next thing I saw was flames shooting out into the stables, which is when I ran and got you and Mr. Bingham."

"You did a good job, lad." Steven looked over at his manager. "Where is this Alain?"

Wearing a mask of soot and a fierce frown, Mr. Bingham led the way toward the adjoining barn where the stableboys slept. As they rounded the corner, a young man began to run toward them. "What happened?" he asked, skidding to a halt beside them. "I was asleep and . . ."

"You were seen earlier in the barn, Alain," Mr. Bingham said grimly.

Even in the darkness, Steven could see the man blanch. "What's that?"

Fury pulsed through Steven at the realization that this sorry excuse for a man could have destroyed his only chance for redemption. Grabbing hold of his jacket lapels, Steven dragged Alain forward, until his face was mere inches away. "Why did you try to burn down my barn?"

"I—I—I—"

He gave the man a shake. "You could have killed all the horses, do you realize that?"

"I wouldn't have hurt the horses," Alain almost whimpered. "I love the beasties."

"If you love them, why set fire to their stables?"

Alain's head dropped forward until his chin rested against his chest. "For the bloody money."

"Someone paid you to set fire to my barn?" At Alain's nod, Steven shook him once more. "Who was it? If you tell me, I won't set the magistrate on you."

After a long moment, Alain finally answered. "Some laird fellow."

Stunned, Steven loosened his grip upon Alain. "Laird MacWilliam?"

"That's it," Alain replied in a surprised tone.

"He paid you to burn down my barn?"

"And, if that didn't scare off those gentry folk you had here this morning, I was to destroy some fences." He glanced around, obviously reading the hostility in the faces of his former coworkers. "Can I pack my things and be off then?"

Steven jerked his head toward Mr. Bingham. "Mr. Bingham will accompany you to your bunk, watch while you pack, and make certain you are off my property by dawn." He fixed a steely gaze upon Alain. "If I ever see you near my property again, I promise I'll have you tossed into prison for so long you won't remember what it feels like to be free."

Obviously shaken, Alain hurried off with Mr. Bingham directly behind him. "Let's clean up the stables so we can return the horses to their stalls."

As the stable hands hurried to do his bidding, Steven considered his most recent problem. Apparently Laird MacWilliam was out to destroy him, first with buying his vowels and now this.

He'd leave for London at first light . . . and the moment he got into town, he'd find this Laird MacWilliam.

As Steven rode into London, he remembered how just a short while earlier, he'd hated the very thought of coming to town. Yet now he eagerly entered the city . . . because Harriet was there. He'd never before realized that sometimes it was a person that made a place home. Wanting to settle this nasty business with this Laird MacWilliam person so he could focus on important things like marrying Harriet, Steven nudged his horse into a cantor.

Barely noticing the welcoming calls, Steven tossed his reins to a footman before heading into his house, taking the front steps two at a time. After handing off his gloves, hat, and cape to his butler, Steven made his way to his study to see if his solicitor had provided the name of MacWilliam's man of business. He stepped into the room . . . and bumped into Harriet.

"Harriet!" he exclaimed, automatically reaching out to catch hold of her.

"You're back!" She threw her arms around his neck, pressing kisses all over his face. "I've so much to tell you, so much to . . ."

He cut her off as he captured her mouth beneath his,

too hungry to talk. "Missed you," he finally murmured as he shifted his mouth downward, along the elegant line of her neck.

Without hesitation, she tilted her head, giving him greater access to the tender flesh at the nape of her neck. When he'd left, she'd been somewhat prickly, though she'd promised to try and trust him. Now that he'd returned, it was as if he'd come back to the Harriet who had shared those magical days at the cottage with him.

"Harriet," he murmured, lifting his head. "I thought you were angry with me."

"Shhh," she whispered, nipping at his lower lip. "Later; just kiss me now."

Not questioning his reversal of fortune any further, Steven fulfilled her request, claiming her mouth with his own as he maneuvered them forward until he could kick the door shut behind them. He undid the fastenings at the back of her gown as swiftly as possible, needing to touch her softness. Harriet returned the favor, tugging off his cravat before setting to work on his shirt.

Pausing to slip her arms free of her gown and chemise, Harriet moved forward, the tips of her aroused breasts catching in the whorls of his chest hair. Matching moans of satisfaction escaped them. Hunger clawed through Steven as he bent Harriet back over his arm to feast upon her breasts.

Her fingers slipped into his hair, clasping him against her as cries of pleasure ripped from her. Desperate to be inside her warmth, Steven lifted his head long enough to lower her into a wing-back chair. As he leaned forward to claim her mouth for another kiss, he lifted her skirts to her waist and slipped off her under-garments.

Voraciously he devoured her, feeding off her desire until he was mad to have her. He swept one hand boldly along her womanhood, his fingers curving inward to ca-ress her inner folds. Another cry of passion burst from her as she arched upward, offering him her breasts. Accept-ing the invitation, Steven lowered his mouth, trailing moist kisses along her neck and finally onto her pointed breasts.

With his other hand, he ripped at his breeches, desper-ate to free himself from the confines of his clothes, con-sumed with the elemental need to join with this woman. As soon as he sprang forth, Steven clasped Harriet's hips, sliding her downward on the chair until her buttocks touched the very edge of the cushion.

Stroking forward, Steven drove into her, groaning at the overwhelming sensation of her warmth closing over him, surrounding him in wet heat. Instinctively, her legs lifted, wrapping around his waist to deepen his penetra-tion. Despite all the women he'd enjoyed, Steven had never felt anything like being in Harriet. It was as if she'd been made for him, a perfect fit for him alone, drawing him inward.

Her hands clutched his as she arched her pelvis into him. Needing no further encouragement, he began to move in bold, fast strokes, driving them both into a hard rush for completion. Harriet's breath rasped out of her as she held onto him, eagerly riding toward the end, until fi-nally a scream broke from her, her body arching upward as her orgasm crashed through her.

Almost . . . almost . . . Steven's thoughts splintered as he exploded, pouring his soul into Harriet. His entire body shook with release as he dropped forward, bracing himself against the arms of the chair. "Lord, Harriet," he murmured when he could find his voice. "The things you do to me."

Wrapping her arms around him, she practically purred in contentment. "So happy to be of service, my lord."

Steven turned his head to press a kiss against the side of her breast. "I didn't mean to launch myself at you like that."

"You won't hear any complaints from me," she countered, curving her hands into his hair. "In fact, being in your arms is the crowning touch to a few glorious days."

"Glorious?" he asked, raising his head. "Are you referring to the fact that I wasn't around?"

"Don't be ridiculous." Steven found himself blinded by the brilliance of her smile. "While you were gone, I gathered enough money to repay all your debts."

Steven's heart froze within his chest. "What was that?"

"I said I gathered . . ."

"I heard that part," he interrupted. "But since money doesn't grow in convenient bunches like nuts to be gathered, I don't understand where you foraged for the funds." Suddenly chilled, Steven shifted backward, pulling free of Harriet's embrace. Rising, he adjusted himself and secured his breeches.

As he tugged his shirt closed, Steven noticed Harriet smoothing her skirts downward and pulling up the bodice of her dress. "You make it sound as if I did something wrong." She rose as well, reaching around her back to refasten her gown. "Your mother and I . . ."

"My mother was in on your grand scheme as well?" Steven snapped, feeling colder by the minute.

Anger replaced the affection in her expression. "There was no 'scheme,' Steven," she retorted, her hands fisting at her sides as she abandoned the last few fastenings. "All we did was contact a few close friends and borrowed the money in small increments so no one could know the true amount of your debt."

The tiny spark of hope flickering inside of him died.

Chapter Twenty-Three

"You said you believed in me."

The flat tone in his voice alarmed Harriet. "I do," she replied, not understanding what one had to do with the other.

"No, Harriet. You don't." His movements were stiff as he fastened his shirt. "If you did, you wouldn't have begged for money from everyone in town."

Offended by the unjustified accusation, Harriet abandoned her attempts at straightening her clothes. "Asking a few close friends for help hardly constitutes begging all over town," she retorted. "I thought I was helping you."

"I asked for your trust, not your help."

His sharp reply slapped at her. "I didn't realize I had to wait for your permission as if I were your personal servant. As your future wife, it is my right to help you."

"This from a woman who claims that the engagement is only temporary until you discover if you're carrying my child or not?" roared Steven, his cheeks stained red.

Her hand trembled as she held on to the chair. "You know perfectly well, Steven, that the only reason I didn't want to marry you is because I didn't wish to be another burden," she said, striving to control her hurt and anger. "You have no reason to attack me."

"I have every reason." A harsh rasping breath rushed from him. "How in the bloody hell am I supposed to walk with my head up now?"

The flatness of his voice pierced her own emotions, making her understand that she'd wounded his masculine pride. "Steven, no one will say anything to you," she said softly, speaking in a soothing tone.

"Perhaps not, but they'll bloody well be thinking about it." Thrusting both of his hands through his hair, he began to pace. "Dammit, Harriet, I'd found a way to pay off the debt."

"Your plan to race horses seemed somewhat precarious," she replied vaguely, hoping to calm his rage.

"I know." A harsh laugh escaped him. "Foolish me, I actually listened to you when we spoke in your garden. When you mentioned that my plan might be somewhat uncertain, I heard you and altered my idea accordingly. I'd found another way, a guaranteed way, to recoup my fortune." He dropped into a chair. "And all I asked for in return was a little faith."

Harriet's throat tightened as she realized the enormity of her mistake. "I was only trying to help," she repeated.

"You know what would have helped me, Harriet?" he asked loudly. "It would have been of great comfort to me if I'd had your unwavering support, your unconditional loyalty."

Helplessly, she tried to fix this problem. "What if we simply return the money?"

"Will that stop people from talking about it?" Another bitter laugh rumbled from his chest.

"Steven, I . . ."

"Enough!" Steven slammed both of his hands against the mantel. "I don't want to hear any more excuses. If you'd believed in me, you wouldn't have taken matters into your own hands." Turning away, he presented her with his back as if he couldn't stand the sight of her. "Just leave, Harriet."

How had they gone from I-missed-you-so-much-I-can't-wait-another-moment-to-make-love to just-leave? Because she'd stripped him of his pride, leaving him bare to the tongue-lashings from the ton. Harriet squeezed her eyes shut, hoping to shut out that nasty inner voice as easily. All she'd wanted to do was help him . . . and herself.

Harriet's heart cracked as she wondered if that might be true. Steven had been willing to marry her, but she'd refused, not wishing to become a burden. Instead, she'd found a way that she could marry him without feeling like just another responsibility, but her way had sacrificed Steven's pride.

And she'd lost him anyway.

Fighting off the urge to break down into a torrent of tears, Harriet walked out of Steven's study, leaving him alone. She'd managed to do the one thing that all his creditors had failed.

She'd found a way to defeat him.

* * *

"Steven?" His mother called as she peered into his study. "Are you in here?"

Steven remained seated, his head leaning back against the cushion as he sipped from his brandy glass. "I'm here," he said finally.

"When did you get back?" she asked as she entered the room, heading over to light the candles on the mantel. "And what on earth are you doing sitting here in the dark?"

Deciding to answer the easier of the two questions, Steven replied, "I returned home a few hours ago."

"Then you must have just missed Harriet."

The coldness inside of him deepened. "I didn't miss her."

Sitting upon the stool in front of his chair, his mother beamed at him. "Did she tell you our wonderful news? We're saved! Harriet and I sent notes to . . ."

"She told me," he said flatly.

Her smiled faded. "You don't sound excited."

"At the prospect of having our family name destroyed?" Steven lifted a brow. "Imagine that."

"Steven!"

"You sound shocked, Mother," he drawled, taking another sip of his brandy.

"That's because I am," she countered, spreading her hands wide. "All of this was threatened until Harriet came up with her idea to ask for money from many different people, thereby concealing the true amount owed." As Steven opened his mouth to argue her point, she cut him off. "I know that you'd also devised a manner in which to save our estate, Steven, but, as Harriet pointed out, it was less than a guaranteed success."

"Your overwhelming faith in me is very touching, Mother," he said as he drained his glass.

"Oh, Steven," his mother said softly, tears glimmering in her eyes. "It's not that we didn't believe in you; it's just that Harriet's plan seemed so sound, and we both just wanted to help."

"Dammit, Mother," he ground out, thrusting to his feet. "Did you ever stop to think for one moment that I didn't need your help?"

His mother scowled at him. "No, Steven, we didn't. We were too busy trying to decide how best to help someone we both love."

"As the one who is going to face mocking scorn, forgive me if I don't thank you."

"I find your attitude most ungrateful, Steven." Clasping her hands together, his mother stared at him. "So where does this leave your engagement to Harriet?"

Steven remained silent.

Slowly, his mother rose to her feet, gazing at him with what looked like pity in her eyes. "Then I shall leave you to your thoughts," she murmured. "But consider this as you're contemplating your engagement: Perhaps you're right. Perhaps Harriet and I should have believed in you and not gone ahead on our own. But does righteous anger make a comfortable bedfellow?" She shook her head. "It appears to me that you have a simple choice, Steven. You can be right . . . or you can be married to Harriet."

As he watched his mother walk from the room, Steven held his tongue, wanting to shout out his frustrations. Bloody hell, just how much was man supposed to take from interfering females?

Especially from ones he happened to love.

That thought knocked the breath from him. God help him, he loved Harriet. He made his way over to the sideboard and poured himself another glass of brandy.

Lord, he'd been so smug about his assumption that he found Harriet comforting and refreshing, which was why he desired her so much. But he'd been fooling himself.

He loved talking to her, flirting with her, just spending time with her because he loved her.

Snorting, he took a sip of his brandy. How ironic it was that his realization only enraged him more.

Pacing the confines of his study, he felt as if the walls were closing in on him. He needed to break free, escape his own thoughts, forget about everything—Harriet, his finances, the incident at the stables, the . . .

Steven skidded to a halt. That was it! He might not have any answers about how to handle his problems with Harriet, but he might be able to solve the problem of who Laird MacWilliam was and why he seemed bent on destroying the Heath estates.

Drawing in a cleansing breath, Steven strode from the room, relieved at having something to focus his energy and thoughts upon, eager to accept the challenge of unraveling this mystery. First off, Steven would call upon Royce to see if he'd heard of the bloke. After all, the Van Cleefs had remained in London during the years when Steven was happily spending time at his country estate, so Royce would know most everyone in society.

With every step Steven took, he felt more and more relieved. It was much easier focusing on finding Laird MacWilliam than it was to sort through the problem of Harriet.

* * *

"I hear congratulations are in order," Royce commented as he led Steven into his study.

Lord, did everyone want to talk about his uncertain engagement to Harriet? "Thank you," Steven said curtly.

Royce's brows lifted. "Is something the matter?"

Yes! He'd come here to escape his thoughts of Harriet, not to discuss her. Still, to Royce, Steven replied, "Sorry. I'm distracted over a near-tragic incident up at my northern estate."

"What happened?"

Launching into the tale of the stable fire, Steven finished, ". . . and when I learned the man who arranged for the fire was the very same man who purchased all my vowels, I came back to town immediately to find the fellow."

"I can well understand why," Royce agreed.

Watching Royce pour himself a brandy, Steven clarified his story. "Apparently, the order was that no horses were to be harmed. This Laird MacWilliam didn't . . ."

Royce's hand jerked, sending brandy spilling onto the floor as he spun to face Steven. "Laird MacWilliam?"

Steven took a step forward. "You know him then?"

"Not personally," Royce said, his expression grim as he set down the snifter. "But he's the one who accused me of stealing from my fellow investors; he's the one who caused my accounts to be frozen."

All the disjointed pieces began to fall into place. "First my mother has multiple, bizarre accidents that cost us a fortune, then I discover all the vowels have been bought up by this MacWillaim. I try to borrow funds from you, and we learn your accounts have been frozen by this very same man. Finally, when I figure out how to repay all my debt, there is a fire in my stable caused by him."

"I'd say you have yourself an enemy, Steven."

"That much is obvious . . . but what I can't understand is why? I don't even know Laird MacWilliam. What could I possibly have done to offend someone badly enough that he vowed revenge? Besides, I've barely spent any time off my estate in the past few years, so unless it's the gardener I angered, I don't know of anyone who would wish revenge."

"And what of your years in town before you decided to live like a hermit?" Royce countered swiftly. "With all the carousing you did, it's highly likely that you offended someone somewhere along the line."

While Steven didn't deny that possibility, it didn't make much sense to him. "If I'd offended someone badly enough that he sought to destroy me, I can't imagine his waiting so long to seek his vengeance. Either way, the riddle will be solved as soon as we discover Mac-William's identity." He thrust his hands in his pockets. "I was hoping you might know more about the fellow."

"Unfortunately, I don't," Royce said, before snapping his fingers. "However, I'd asked my solicitor for all the information he could find on Laird MacWilliam. Unfortunately, he hasn't discovered the man's identity."

"I know someone who might have some information," Steven began. "Edward Longley, one of the fellows who's trailing after my mother, is supposedly connected with MacWilliam." He fisted his hands. "I say we find this Longley fellow and see if he knows anything."

"It's a plan."

* * *

"Laurel, you really shouldn't have come to call upon me," Harriet protested, helping her very pregnant friend into a chair. "You are due to deliver any day now. The last thing you should be doing is traipsing about town to visit me."

"You left me no choice," Laurel countered. "I sent you a note asking you to call."

"To which I replied that I was too busy at present to spare a moment, but that I would call upon you as soon as I possibly could."

Laurel folded her hands over her rounded belly. "I know what your note said, Harriet, but I felt it most important that I speak with you about all the rumors flying about."

"Rumors?" Harriet sank down onto a chair.

"About you and Lord Heath." Having caught Harriet's full attention, Laurel got straight to the point of her visit. "Lady Hampton called upon me the other day and imparted a bit of gossip I found difficult to fathom. Apparently, Lady Camilla is claiming that you are about to break your engagement to Lord Heath because he is too much of a man."

Horror filled Harriet as she realized Lady Camilla hadn't kept her confidence. All Harriet had wanted to do was keep the heiress interested in Steven until they determined whether or not she was expecting. Yet Lady Camilla had fed Harriet to the gossipmongers, leaving them to tear her and Steven apart.

"Then Lady Bloomsbury called upon me to tell me that you'd been writing to everyone asking for small sums of money. She also explained that Lady Heath was doing the exact same thing." Laurel arched her back as if working out a kink. "Naturally, I suspected this rumor was truth, but I didn't let on. I merely made a comment that I hadn't spoken to you in a few days."

Dropping her head into her hands, Harriet prayed for the earth to open up and swallow her. How much worse could things get? Steven's greatest fears had been realized; all the ton knew about her attempts to recoup his funds. And she could only imagine his reaction when he heard the bit of news Lady Camilla had shared.

Before Harriet could reply, she heard a slight scuffle outside the salon. Lifting her head, she blinked in surprise as Lady Heath hurried into the room, followed by her admirer, Mr. Connor. "Pardon the intrusion, Harriet, but I simply had to see you right away."

Reassuring her harried butler that Lady Heath was welcome, Harriet rose to greet them. "This is an unexpected surprise," she murmured, straining her already taut nerves to behave as if nothing untoward had just happened. "Mr. Connor," she said with a bow of her head.

"I hope you don't mind that I brought Robert along," Steven's mother said. "After speaking with Steven, I needed to see you right away, so when Robert called to see me a few minutes later, I asked him to escort me here."

"You're both welcome." Forcing a smile onto her face, Harriet gestured toward the chairs. "Won't you have a seat? Tea should be here any moment."

"Don't fuss about the tea; I need to speak . . . Oh!" gasped Lady Heath when she finally spotted Laurel. "Goodness, Lady Tewksbury, I didn't realize you were in here." Awkwardly, she glanced back at Harriet. "I didn't mean to interrupt, dear."

"It's quite all right," Laurel said, answering for Harriet. "We were just catching up on a bit of gossip."

Lady Heath paled. "Gossip?" she said, obviously struggling for a nonchalant tone of voice . . . and failing miserably. "What sort of gossip?"

Now it was Laurel's turn to feel awkward and look toward Harriet for a reply. Unfortunately, Harriet felt as much at a loss for a reply as Laurel did. Feeling like a stammering fool, Harriet glanced pointedly at Mr. Connor. It was one thing to air personal business with Laurel or Steven's mother, but quite another altogether to do so in front of a virtual stranger.

"Does the gossip pertain to the money you've borrowed recently?"

All three pairs of feminine eyes turned their stunned gaze upon Mr. Connor. "Pardon me?" Harriet asked in a choked voice.

He clutched his gloves, squeezing them between his hands. "I didn't mean to offend you, Miss Nash. It was my intention to reassure you that you needn't feel hesitant about discussing the Earl of Heath's financial troubles with me as I've already heard the gossip."

Swaying, Harriet reached out to steady herself against the back of Laurel's chair.

"How did you hear about that?" Lady Heath asked in a strangled tone.

He shrugged his shoulders. "I can't really remember, Caroline, but it seems as if everyone is talking about it. You must remember that sometimes it seems as if the walls have ears with the way rumors spread through the ton." Offering Lady Heath a smile, Mr. Connor leaned over to pat her hand. "Even if you did borrow money because the Morris coffers are empty, there's nothing to be ashamed of, Caroline."

A soft moan escaped her. "Of course there is, Robert. This is all my fault."

"None of those costly accidents were your fault," Mr. Connor stated firmly.

Lady Heath looked ill. "That is sweet of you to say, Robert, but I'm afraid you're being overly kind. After all, it was my foolhardy actions that cost Steven his inheritance."

Leaping to her defense, Robert shook his head. "No, Caroline, that's not . . ."

"Harriet!"

Her father's booming voice echoed down the hallway into the salon.

Wearing a broad grin, her father stepped into the room and flung his arms wide. "Harriet, my girl, you're rich!"

Chapter Twenty-Four

"Papa," she began, thinking that if one more person mentioned the gossip about town, she'd scream. "You know the money I borrowed was to . . ."

"I'm not talking about that," he said, cutting her off. "I'm telling you you're rich, Harriet."

"How's that, Papa?"

"Your investment, girl!" Pulling her into a fierce hug, he twirled her around. "Your investment!" he repeated.

"The fertilizer?"

Pulling back, her father nodded down at her. "Precisely. After I spoke to Mr. McKenny about your financial worries, he decided to approach investors immediately." He held up a wrinkled note. "Mr. McKenny just wrote me to let me know that everyone he showed his results to wanted to purchase all the fertilizer he'd made with your investment as well as put money into the company you started with Mr. McKenny."

The news was so unbelievable Harriet had a hard time getting her mind around it. "So you're telling me that I made back my investment plus a little more?" she asked hopefully, praying that it was true.

"No, Harriet," her father began in a patient tone. "I'm telling you that you made over three times your investment."

An intoxicating mix of pleasure, excitement, and pride overwhelmed Harriet, stealing away her very breath.

"Oh, Harriet!" exclaimed Lady Heath. "This is such wonderful news."

"Indeed it is," Laurel agreed from her chair. "I'd jump up as well if I thought I could get out of this chair by myself."

"Everything will be fine now," she murmured, allowing herself to hope for the first time since leaving Steven's home. How ironic that she, who had always lamented that gentlemen from the country wanted to talk about fertilizer, had made a fortune off of it. Perhaps their conversations had been more edifying than she'd realized.

Lady Heath reached out to clasp Harriet's hands. "You can use the money you've earned to pay off the debtors and return all the money collected from friends."

An image of Steven, his back turned toward her, killed her wavering hope. She was only fooling herself if she thought this newfound fortune would help her or Steven. The damage done was irreparable. While she could return all the money, how could she ever hope Steven would forgive her?

Her heart wept at the realization that he was gone to

her forever. "Please excuse me," she whispered in a tear-laden voice as she rushed from the room.

"Oh, dear!" Lady Heath pressed her hands to her cheeks. "I don't understand what's wrong."

Harriet's father patted Lady Heath on the shoulder. "She was probably undone by joy and needed a moment to collect herself."

Silently taking in the scene for a moment, Mr. Connor finally stepped forward. "I can see that this is a private moment," he said gently. "If you'll excuse me, Caroline, I shall take my leave."

"There's no need to go, sir," protested Harriet's father.

Mr. Connor bowed respectfully. "While I appreciate your kind welcome, I really feel it best if I withdraw."

With a smile for Lady Heath, he left the room.

"Ouch!" Laurel's exclamation drew Mr. Nash and Lady Heath's gaze to her. "Sorry," she murmured as she rubbed her stomach. "The baby has been very active today."

"Can we get you something to make you more comfortable?" asked Lady Heath.

"No," Laurel said with a smile. "Though I would appreciate a hand up. Standing can be something of a challenge to me these days." Holding out both her hands, she allowed Harriet's father and Steven's mother to help her up. "I'm going home now."

"Allow me to see you home," offered Mr. Nash.

Laurel smiled at Harriet's elderly father. "I thank you for the offer, Mr. Nash, but you should see to Harriet."

"I'll see to you first," he insisted firmly. "When my wife was about to deliver Harriet, she felt much as you do now, and I'll not be sending you off on your merry way to leave you to give birth alone in the back of your carriage. Lady Heath can accompany us."

"But, Mr. Nash . . ."

He fixed a steady gaze upon Laurel. "Haven't you learned yet that it's useless to argue with old men? We have more time and patience than you can imagine. If we don't have a logical argument, we'll simply continue to argue until we wear you down."

Laughing, Laurel accepted his arm. "Hate to spoil your theory, Mr. Nash, but as a married woman I can testify that stubbornness isn't limited to old men."

Mr. Nash joined in her mirth. At the door, Harriet's father paused to speak with the butler. "If Miss Harriet asks, please tell her that Lady Heath and I will return after we escort Lady Tewksbury home."

"I shall tell Miss Nash when she returns," the butler replied smoothly.

Drawing to a halt, Mr. Nash frowned. "What do you mean by when she returns?"

The butler nodded once. "She left a few moments ago with the other gentleman, sir."

"Mr. Connor?" Lady Heath looked at Mr. Nash and Laurel in confusion. "That seems a bit odd. I didn't think Harriet knew Robert other than as a casual acquaintance."

Just then an odd pain shot through Laurel's lower back, gripping tightly and releasing. "I need to go home now," she murmured, interrupting Mr. Nash's conversation.

"You'll be holding your second son before the next daybreak," Mr. Nash predicted as he resumed helping

Laurel out to her carriage. "Come along, Lady Heath. We'll sort through this situation after we return Lady Laurel home."

Standing before the unassuming town house, Steven checked the address he'd gotten from his mother. "This is the place," he said, taking the front steps two at a time and knocking on the front door.

Longley's butler showed them into the front salon. Only a few minutes had passed when Longley waddled into the room. "Lord Heath," he exclaimed with a jovial smile. "This is an unexpected pleasure." As he glanced toward Royce, his brows lifted. "And the Earl of Tewksbury as well?" Longley patted his stomach. "I'm truly honored."

"I'm glad you think so, because we'd like to ask you a few questions," Steven said politely, not wanting to upset Longley in any fashion. He'd be far more likely to talk to them about MacWilliam if he wasn't angry. "If that's all right with you, of course."

"Fine, fine," Longley assured him, waving them into chairs. "Please sit and relax while I ask my butler to fetch us some tea."

Shaking his head, Steven remained standing. "That won't be necessary."

Longley tucked his hands into the pockets of his waistcoat. "This must be urgent business you're about then."

"Indeed it is," Steven agreed. "I'm trying to find information on Laird MacWilliam."

Alarm flashed in Longley's eyes. "MacWilliam?" he croaked. "Don't believe I know anyone by that name."

"That's curious," Steven replied in a considering tone. "According to Lord Hampton, you're business associates."

Longley made a gurgling sound. "I—I . . . that is . . ."

"That's an interesting shade of red you're turning," Royce said, speaking for the first time, before turning his gaze on Steven. "I think the man is trying to hide something from us, don't you?"

Rocking back on his heels, Steven nodded in agreement. "Looks like it."

"I don't want to get involved in this," Longley said, raising both his hands. "It was a simple business arrangement, that's all."

"I think I'd like to hear some details about this arrangement, wouldn't you, Royce?"

Royce smiled coldly. "Absolutely."

With a frantic shake of his head, Longley stumbled backward, bumping into a chair. "I can't tell you anything."

"Because you're afraid of what MacWilliam would do to you?" Steven asked. At Longley's nod, he glanced at Royce. "Seems like this MacWilliam is a dangerous fellow, Royce."

"What Longley here has failed to realize is that we can be dangerous to his well-being, too," Royce finished.

Crossing his arms, Steven returned his gaze to Longley. "It's true," he said to the portly man. "We could ruin your life here. One word from either of us, and you wouldn't be welcome at any affair."

"And if I'm assuming correctly, you've leased this town house." Longley's eyes flared. "One conversation with your landlord, and we could have you tossed into the street."

"That's just the start of what we could do," Steve threatened. "Do you think we're dangerous enough now?"

Longley's hands shook as he sank into a chair. "I don't want any trouble," he mumbled. "It was just business, I tell you. When MacWilliam first approached, I thought it would be an easy way to make some blunt. Besides, your mother wouldn't accept my proposals, so what could it hurt?"

"What does this have to do with my mother?"

"I just told you," Longley exclaimed, slapping his hand against his leg. "At first MacWilliam just wanted me to cause a few minor accidents."

The pieces were beginning to fit together. "Like knocking over Lady Hampton's china."

"Precisely." Longley shrugged. "What was the harm?"

Remembering his mother's distress, it was all Steven could do to keep from throttling the man. "What else did you do?"

"While in Europe, I caused a few mishaps there, but nothing of importance."

Steven's definition of importance greatly differed from Longley's.

"Most recently, MacWilliam wanted me to become more aggressive in my proposals," Longley finished. "As I said, it was easy work."

"You bastard."

Longley flinched at Steven's insult. "It was simply business," he repeated, as if that perfectly justified his actions.

"Why would MacWilliam wish to harm Lady Heath?" Royce asked, his voice a calming influence on Steven.

"Haven't you figured it out yet?" For the first time since they'd inquired after MacWilliam, Longley laughed shortly. "I thought you were clever fellows."

"There were three of you following my mother."

"Now the lad's coming around," Longley murmured.

"Since Windvale is penniless, he couldn't possibly have paid you, so that would leave . . ." Steven looked at Longley. ". . . Connor."

Longley clapped three times. "Excellent deduction, my lord. I do believe you missed your calling."

"What I don't understand is why he'd caused all those accidents in the first place and why pay Longley here to be an overly ardent suitor?" Royce asked.

Longley smiled at Steven. "Care to take a guess at that answer? A hint is that there is only one answer to both questions."

All the pieces of the puzzle had tumbled into place. "Because Connor wanted my mother to marry him." Turning toward Royce, Steven explained. "First, Connor wanted my mother to be in a dire financial situation, so she would wish to marry for money. He knew Windvale wasn't a threat by reason of his lack of funds, so he paid Longley here to step back and allow him an easy path to my mother."

"So when I offered to loan you the money necessary to repay your debts, he tied up my funds as well, making it impossible for me to help you," Royce concluded.

"Exactly." All of Steven's anger hardened into a knot in the pit of his stomach. "Let's go find Connor."

* * *

"What was the urgent, troubling matter you needed to speak with me about?" Harriet asked as she turned toward Mr. Connor. "Is it about Steven?" Steering the horses down a narrow street, Mr. Connor remained silent. Suddenly, Harriet noticed their surroundings. "Where are we going?"

As Harriet watched, Mr. Connor reached into his coat pocket and withdrew a pistol. "I'm terribly sorry about this, Miss Nash."

The formality while he was holding a gun on her would have struck Harriet funny if she hadn't been so afraid. Deciding the best way to handle this situation was to brazen it out, she glared at the little man. "What is the meaning of this, Mr. Connor?"

"I'm sorry," he repeated. "I just can't let you marry Lord Heath."

Her topsy-turvy world had just begun to spin out of control again. "I'm afraid I don't understand," she said softly, hoping to keep Mr. Connor calm.

"I'm so close," he muttered, more to himself than to her. "I've worked so hard, and my dream is about to come true." He shifted his attention between her and the street. "I can't allow you to marry Lord Heath and give him all your money."

"I still don't understand," she said, noticing that Mr. Connor kept looking back at the road. This might be her only chance, she realized, trying to calm her jittery nerves.

The next time Mr. Connor glanced away, Harriet made her move, lunging forward to knock the gun from his hand. Panicked, Mr. Connor pulled back on the reins, causing the carriage to career sideways, sending Harriet off-balance. As she tumbled onto the floor of the carriage, her head struck the front wall, sending pain shooting through her.

As darkness closed in, Harriet heard Mr. Connor murmur an apology . . . then she heard no more.

On their way to Harriet's town house, Steven and Royce came upon the Tewksbury carriage. Pulling their horses to a stop, Royce leaned forward to tell his wife where they were going. One glance inside caused all the color to drain from Royce's face. "Laurel?" he whispered, sliding off his horse. "Are you ill?"

"Nothing that a few hours of labor won't cure," she muttered in between panting breaths.

Ripping open the door, Royce began to enter the carriage when he stopped, one foot on the riser. "Damn," he muttered, swinging around to look at Steven. "You'll need to find Connor on your own. Just save a piece of him for me."

"Are you speaking of Robert?" Steven's mother asked, leaning forward to look out at her son. "What do you want with him?"

"He's Laird MacWilliam."

His simple explanation caused his mother to gasp in shock. "Not Robert," she whispered, pressing two fingers to her lips. "Why would he do this to us?"

"I don't know," Steven admitted, "but I intend to find out."

"Excuse m-m-me." At Laurel's interruption, everyone turned their attention to her. "I don't mean to be a pest, but your son isn't going to wait for us to finish this conversation," she said to Royce. "Now why don't you climb in here and let Mr. Nash go with Steven to track down Mr. Connor and Harriet?"

Immediately, the men jumped to do Laurel's bidding. Sitting atop his white stallion, Steven couldn't hold back a grin as the carriage rolled off. "That sharp tongue of Laurel's was why we picked her for our wager."

"What wager is that?" Mr. Nash asked.

Thinking back on the unusual courtship of his best friend, Steven shook his head. "That's another story for another time."

"I quite agree," Mr. Nash said as he mounted Royce's chestnut stallion.

Something Laurel said stuck in his mind. "What did she mean by we're going to have to track down Connor and Harriet?"

Mr. Nash clutched the saddle. "Dear Lord, in all the excitement, I'd forgotten," he began, meeting Steven's eyes. "They went for a ride in his carriage earlier."

Alarm grabbed hold of Steven's throat, threatening to squeeze the very breath from him. Harriet with Connor. While the man hadn't made any physical threats to him or his family, Steven worried that an act of violence might be his next step. How much would it take to nudge him over the edge?

Steven clenched his teeth. By God, he wasn't going to risk Harriet. She was far too precious to him. Finally, Steven understood what it was to have everything taken away from him.

"Where did they go?" Steven asked Harriet's father.

The elderly man shook his head. "I don't know."

Panic threatened to overwhelm him, but Steven fought

it back. Where would Connor take Harriet? Unaware that Steven knew his true identity, Connor would still feel safe and well hidden.

He'd head for home.

"I think I know where they're headed." Steven tossed the piece of paper containing Connor's address to Harriet's father. "I'm going to be riding fast; if I lose you, just head there."

Not waiting for a reply, Steven kicked his stallion into a full gallop, thankful that the horse had been bred for speed.

Chapter Twenty-Five

Slowly, Harriet became aware of sounds—the chirping of the birds, the ticking of the clock, the breathing of . . .

Her eyes flew open as she struggled to overcome the fog still clouding her thoughts. "Mr. Connor," she murmured, fear mounting as her memories came tumbling back. As she sat upright on the bed, she realized her wrists were bound, tying her in place. Being bound to a bed terrified her, but she'd fight to the death before she'd allow him to touch her. "Release me at once," she demanded, deliberately hiding her fear.

"I wish I could, but we've gone too far for me to let you go."

The conversational tone of his voice startled her. "You can release me," she said, trying for a friendly pitch this time. "Then we could talk about what's troubling you."

He appeared to consider her suggestion for a moment, before shaking his head. "I'm truly sorry, Miss Nash, but

I simply can't take that risk. Your actions in the carriage were most telling."

"Then what are you going to do with me?"

A sad expression turned down the corners of his mouth. "I'm not quite certain yet, but I fear the only solution will not bode well for you. When your father burst in with the news about your newfound wealth, I knew I had to act immediately, so I took you without carefully planning it out." He nodded solemnly. "I'm usually most meticulous in my planning." Placing his hand on his chest, he closed his eyes as if saying a pledge. "If you fail to plan, you plan to fail." His lids lifted. "Unfortunately, I panicked, and now I'm afraid the results will be disastrous."

"For me," Harriet finished as she realized in that moment that Mr. Connor was mad.

Mr. Connor nodded again. "Please believe me when I say I am truly sorry."

Again, fear threatened to overwhelm her, but she pushed it back. No one even knew she was out with Mr. Connor. If she were going to get out of this dire situation, it would be up to her to think of a way. She needed to keep him talking, she realized, keep him too busy to notice anything she might do.

"Why did my turn of fortune alarm you?" she asked as she surreptitiously moved her arm forward, testing her binding.

"Because if you gave your fortune to Steven, he would no longer be in a financial bind," he explained slowly, as if speaking to a child.

Feeling a slight give in the knot, Harriet tugged again. "Why is it important that he remain in debt?"

"Because if I don't remain debt-ridden, then my mother will have no reason to marry."

"Steven," she whispered, part of her wondering if he was a mirage conjured up by her desperate mind.

"No!" shouted Mr. Connor as he jumped up from his chair and pointed the gun at Steven. "You can't be here!"

Unarmed, Steven took a step into the room. "Ah, but I am . . . Laird MacWilliam," he replied smoothly.

Mr. Connor's eyes widened. "How did you find out?"

"Once I'd begun to piece it together, it was really quite easy." For a second, Steven glanced toward her, his gaze sweeping over her as if to assure himself she was safe, before shifting his attention back to Mr. Connor and his gun. "If you hadn't gotten sloppy, it might have taken me a while longer to figure it all out."

"Sloppy?" he raged, his hand shaking. "My plans have been flawless, right down to the minutest details."

"I believe, Connor, that you're missing one very important point." Steven took another step into the room. "If your plans are flawless, then how did I find you?"

Mr. Connor twitched as he swung the gun toward Harriet. "One more step, and I'll shoot her. I swear I will," he vowed.

Immediately, Steven stopped moving except to lift his hands in a sign of surrender. "If you harm her, I swear you'll know Hell."

"I don't want to hurt her!" he shouted, his face flushed and his eyes wild. "All I want is for Caroline to marry me."

Steven lowered his hands. "But if you shoot either me or Harriet, she'll never marry you."

A sly smile twisted Mr. Connor's mouth. "She'll never

have to know that it was I." He pressed a hand to his chest while keeping the gun trained on Steven. "As her friend, I shall console her, offer her my sympathies, and never tell her that you both died by my hand."

"Again, your plan is perfect except for one detail," Steven said calmly. "My mother already knows you're Laird MacWilliam."

"No, no, no," he muttered under his breath. "This can't be happening. I'm so close, so close." With Mr. Connor lost in his thoughts, Harriet took a risk, jerking her arm sharply, once, twice, until she felt her binding slip. Almost free, she realized, preparing to tug again until she realized Mr. Connor had his gaze fixed upon her. "I know what I'll do," he said finally. "I'll lock you away at one of my other homes and keep you alive as long as your lord here remains silent about all this."

"Did you hear what I said, Connor?" Steven asked loudly, obviously trying to draw Mr. Connor's attention back to him. "My mother already knows your identity."

"Yes, yes," he said with a gleeful smile. "But what does she know? That I purchased your vowels? Perhaps she knows about my freezing Tewksbury's accounts. Or did you tell her that I was the one behind the tragic fire at your stable?" His high-pitched laugh was tinged with madness. "Your mother's a beautiful, charming, but unbelievably naive woman, Lord Heath. Even if Caroline knows me as Laird MacWilliam, she'll believe me innocent of everything if I spin my tale well enough."

Steven shook his head. "You underestimate my mother."

Worrying his lip between his teeth, Mr. Connor stared at Steven. "Perhaps you're right," he said slowly, his hand steadying. "I can't take the risk that she'll find out the truth."

The tension in the room grew, frightening Harriet even more as she realized something dreadful was about to happen.

"Perhaps I should kill you, then kill Harriet and make it look like some sort of lovers' quarrel." His eyes began to gleam as he warmed to his new plan. "Yes, it would work splendidly. The ton already believes your sexual appetites frighten your affianced."

At that remark, Steven threw Harriet a confused glance before returning his attention to Mr. Connor.

"I can leave her tied to the bed, freeing one hand that can be holding the gun." He waved the pistol toward Harriet. "I can shoot you first, then her, making it look as if she killed you because of your debased sexual preferences, before turning the gun on herself." Wearing a pleased expression, Mr. Connor nodded firmly.

As if sensing the situation was spiraling out of control, Steven advanced farther into the room. "But how long will you be able to keep your secret? How many times will you be able to look at my mother and not see my face before you?"

"Thousands," Mr. Connor said with a laugh. "I won't even think of you once you're gone. I'll simply pretend that you never were."

"You're insane," Steven rasped.

Mr. Connor shook his gun at Steven. "No! I'm in love!" He grinned wildly. "Mad with it, perhaps, but it is love that drives me."

For a moment, Harriet felt empathy for Mr. Connor. How far would she go in the name of love? There was no denying Mr. Connor was mad, but did unrequited love do that to a person? Harriet prayed she never learned the answer.

"Have you considered that even if you kill Harriet and me, the possibility remains that my mother will still refuse to marry you?"

A tremor rocked Mr. Connor's entire body. "If she refuses me again, I'll have to claim her life along with mine, joining us in death as we could never be joined in life."

"Connor, you are . . ."

"Enough!" His shout echoed in the bedchamber. "Enough talk, enough discussion; it's time to fulfill my dreams." He waved the pistol toward Harriet. "Say farewell to your love."

As Mr. Connor cocked back the pistol, Steven raised both of his hands. "Wait!" Gesturing toward Harriet, he beseeched Mr. Connor. "At least let me kiss her farewell." He paused for a moment. "If our positions were reversed, wouldn't you want one last kiss from your Caroline?"

"Yes, oh, yes," he said breathlessly before nodding to Steven. "You may kiss her one last time. If you try anything, I'll kill you first."

Shifting his gaze to Harriet, he moved toward her, easing his hip onto the bed near her bound hand. He braced himself with one hand as he leaned over her. Mere inches from her mouth, knowing his lips were hidden from Connor's view, he whispered, "I'll untie you, then you roll off the bed."

Using his body to block Connor's unswerving gaze, Steven swiftly undid the binding she'd loosened. He lifted his head to stare down at her. "Harriet," he finally said, the one word vibrating with emotion.

If this was her last moment on earth, she needed to speak the words in her heart. "I love you, Steven."

His eyes flared, a burning intensity darkening them into deep blue. "Harriet, I . . ."

"That's enough," Mr. Connor announced, cutting off Steven's words, snatching his declaration from Harriet's grasp. "Now stand up and get over there."

Steven's muscles bunched as he launched himself backward, slamming into Connor with a force that knocked the older man into the wall, causing him to pull the trigger, firing a single shot toward the bed.

"Harriet!" Steven screamed as he rammed Connor against the wall again, knocking him unconscious. Releasing Connor to slump to the floor, Steven raced toward the bed, waving aside the mass of floating feathers to search for Harriet.

A foot from the bed, he tripped over a large object.

"Ouch!"

His breath slammed into his chest as he dropped to his knees. With a shaking hand, he reached out to touch Harriet. "Are you hurt?" he asked, the question torn from him.

"Only where you stepped on me." An instant later, she was in his arms.

Safe and where she belonged.

Burying his face into the curve of her neck, Steven enfolded her close. "I thought I'd lost you."

"I'd rolled off the bed like you said." She tugged at her remaining binding. "But I couldn't get any farther than this."

Giving a shaky laugh, Steven untied the rope, freeing

her at last. "God, Harriet, if anything had happened to you . . ."

Drawing back her head, she gazed into his face, ignoring the feathers that drifted down onto them. "Will you ever be able to forgive me?"

His eyes darkened again as the love he felt for her swelled up inside of him. She asked if he would forgive her, he thought. Didn't she realize how he felt at this moment? All that mattered was Harriet was alive and well . . . and in his arms.

Needing to reaffirm himself in her, Steven lowered his head.

Downstairs a door slammed open. "Would someone please tell me what the devil is going on around here?" bellowed Harriet's father.

Steven grinned down at Harriet. "The reinforcements have arrived."

Chapter Twenty-Six

"She's absolutely beautiful," Harriet cooed, bending down to kiss Laurel's newborn daughter on the head. "Welcome Christina Noelle." Leaning forward, Harriet kissed her dear friend on the cheek. "Well done, Laurel. Once again, you make motherhood look far too appealing."

"Come round when Christina's screaming, and you'll see the other side of motherhood," Laurel replied with a laugh.

"I'm confident you'd handle that with as much grace as you accept your good fortune."

"Speaking of good fortune," Laurel countered, "I hear Steven has his back."

Just the mention of his name caused a pang in her heart. It had been three days since their ordeal at Mr. Connor's house, and she hadn't heard a word from Steven. While she realized he had a mess to sort out, she found it difficult to believe he couldn't spare a moment to see her . . . so she hadn't been able to tell him that she'd started her monthly courses. "Indeed he does," Harriet confirmed. "Mr. Connor was arrested and Steven petitioned the courts for restitution. His petition was granted yesterday."

"And from what Royce tells me, the entire story has sent all the gossips abuzz." Laurel kissed the downy hair at the top of Christina's head. "He says that everyone is calling Steven a hero for protecting his family and his honor at all costs." She lifted a brow. "They even say that his asking friends for help is a sign of his self-confidence. After all, only a man who possessed a great deal of confidence could set aside his pride and ask for help in order to save his family."

"Then all has been set aright," Harriet concluded. "People have finally seen him for the wonderful gentleman he is and forgotten all about his rakish past."

"You're mistaken," Laurel said, shifting the baby to her other arm. "When Royce returned from his club yesterday, he said that the men are already placing wagers on which lady Steven will seduce first after he weds you."

Harriet frowned at the very notion of Steven securing a mistress after he'd married.

"Naturally, Royce placed a large wager that Steven would remain faithful and true to you throughout the days." Laurel grinned wickedly. "My darling Royce has been well trained."

Harriet laughed out loud. "Just don't let him hear you say that."

"I'm no fool," she countered, glancing toward the door to ensure Royce wasn't listening. "As I was saying, all of society is abuzz about Steven's rakish ways and how he's so lustful that you find him overwhelming." Looking at her daughter, Laurel whispered to the baby, "Don't listen to this part, Christina." Her gaze lifted to settle upon Harriet with determination. "Are the rumors true? Is Steven an absolute rogue in bed?"

"Laurel!" gasped Harriet, unable to believe her friend's question. "You're a married woman who has just given birth."

"All the more reason to live vicariously through you." She tucked a strand of hair behind her ear. "So tell me if the rumors are true."

Wonderful memories of the sensual hours spent at the cottage filled Harriet's mind. If she closed her eyes, she could almost imagine she was back in the beautiful house, spreading scented oil all over Steven's body, trailing a feather along his torso, downward to swirl the softness over his hardened length, before sinking down on her knees and . . .

"Harriet?"

Harriet jumped at the sound of Laurel's voice. "Sorry; I got lost in thought."

"If the blush on your face is any indication, I'd say they were absolutely delicious thoughts." A corner of her mouth turned upward. "Care to share?"

"No, thank you," Harriet said firmly. "Suffice it to say, Laurel, that it doesn't matter if the rumors are true or not. All that counts is that we won't be getting married."

Every trace of teasing left Laurel's expression. "Why not?"

"Because there's no longer a reason for Steven to marry me," Harriet explained, ignoring the painful knot in her stomach. "His fortune is again intact, his name has been restored to its former glory, and my courses began yesterday." She'd ticked off the points on her fingers. "So you see, Laurel, he has no reason to marry me."

"None other than the fact that he loves you," she retorted, tossing a small pillow at Harriet.

"Does he?" Harriet wouldn't even allow herself to dream that possibility. "I'd be happy if he would simply forgive me."

Laurel frowned. "What have you done that you need his forgiveness for?"

"First off, I seduced him using a version of Royce's theory, then I caused him to announce our engagement because my aunts had us followed and learned of our affair, and finally, I borrowed money to repay his debts, showing a lack of faith in his ability to handle his own affairs."

"Poppycock!" Reaching out, Laurel rang for the nursemaid and handed over Christina. The moment the maid left the room, she fixed a stern eye upon Harriet. "Let's address your sins one by one, shall we?" Lifting her index finger, she began, "One. You say you seduced him, but Steven would thank you for your efforts rather than hold them against you." Another finger joined the first. "Point two. Steven knew the risks involved in meeting you at his cottage and felt you were worth it. If I recall correctly, he was the one pushing for the engagement."

"Only because he feared I might be expecting his child," Harriet interjected.

"For a gentleman being forced into announcing his

engagement, he certainly seemed content with the idea of it every time I saw him."

Harriet rolled her eyes. "Naturally he wouldn't behave any differently around you, Laurel; you are my best friend after all."

"And I don't even think we need to discuss your third comment as your actions of borrowing money only made Steven look more noble in the end."

Falling back into her chair, Harriet stared at Laurel. "Every time I speak to you, you always seem to counter my every argument."

"It's a gift," she said with a grin. "So tell me, Harriet, what will you do if Steven asks you to marry him?"

Leap for joy? Shout it from the rooftops? Drag him back to the cottage? Now that idea had merit. "I'll thank him . . . then refuse him."

"What?"

"You heard me perfectly well," Harriet said concisely. "If Steven happens to ask for my hand again, I shall turn him down." Knowing she'd confused her friend, Harriet tried to explain. "I used to believe I was plain and ordinary. Don't you remember that I'd describe myself as remarkably unremarkable?" At Laurel's nod, Harriet continued, "But then that changed; I changed. Steven helped me see that I was more than just 'a best friend'; he showed me that I could be adventurous, outrageous, and incredibly desirable."

"Then why won't you marry him?"

"Because I deserve more," she said simply. "I deserve to be married for love, to be married because that person would rather live without food, clothing, or shelter than live without me. And since he hasn't sought me out these last few days, I fear he doesn't feel that way about me." Blinking back the tears, Harriet smiled softly. "The most ironic thing of all is that it is Steven himself who changed me. Before he came along and made me realize I was more than plain Harriet, I would have jumped at the chance to marry him, not caring as to his reasons for his proposal."

Laurel remained silent for a long minute. "I think you're making a huge mistake," she said finally. "You're forgetting one of the most important rules in any marriage."

"And that would be?" Harriet asked, her curiosity getting the better of her.

"He's a man, darling Harriet." Her lips curved upward into a wide smile. "Which means he's trainable."

"Come in, Royce," Steven said, abandoning the ledgers in front of him to greet his friend. "I'd hoped to call upon you later in the week."

Gesturing toward the desk, Royce asked, "Am I intruding? If so, I'll apologize now for not being able to leave you to your work."

The fact that Royce wasn't willing to come back another time could only mean one thing. "Laurel sent you."

A grin brightened Royce's face as he slapped Steven's back. "See how well you know me?"

"Not only you, but that wife of yours as well." He reached out a hand. "Congratulations on your daughter, Royce. My mother tells me she's beautiful."

"Like her mother," Royce said, beaming with fatherly pride. "My Ryan adores his little sister, but he wants to know when she'll be old enough to run around with him."

"Lord help you both then." Heading over to the sideboard, Steven poured two brandies. "I imagine Laurel sent you over here to speak with me about Harriet."

Accepting his brandy, Royce raised the glass. "Always knew you were a bright fellow."

"Undoubtedly she wants to know the status of our engagement."

"With your current streak of luck, you might want to play the tables today," Royce murmured, taking a sip of the amber liquid.

Gazing down at his glass, Steven swirled the brandy around. "Tell her that I don't know."

"Don't know what?" Royce asked, an incredulous note coloring his voice. "Whether or not you're engaged?"

"Precisely." Steven met Royce's eyes. "I don't know if Harriet still wishes to marry me."

"Oh, for heaven's sake," Royce muttered. "She says the same thing to Laurel, and between the two of you, my wife and I can't get any peace." He drained his glass. "Has it occurred to you, Steven, that you might actually talk to the girl about the matter?"

"Of course it has." He paused for a moment, before finally admitting, "I didn't want to see her until I'd thought things through."

"What's there to think about? You've been interested in her from the start, and now that you don't need to marry for money, you can claim her without having to lose your estate." Royce shook his head in confusion. "I don't understand what there is to think about."

Steven took a sip of his brandy. "Harriet claims to love me," he began, feeling that incredible swirl of warmth inside of him at the words. "Yet when everything was falling apart, she didn't have any faith in me."

Setting his glass down with a loud clink, Royce glared at Steven. "Do you know what your problem is, Heath? You think too much sometimes." He tossed his hands up into the air. "Just because Harriet devised a plan of her own to pay your debts doesn't mean she didn't have faith in you to come up with the money."

"That doesn't make any sense, Royce."

"It's not supposed to . . . it's women's logic." Royce chuckled softly. "Isn't that a contradiction right there?"

Steven took another swallow. "I still don't get your meaning."

"It's very easy, my friend. The problem here is you believe Harriet thinks like you, which is why you consider it a lack of trust that she went ahead with her own plans." Laying a hand on Steven's shoulder, Royce shook his head. "But that's not true. It's not that she doesn't believe in you; it's that she's a woman, and women do things like that all the time. They're fixers—they see a problem, and they want to fix it or, at the very least, help you to fix it." He squeezed Steven's shoulder once before releasing him. "So you see, it's not a matter of faith, but rather a matter of women thinking differently than we consider logical."

Royce's argument made a lot of sense. Sweet, kind

Harriet, beloved by children and the elderly alike, would always want to help fix a problem . . . whether anyone asked her to or not. "My God," Steven said softly. "How could I have been so blind?"

Royce scowled slightly. "Laurel tells me that being blind is what we men do best."

Placing his glass on the table, Steven tugged down on his vest. "Please excuse me, Royce. I've got to see Harriet right away."

As Steven headed for the door, Royce poured himself another brandy. "Can I offer a word of advice?"

Steven paused, turning to look at his friend. "I'd welcome it."

"Grovel," Royce said with a smile, lifting his glass again. "Prepare yourself for public humiliation and pray she forgives you."

"That doesn't sound very enticing."

"It's not." He shrugged once. "But it works."

"Hopefully I won't be pushed to that level."

A booming laugh escaped Royce. "I wouldn't count on that hope if I were you."

"Wish me luck."

"No, I'll wish you one better." Royce bowed. "Happy hunting, Lord Heath."

A broad grin creased Steven's face. "Tally-ho, Lord Tewksbury."

Grovel.

I can do that, Steven decided. He still remembered how Royce had groveled for Laurel, making a bloody spectacle of himself, but it had done the trick. Laurel had run into his arms and never left. If groveling would have the same effect on Harriet, he'd even get on his knees to do it. Hell, he'd do whatever it took to convince Harriet to marry him.

Taking a deep breath, Steven looked up at the imposing structure of the Hammersmith town house. After calling upon Harriet, he'd been told that she had accompanied her aunts and parents to Lady Hammersmith's for a farewell tea. When he'd learned she was preparing to return to the country with her parents, he'd hurried over to the Hammersmith town house without delay. Now all he had to do was walk into the Hammersmith parlor and sneak Harriet away for a private moment. He could declare his love for her and she would fall into his arms.

No problem.

After being admitted, Steven strode confidently into the crowded salon . . . and stopped cold as all attention shifted to him. Instead of the small gathering he'd expected, Lady Hammersmith was hosting a full-blown party with close to fifty people in attendance.

And each and every one of the partygoers was now staring at him.

Feeling as if he'd forgotten to put on his breeches, Steven smiled in greeting. "Good afternoon," he said jauntily, hoping that everyone would return to their own business.

Unfortunately, they simply replied in kind and continued to stare at him. Beside him, a young chit barely out of the schoolroom leaned over to her friend, and whispered, "That's Lord Heath. He's the one."

The one what? Steven wondered. Perhaps she was referring to the recent arrest of Mr. Connor. Spotting Harriet, he slowly worked his way through the now-quiet room, aware of every eye following his move. "I suppose everyone's heard of my recent mishaps with Laird MacWilliam."

Again, the crowd murmured in agreement, but didn't begin to converse amongst themselves. How the devil was he supposed to sneak Harriet away if everyone was watching him so closely? Desperate, he tried again. "Did you hear that the Earl and Countess of Tewksbury have a daughter?"

Having reached Harriet's side, he prayed they'd take his last gambit. "Harriet," he murmured, his voice sounding unnaturally loud in the silent room. Glancing around, he realized he'd simply have to ask to speak with her in private. While it might be scandalous for them to head off privately, Steven was beyond caring. He needed to speak with Harriet, to secure his future with her, and if it meant being the topic of conversation for the gossips, well, so be it.

"Might I have a word with you?" he asked quietly.

She kept her gaze fixed forward. "No."

He blinked twice. "No?"

"I believe I spoke clearly."

Cupping her elbow, he bent closer. "But I need to speak with you privately about a most urgent matter."

"I'm afraid that is impossible, my lord," she said, her voice sounding oddly tight. "My parents and I are leaving for the country within the hour, and I wished to say good-bye to my . . ."

"That's one of the things I needed to speak with you about," he said firmly. If he was going to convince her to stay, he needed to do it quickly. "Please, Harriet, I just need a . . ."

"I'm sorry, Steven, but we have nothing to say to one

another," she said softly, before turning her back on him.

Anger began to boil inside of him as he struggled to retain hold of Royce's advice. Grovel. "Harriet," he said again, tapping her on the shoulder. "Might I have . . ."

"No!"

Her sharp response stunned him, blasting away all of his good intentions. "What do you mean 'no'?" he countered, not even bothering to lower his voice. "After all we've been through I deserve a moment of your time."

As if finally realizing that they were being watched by everyone, Harriet lowered her voice. "Steven, this is neither the time nor the place."

"Well, that's just too bad because it's going to have to do." He crossed his arms over his chest. "Might I remind you that you'll be leaving within the hour?"

"That's right," she said calmly. "Perhaps I should go find . . ."

Immediately, he cupped her elbow. "You're not going anywhere until we sort this entire mess out."

"Mess?" she exclaimed, tugging free of his grasp but no longer making any attempt to leave. "Is that what you've reduced our relationship to?"

"Don't be ridiculous."

She gasped loudly. "So now I'm some sort of silly twit you'd like to forget about?"

That did it.

He'd been willing to be reasonable, but to accuse him of forgetting about her was unacceptable. After taking one look around the room, Steven dismissed the people who sat there watching them with avid curiosity like they were premier actors putting on a play.

"If you think that I'm . . ."

"That's just it, Steven," she said, poking him in the chest with her finger. "I don't know what to think anymore. I don't hear from you for three days following one of the most traumatic experi . . ."

Snapping, he grabbed hold of her shoulders and dragged her against him for a kiss. Not the sweet kiss he'd planned on giving her just before he told her he loved her, but rather a hungry, raw kiss that spoke of his frustrations, his desire, his love.

As he lifted his head to look down at her, Harriet opened her eyes. He smiled softly. "I love you," he whispered, setting free the words in his heart.

Pain flickered in her eyes as she pushed away from him. "Don't," she murmured brokenly.

Confused, Steven tried to reach for her again, but she stepped back. "Don't what? Tell you of my love."

She flinched as if he'd struck her. "You're very sweet for saying it, but I don't want you to use those words in order to make me happy. You don't have to marry me anymore."

"You say that as if it's some sort of obligation."

"Isn't it?" She squared her shoulders. "But you don't need to feel obligated anymore, Steven." Bracing against his chest, she went up on her tiptoes to whisper in his ear. "I got my monthly courses the other day."

"What does that have to do with anything?" he asked, catching a glimpse of Lady Hammersmith out of the corner of his eyes as she sat nibbling on a scone, not taking her eyes off of them.

Harriet's expression darkened with frustration. "It has everything to do with this discussion." Fisting her hands upon her hips, she shouted, "You don't need to feel honor-bound to marry me anymore."

"And why's that?"

"Because I'm not enceinte!"

"Don't worry, Harriet; I can take care of that little problem after we're married," he promised her smoothly.

Titters of laughter spread across the room before everyone fell silent, unwilling to miss even one word of the entertaining exchange.

"We aren't getting married!"

"Yes, Harriet, we are." He grinned wickedly at her, the look in his eyes reminding her of all the time they'd spent in their cottage hideaway. "Don't forget that I thoroughly compromised you," he announced to the room, drawing out the word 'thoroughly' to entice their audience.

Gasping, Harriet gestured toward the crowded room.

"If you didn't want everyone to overhear our discussion, you should have agreed to speak with me privately."

Stiffly, she nodded once. "Very well then. Let's find a . . ." At the shake of his head, she fell silent again.

"It's too late for that, Harriet," he pronounced with a grin. "Why can't you understand that I love you?" He gestured toward her brow. "I love the way you scowl at me when you don't agree with what I'm saying." He waved his hand toward her body. "I love how you make me feel when you hold me close and gift me with yourself." Stepping closer, he trailed his fingertips down the curve of her jaw. "And I love the way you make me feel . . . whole."

A collective sigh broke from their audience as Harriet struggled to blink back her tears. "Oh, Steven," she murmured, launching herself into his arms. "I love you so much."

Meeting her halfway, he captured her lips with his own, kissing her softly as a promise of his love. Finally, he knew what it meant to be wealthy. As long as he had Harriet in his arms, he'd never worry about his good fortune again.

Cheers and well-wishes filled the salon as Steven bent to lift Harriet in his arms, leaving her long skirts to trail over his arm, as he turned and strode out of the room. As they passed the young girls, the dark-haired one sighed dramatically. "I told you he was the one."

"You realize you'll never live this down," Harriet murmured as she smiled up at him, love illuminating her features.

"Ask me if I give a damn," he retorted, grinning like a perfect fool. "As long as you're living with me, I think I'll be able to handle anything."

"Even having young girls sigh as you walk by and declare you the one?"

He glanced down at Harriet. "The one what?"

"The one who is too much of a man, the one who seduces innocent young ladies, the one who is a true rogue."

Pausing, Steven grinned down at his future bride. "As to the first, I've never been too much for you to handle; secondly, you're the only innocent I plan on seducing in the future; and as to the last count, what can I say? You bring out the rake in me, Harriet Nash."

"Ha!" She shook her head. "Your past says otherwise."

"Harriet," he murmured, bending down to kiss her sweetly on the lips, "with you in my arms, I can't be bothered to think about my past." He tucked her closer against him. "You're my future."

"I wouldn't be so quick to dismiss your past, Lord Heath," Harriet replied cheekily. "After all, I've become quite fond of your roguish ways."

His laughter echoed in the Hammersmith foyer as Steven stepped out the door and into the sunlight.

Epilogue

One year later

"*T*his is really very naughty of us," Harriet murmured as she leaned back against her husband, lifting her leg out of the water to lay it along the edge of the tub. "We just left our son with your mother and snuck off for the day."

"I don't think it was naughty at all," Steven returned, skimming his hands upward to cup her breasts. "After all, we do have a reputation to uphold."

Laughing, Harriet arched upward. "Indeed we do, and it's all your fault."

His thumbs flicked over her turgid nipples. "My fault? And how did you reach that conclusion?"

"Who was the one that pulled us into a closet at the Hampton ball only to be discovered in dishabille by a maid?"

Steven's hands stilled for a moment. "I'll lay claim

to that," he conceded. "But who was the one that insisted we have a dalliance in the maze hedge during the Sommer garden party without realizing that Lord Sommer was conducting a tour of that maze for his garden club?"

Harriet couldn't help but laugh at the memory of poor Lord Sommer bobbling his eyepiece when he'd come upon them with their clothes in disarray. "It's true," she sighed. "I can't help myself though. You seem to bring out the wanton in me."

"Lucky me," he murmured as he slid his hands lower. "You're so beautiful, Harriet."

Dropping her leg back into the tub, she twisted until she was facing him. "You make me feel beautiful."

Reaching up, he cupped her face, smiling into her eyes. "I'm glad."

His simple answer touched her as Harriet moved closer, leaning in to kiss him as she straddled his lap. Steven's hunger for her continued to amaze her, but she wasn't about to question her good fortune. She'd been blessed with a passionate, loving husband who made her feel special. She'd never known love would be this wonderful.

"Harriet, my love," Steven murmured, pausing in his nibbling along her neckline. "Are you planning on just sitting there all day, or are you going to ravish me?"

Only Steven could give her this wonderful mixture of erotic lovemaking and laughter. Wearing nothing but a sensual smile, she shifted downward, enveloping him in her warmth as she settled onto his lap. Steven wrapped his arms around her, thrusting upward to deepen the connection, before growing still again.

Using only her inner muscles, she caressed his length, milking him deep into her, as she toyed with his lips, rubbing the tips of her breasts against his chest. A groan broke from Steven as he murmured, "You're killing me, Harriet."

"But what sweet death." Slanting her head, she kissed him deeply and finally began to move. Steven's fingers dug into her hips as she arched into him. Groaning softly, Steven drove upward, lifting her almost out of the water as he pumped into her, stroking her deeply, sending her plunging over the edge before joining her in the bliss of satiation.

"Is it still supposed to feel this good?" Harriet asked.

"I never question my good fortune," Steven mumbled, his head resting against the back of the tub.

Gazing up at him, she asked one more question. "If lovemaking is this wonderful between married couples, why would any husband take a mistress?"

Steven slanted open an eye. "Because only a few lucky couples ever find the magic that we've found, Harriet, my love."

His answer warmed her. Smiling, she snuggled back against his chest, closing her eyes to float along in a blissful haze.

"Did I ever mention all the many pleasures you can find using a silken tie?"

Turning to press a kiss upon her husband's chest, Harriet thanked her lucky stars for giving her Steven. "No, darling, I don't believe you have," she finally answered.

His hands trailed over her back as he began to list the various sensual uses of a silk scarf. "Other than using it with our chair, you can slip it between your legs and . . ." He paused for a moment. "Would you prefer a demonstration?"

Lifting her head, she smiled up at the golden Adonis she'd married. "Need you ask?"

**Visit the Simon & Schuster
romance Web site:**

---

www.SimonSaysLove.com

**and sign up for our
romance e-mail updates!**

Keep up on the latest
new romance releases,
author appearances, news, chats,
special offers, and more!
We'll deliver the information
right to your inbox—if it's new,
you'll know about it.

POCKET BOOKS

2800.02